BEST WOMEN'S EROTICA OF THE YEAR

VOLUME SIX

BEST WOMEN'S EROTICA OF THE YEAR

VOLUME SIX

Edited by

RACHEL KRAMER BUSSEL

Published in the United States by Cleis Press, an imprint of Start Midnight, LLC, 221 River Street, 9th Floor, Hoboken, NJ 07030.

Printed in the United States.
Cover design: Jennifer Do
Cover photograph: Shutterstock
Text design: Frank Wiedemann
First Edition.
10 9 8 7 6 5 4 3 2 1

Trade paper ISBN: 978-1-62778-301-9
E-book ISBN: 978-1-62778-514-3

CONTENTS

INTRODUCTION: SEXUAL ADVENTURERS AT HOME AND AWAY

Asking authors to get "adventurous" in an erotica anthology can be a tall order. After all, what's "adventurous" to one person may be totally mundane to the next. However, I feel safe in saying that the twenty stories you're about to read in *Best Women's Erotica of the Year, Volume 6*, are totally bold and refreshing. Whether single or partnered, straight or queer, vanilla or kinky, close to home or traveling the world, the characters in these stories are the opposite of meek.

What drew me to the theme of adventure is that in my mid-forties, my day-to-day life often looks pretty familiar: wake up, make coffee, take vitamins, eat breakfast, get to work. Whereas my younger single days were freewheeling, where I felt like I could wind up in the bed of anyone at any time, I've now been with the same partner for almost nine years. My concept of adventure and what it means, both in and out of the bedroom, has changed, and I wanted to see characters who were also grappling with how sex and adventure mingle, mix, and dance together.

Contemporary erotic romance author Shelly Bell kicks things

off with "New Year's Chance," where Dara encounters her old bad boy crush, Haydon. Next, the story "Inked on My Skin," by Naima Simone, who also writes the must-read Sin and Ink series, sizzles on the page and is so hot, while also being tender, I'm pretty sure you'll want a tattoo of your own by the time you're done.

Historical romance author Olivia Waite travels into the past to deliver the stunning f/f story "Cabinet of Curiosities," a prequel to her sexy novel *The Lady's Guide to Celestial Mechanics,* in which widows Phoebe and Harriet explore Harriet's collections from her travels before quite thoroughly exploring each other. If you think women who slept with and lusted after women in previous eras were at all dainty and demure in bed, you'll be pleasantly surprised by the ardor fueling their can't-get-enough-of-each-other sex.

Adventure sometimes takes place outside the constraints of the real world, such as in "Blues," by Amy Glances, in which a mermaid seduces a human. Even though she can't have everything she desires ("I wanted his whole body close to mine, but I knew that wasn't possible"), she's willing to go after the object of her affection, despite the constraints. In the magic realism of "Magia," by D. L. King, Anita gets lost in the New Mexico desert, and the being who helps her find her way offers her an encounter that will leave you breathless.

Sometimes we find adventure, and sometimes it finds us. There's a little bit of both in the totally sensual motorcycle clubhouse adventure Katrina Jackson takes readers on in "Easy Ride." If you've ever had a partner who tried to make you smaller, quieter, and less yourself, you'll be thrilled for Tysha, divorced from a man who did just that, when she enters this hidden setting on the "wrong" side of town and goes after what she truly wants in the form of a very sexy biker. "I've never felt anything like his body against mine. Everywhere he touches me is like sensory overload," Jackson writes.

An adventure doesn't have to be totally spontaneous to be sexy. In "Spring Fling," by Kyra Valentine, Jennie, Ewan, and Meghan meet at a restaurant to discuss a possible tryst. Their threesome is all the hotter for the negotiation that led up to it.

Parenting is its own kind of life adventure, and several moms in these stories seek out ways to access their sexy sides amidst the chaos. In "The Eighth Wonder of the World," by Mia Hopkins, the divorced single mom narrator puts her needs first with a steamy romp with her vacation tour boat operator. Jeanette Grey also explores the need for sex and passion to reawaken a mother's sense of self in "Adult Time."

Just as travel provides the perfect opportunity to cast off their everyday concerns in the two stories mentioned above, in "Far Side of the World," by Zoey Castile, a hike along the Scottish coastline becomes the perfect backdrop for Graciella to accept a sexy stranger's help—and affections. If you've ever attended a business conference and were bored out of your mind, you'll appreciate the chance to live vicariously through Shalini in "The Conference," by Anuja Varghese.

Sometimes an adventure can even happen alone, in our minds, where we are totally free to act on our desires and be our most wild and wanton. In "Meat Cute," by Jane Bauer, a passionate vegetarian discovers a whole new kind of passion when she lusts after her local butcher. Instead of seducing him, she has an intimate experience cooking herself a dinner that unleashes something new and unexpected. Brit Ingram shows how exciting exhibitionism can be in "Cooling Off," as the narrator gives firefighter Caleb a sexy shower show he won't soon forget.

BDSM plays a prominent role in many of the stories here, with kinky adventures helping push characters to try things they've never tried before, whether that's saying yes to a new lover in "Sweater Weather," by Elia Winters, or stepping into the unknown in closing story "The Escape Room," by Elizabeth SaFleur. In "Calyx," by Margot Pierce, Claire reclaims the former fierce and fiery part of herself when she enters a hotel room to join Matteo. As she gets comfortable with her dominant side, defying the ex who kink shamed her, she in turn makes space for Matteo to revel in his submissive side, a perfect melding of needs and wants. In "Change of Season," by Leah W. Snow, an empty nester finds more time and room to explore D/s with her husband, her Sir, during a football game that takes a decidedly kinky turn.

From exploring a powerful fetish in "Inflated Egos," by Evie Bennet, to indulging a partner's fetish and finding out just how arousing it can be in "The Instruction Manual," by Alexis Wilder, to discovering the power of porn in "Cream," by Saskia Vogel, the characters you'll read about here aren't afraid to explore in every sense of the word. They aren't constrained by what our culture thinks women "should" do, and instead reach boldly into their personal arousal arsenals to follow the directions their inner erotic compass is pointing them.

We all deserve adventure in our lives. Maybe not every day (though I applaud you if you manage it), but at some point. We all deserve a lover with the enthusiasm of Bell's Haydon, who tells Dara, "I want to get to know this pussy a little better. What it likes. What it doesn't. All its different flavors." We all deserve an attitude like that of Tysha in Jackson's "Easy Ride," when she reclaims herself from her dismissive ex: "I look at myself and know that I want more, because Neil always wanted less." We all deserve pleasure, passion, and moments that make us think to ourselves, *Is this really happening?*

I hope this erotica collection sparks an adventure for you!

Rachel Kramer Bussel
Atlantic City, New Jersey

NEW YEAR'S CHANCE

Shelly Bell

I parked my car in front of the obscene Christmas display. How my town had missed that wrapping palm trees with Christmas lights made them look like giant orgasming penises was beyond me. Then again, I hadn't had sex in almost three years. Maybe I just had penises on the brain.

Holding my purse close to my chest, I strolled through the sliding glass door of the supermarket.

Just as I'd predicted, the store was dead.

Thank goodness.

The last thing I needed was to run into someone I knew tonight. In lieu of a bra, I'd thrown my comfy button-down plaid shirt on over my white ribbed tank. Jean shorts and flip flops completed the ensemble. Despite it being southwestern Florida, it was a bit on the chilly side now that the sun had set. No one needed to see the outline of my nipples through my shirt.

With the store about to close, I had ten minutes to get the essentials—a bottle of non-alcoholic champagne, one pint of ice cream, and a box of assorted frozen canapés. I'd been intent on celebrating New Year's Eve by myself this year, but that didn't mean I had to forego the traditional holiday treats.

It was the first New Year's Eve in eighteen years that I didn't have Riley by my side. My daughter was spending the holidays with her girlfriend. And I was happy for her. I really was. That's why I'd insisted that we celebrate the first night of Chanukah together, so that she could fly out the next morning and make it to Connecticut for the rest of her break from college.

It was also why I'd lied about having plans tonight.

I mean, I do have plans. Just not with other people.

My coworker, Joe, had invited me to ring in the new year at our local bar over watered-down beer and all-you-could-eat chicken wings. I'm sure he was hoping we'd end the night together in his bed again, but a choice between sex with Joe and a night by myself wasn't really a choice at all. I much preferred my own company to his.

I snatched the bottle of fake champagne from the display at the front of the store and then steered myself toward the frozen foods. For such a small store, they had a decent selection of ice cream. As I stood in front of the freezer, I weighed my options. The biggest decision I'd be making tonight was what flavor to consume. It could set the entire tone for the year. I didn't want to screw it up.

I bit my bottom lip. Maybe I didn't have to decide. After all, I'd been the one to set the rules all those years ago. What was keeping me from changing them now? Would the world end if I ate more than one flavor of ice cream tonight?

Cold air blasted my cheeks as I opened the freezer. Holding the champagne in my left hand, I propped the door open with my hip and grabbed two pints with my free arm. *Ha, I'm such a rebel. If only Riley could see me now.*

"Dara?"

I jumped at the unexpected voice coming from directly behind me, dropping both pints of ice cream to the floor with a thud.

No fucking way. I hadn't heard that voice since graduation night twenty-one years ago. Full of gravel and sin, it was a voice I'd never forgotten.

Haydon Cross.

Our town's resident bad boy. Well, at least he had been the resident bad boy two decades ago.

I didn't even think he knew my name.

If my nipples hadn't already been pebbled from the freezer, Haydon's voice would've had the same effect. It always had.

I flipped around and came face to face with my old crush from high school.

Oh, and what a face it was. Time had only worked in Haydon's favor. He still had that thick black hair of his but he wore it shorter now, framed in a way that enhanced his high cheekbones and full lips. As if he spent every day laughing, he had those crow's feet at the corner of his cocoa brown eyes.

"Haydon. Wow." I wasn't sure whether to hug him. It felt like the thing one did in this situation, but just like back in high school, I was too shy to make a move. Instead, I picked up the pints of ice cream from the floor and returned them to their shelf in the freezer so that they didn't melt. "What brings you back to Fiddler's Creek?"

"My dad died."

Shit. Even though everyone knew Dean Cross was a shady businessman and a mean drunk, he was still Haydon's dad. "I hadn't heard. I'm sorry."

"Don't be. He was an asshole," Haydon said matter-of-factly. "That's why I left town the day of graduation and haven't stepped foot into Fiddler's Creek since."

I remembered the day as if it were yesterday. After learning through the grapevine that Haydon had split for good, I'd mourned his loss by getting drunk on Sambuca and spending the night with my head in the toilet. I still can't stomach the scent of black licorice.

Haydon leaned his shoulder against the freezer and crossed his legs in front of him. "You know, I've thought about you over the years."

My heart started beating a bit quicker. "You have? Why?"

He grinned at me. "Are you kidding me? You had to know I had the biggest crush on you."

Oh my god. Haydon had liked me? He had to be confusing me with someone else. "What? No, you didn't."

"Why'd you think I was always hanging out by your locker?" he asked.

"I assumed you were there because of your friends."

Now that I thought back on it, I realized none of his friends had a locker near mine. They had just kind of always been there whenever I happened to stop by my locker to exchange textbooks. I'd considered myself fortunate that it gave me a chance to see him, since we didn't have any classes together other than gym one time. I'd had a bad habit of eavesdropping on his conversations once or twice, hoping to hear who he was taking to the prom and praying he'd ask me to go.

"They were there because of me." He pushed off the freezer and took a step closer to me. "I was there because of you."

I shivered—and it had nothing to do with the fact we were standing in the freezer section. "Why didn't you ever ask me out?"

He laughed. "Right. Like the smartest, prettiest girl in school was going to go out with a guy who skated by with a C minus average and didn't even own a car?"

It had never occurred to me that he wouldn't think he was good enough for me. Back then, I hadn't felt smart or pretty. Sure,

I'd had straight *As*, but that was because I'd spent so much time studying. With only a few close friends and no boyfriends, I hadn't had much of a social life . . . which is probably why I got knocked up at nineteen by the first boy I ever dated.

"Those things wouldn't have mattered to me. If you'd asked me out, I would have said yes." Emboldened by his confession, I pressed a hand to his chest. It was just as solid and just as warm as I'd always imagined. "If you don't believe me, you can read all the diary entries I spent poetically waxing on about how much I liked you."

He covered the top of my hand with his own. "Damn. We sure wasted an opportunity, didn't we?" His thumb caressed the side of my wrist. "How 'bout we rectify that right now? Let's ring in the new year together."

His simple touch banished my chill and suffused me with heat. Who knew that my wrist had a direct main line to my pussy? I certainly hadn't, but with each brush of his thumb over my skin, I became wetter and wetter. My clit was throbbing. I'd never gotten turned on so quickly and definitely never from someone touching my hand.

If only I had taken the chance in high school to tell Haydon about my feelings for him. I'd been too afraid of rejection, never considering for a moment that he could feel the same way. After always playing it safe, maybe it was time to find out what it was like to throw caution to the wind. "Yes. I'd love to spend the night with you."

His eyes grew molten. "I'd invite you to my dad's place, but it's filled with moving boxes."

I swallowed the sudden knot of apprehension in my throat. Haydon's words served as a reminder that I shouldn't get attached. We only had tonight. Haydon didn't live in Fiddler's Creek. As soon as he settled his father's estate, he'd return to his life elsewhere.

But I couldn't worry about tomorrow. Not if I wanted to enjoy tonight.

I took a deep breath to steady my nerves. "We could go to mine."

Haydon took the bottle from me and placed it on the floor. Then he linked his fingers with mine and dragged me out of the store. Parked next to my beat-up Ford was a huge black and silver Harley.

The sight of it made my pussy clench. "You still ride a motorcycle."

He stroked the seat, bringing the visualization of him doing the same to me. "There's enough room for both of us on there." He jutted his chin toward my Ford. "Or, if you're not up for it, you could follow me in your car."

"No." In high school, I'd fantasized about him and me on that bike together. "I want to ride you." When he smiled, I realized what I'd said. "I mean, *with* you. On the motorcycle."

And *that* was why I'd never opened my mouth around Haydon. He always had reduced me to a stammering, quivering mess.

He put his hands on my waist to help me up. "Hop on, wrap your arms around me, and hold on tight." Once I was settled, he procured two helmets and handed one to me.

I slid it over my head and leaned forward, plastering my front to Haydon's back and encircling my arms around his tight abs. He smelled amazing, woody and earthy at the same time, and I couldn't help but inhale him into my lungs.

It seemed odd that he had an extra helmet handy for me, but before I could ask about it, we were off, racing out of the parking lot and headed toward my bungalow.

The wind whipped around us as we flew down Fiddler's Creek's main street. Everything around us was a blur, but in actuality, we probably weren't going any faster than thirty miles per hour.

Haydon's muscles rippled beneath my hands. He was like a furnace, radiating heat and keeping me insulated from the wind's chill. The motor's hum caused the seat to buzz between my thighs, increasing my arousal. If my panties weren't already soaked, they would be by the time I got home.

I laughed from the sensation of the lightness in my belly and the staccato beat of my heart. Riding on a motorcycle was exhilarating enough, but riding on a motorcycle with Haydon was literally a dream come true.

I never wanted it to end, but since everything in Fiddler's Creek was less than a five-minute drive away, we pulled up to my house all too soon. How had he known where I lived?

I opened my mouth to ask him, but as Haydon helped me off the bike, standing beside me with a hand high on my ass, I suddenly lost the ability to speak. It was as if someone had released a bunch of hyperactive butterflies inside my belly. He slipped his arm around my waist as we walked to my front porch.

Oh my god.

I was about to have sex with Haydon Cross.

I unlocked the door and led him inside. What was the protocol for a one-night stand? Should we go straight to the bedroom? Sit on the couch and make small talk? "Would you like something to drink? Or eat? I could heat up some leftover lasagna if you're hungry." Too afraid to turn and look him in the eye, I started toward the kitchen.

He didn't let me get far before he caught me. In seconds, he had me trapped between him and the wall. Honestly, I wasn't sure which was harder—the wall or his cock. "There's only one thing I'm hungry for right now and it's not in the kitchen." He framed my face with his hands and then his mouth captured mine.

There was a confidence in the way he took charge of the kiss. All my insecurities were banished with the flick of his tongue. I closed my eyes and surrendered to him. With Haydon, there was no need to worry about what came next. All I had to do was follow.

"I can't believe I finally get to know how Dara Mendoza tastes."

What did he mean by get to know? He'd just had his tongue in my mouth.

He unflicked the button of my shorts and slipped his hand beneath the band of my panties.

Oh . . . that's what he meant.

I whimpered as he cupped my pussy and eased a finger inside of my soaked channel.

"You always this wet, darlin', or is this all from me?" he murmured.

Without waiting for my answer, he withdrew his hand, sank to his knees in front of me, and yanked the shorts to my ankles, thankfully taking my sensible white cotton underwear with them. He lifted my feet, one at a time, and pushed my shorts out of the way before hooking my right leg around his neck and leaning forward until the tip of his nose met my pussy.

Maybe it was because of how pleased Haydon seemed to be at finding me wet, but I wasn't embarrassed about it or the fact he was getting up close and personal with my pussy. "It's all from you." Peering up at me, he gave me one long, slow lick from my opening to my clit. My body went liquid. To give me something to hold onto, I plunged my hands into his hair. "Well, a bit was from your motorcycle," I mumbled, no longer able to concentrate on words or really *anything* but the way his tongue was working my clit in circles.

My thighs tightened and my feet pointed. Ten seconds in and I was already on the verge of climax. It had been eons since I'd been with a man, and even longer since I'd been with one who knew what he was doing.

And Haydon Cross definitely knew what he was doing.

I just needed a tiny bit more pressure and I'd get there. "Don't stop." I pulled on his hair, yanking him forward in hopes of getting that pressure.

Instead of answering my silent prayer, he growled and lifted his head, mouth glistening. "Probably should have discussed this, but I got distracted by the fact I've been dreaming of having you underneath me for about twenty-five years. When it comes to this, I'm in charge. You get me?"

Guess my attempt at getting him to add some pressure to my clit wasn't allowed in his book. I'd read enough romance to know that somewhere in the world existed men who liked to take control in the bedroom. I'd just never encountered one before.

I didn't mind. In fact, after taking care of everybody else's needs for so long, it was liberating to know I could just relax and not worry about what to do next.

I nodded. "I got you."

"Hands flat against the wall," he demanded, without sounding bossy. "I know you were close to coming when I stopped, but I wasn't done with you yet. I want to get to know this pussy a little better. What it likes. What it doesn't. All its different flavors."

Well, since he put it that way . . .

I slapped my palms against the wall. "Maybe I can return the favor later."

He parted my labia and made a point of licking his lips. "You're already doing me a favor, sweetness."

What kind of man considered eating my pussy a favor to *him*? If I didn't know we only had tonight, I could definitely fall in love with Haydon Cross.

He pushed his tongue inside me, the whiskers on his cheeks abrading my sensitive folds and his hair tickling the inner thigh that was wrapped around his neck. The groans and grunts he made as he tongue-fucked me vibrated against my clit. It was almost too much, and yet at the same time, it wasn't enough.

Aching to touch him, I bent my fingers into my palms, digging my nails into the skin. He teased me, alternating between using his tongue and his fingers but purposely staying away from my clit. It drove me crazy, propelling me to great heights while denying me the ability to topple over the edge. I'd never been one of those women who could come without clitoral stimulation. But I had to trust that Haydon would get me there when he was good and ready.

He added a second finger, stretching me wider, and moved his fingers in and out of me, each pass going a little bit deeper. The loud squelching sound of him fucking me with his fingers echoed in the room. Haydon looked up at me with an intensity in his eyes I couldn't understand, his gaze doing just as much to me as his physical touch. At least until he did something wicked with his fingers that felt as if he'd kindled a small fire high inside of my pussy.

A noise I'd never made before tore from my lips, a cross between a sob and a moan.

"Ah, there it is," Haydon said, the pads of his fingers rubbing that magic spot I'd never been able to find. And believe me, I'd searched.

Legs shaking, I nearly hyperventilated as the fire in me swelled to near epic proportions. Soon, I was nothing but a mass of sensation, hyperfocused on a single point low in my pelvis. I couldn't open my eyes, couldn't speak, couldn't think. All I wanted in that moment was to come.

I hoped Haydon wasn't one of those men who demanded I wait for his permission to climax because there was nothing I could do to stop it even if I'd wanted to.

Which I didn't.

Then Haydon added his mouth to the equation, sucking my clit between his lips, and I was a goner. Heat blasted outward from my pussy, rippling through my belly like seismic waves. My pussy and ass clenched and released in blissful contractions. Shuddering, I felt the orgasm everywhere, from my toes to the top of my head.

Haydon unhooked my leg from around his neck, and with his hands firmly on my asscheeks, he lifted me onto his thighs and wrapped my legs around his waist. He rested his forehead against mine. "Almost worth the wait to see you come like that."

For me, there was no almost. That climax had absolutely been worth the wait. If he'd made me come like that in high school, he would've ruined all other men for me. "I feel like I should be thanking you."

"You never have to thank me for taking care of you." He raised his head and caressed my cheek with his thumb. "In fact, throw your arms around my neck. I'm ready to take care of you some more." With that being my only warning, he stood, me hanging on him like a koala on a tree. "Where's your bedroom?"

My bed had never seemed so far away. I pointed toward the staircase. "Upstairs."

One of the perks of having a bungalow was having the entire second story all to myself. Originally, it had been the attic, but the previous owners had converted it into a bedroom right before I'd bought the place. The bathroom and closet were tiny, but the bedroom itself was spacious, which afforded me the ability to have my gorgeous mahogany four-post king-size bed.

Haydon hoisted me over his shoulder and bounded up the steps, smacking my ass along the way. "Sorry. Couldn't resist."

He didn't sound sorry.

Besides, I hadn't minded.

I had a brief moment of panic when I couldn't remember if my room was clean. Then I remembered Haydon wasn't a date I was trying to impress. He was here to fuck. After tonight, I'd probably never see him again. Speaking of fucking . . .

"Did you happen to bring a condom with you?" I asked as he hit the landing of my bedroom. "I think I have some in my nightstand, but since I bought them about five years ago, I'm guessing they've expired."

"In my wallet."

Hallelujah.

He dropped me onto the mattress and tugged his shirt over his head, giving me the first glimpse of his chest since gym class. It had definitely changed—and all for the better. Back then, he'd been firm, but a bit on the slim side, built like a boy rather than a man. Now, he was broader and burly, with a spattering of brown curls on his tan chest and abdomen. Sure, he had a bit of a belly, but that just told me he enjoyed life and wasn't compulsive about his appearance like some people our age.

Feeling emboldened, I spread my legs and leaned back on my elbows to watch him undress. I wanted to memorize each moment I spent with him tonight.

After removing his shoes, he grabbed his wallet from the back pocket of his jeans and procured a square foil from it. His gaze landed between my legs. "Nice view."

I spread my thighs wider. "Right back atcha."

He dragged his jeans and boxers down his legs and stepped out of them, leaving him one hundred percent naked. I soaked in the beauty of his body, the thick thighs and impressive erection curved up toward his belly. His cock was long and cut and, for the rest of the night, *mine*.

Haydon prowled toward me, stopping only when he was between my legs. "You ever been tied up?"

I batted my eyelashes at him and pretended not to understand.

"Once, but I was playing cops and robbers with my daughter at the time."

Shaking his head, he pinched the inside of my thigh. "Not what I meant and you know it."

"I've never been tied up, but I'm not opposed to the idea." If *not opposed* meant completely enthusiastically onboard with it.

The sides of his mouth ticked up. "Got any scarves?"

My arousal shot through the roof. "Top right drawer of my dresser."

He bent and kissed my cheek. "When I get back, I want you lying in the middle of the bed with your head on your pillow."

Leaving me panting, he strode to the dresser while I quickly complied with his instructions. He returned with two of my black scarves in his hands and proceeded to tie each of my wrists to the bedposts. I tugged on the makeshift restraints, testing them, and realized he hadn't tied them tightly. If I yanked hard enough, I could probably get out of them. I trusted him, but at the same time, I hadn't seen the man in more than twenty years. Giving me the ability to escape was considerate and kind. Besides, it was the *idea* of being restrained and helpless that made my body hot.

He straddled my torso and leaned forward until his warm lips covered mine, stealing my breath and making my heart beat faster. His hands caressed my breasts, first tenderly and then, as the minutes passed, more aggressively, pinching the nipples between his fingers and squeezing my flesh. I grew restless and needy underneath him but was unable to move how I wanted, restricted by my bound wrists and Haydon's knees on the sides of my thighs. On and on he kissed me, kissing me so thoroughly and so unhurriedly that when he eventually did lift his mouth off mine, my lips felt bruised and swollen and my pussy was throbbing.

He skimmed his fingers down the slope of my throat. "Now that I have you like this, what should I do with you?"

Make love to me.

I caught myself before I spoke the words out loud. What we were doing tonight had nothing to do with making love. So then why did it feel as though it was?

"Fuck me," I said instead.

Haydon tore open the condom package and rolled the latex down the length of his cock. Gazing at me with tenderness, he draped his body over mine, his weight pinning me to the mattress. "I want to look in your beautiful brown eyes when I bury myself in you for the first time. Wrap your legs around me, Dara."

I crossed my ankles over his tailbone. He slid effortlessly inside of me, stretching me and filling me with his cock. Swiveling his hips, he thrust in and out of my pussy, nudging my clit with every pass. I unconsciously pulled at my restraints, crazed over the inability to do anything but lie there and take what he had to give me. Every part of me pulsated to the wild rhythm of my heart.

A tingling heat gathered behind my clit and all my muscles tightened. The world grew hazy, my focus narrowed to Haydon's face in front of mine and the mounting tension where our bodies were joined.

I didn't want this moment to end. I wanted more of it. More of *him*. I wanted him inside of me forever.

But I didn't have a choice.

I no longer had control of my body. My fingers curled into my palms, my toes pointed, and my legs trembled. I flew over the edge, crying out Haydon's name as my pussy clamped down on his cock again and again. Liquid heat washed over me and spread through my limbs.

Haydon stilled above me. His brows dipped and his lips pursed. "Dara." Groaning, he jerked against me as he followed me over and came.

It took a few minutes before we could catch our breath. I was unsure about how to proceed. Was he staying the night? Or now that we'd fucked, would he get on his motorcycle and ride out of my life for another twenty years?

Surprising me, he didn't roll off and excuse himself to the bathroom or make any attempt to move. He remained right where he was, between my thighs. "I have a confession to make," he said, looking me squarely in the eyes. "It wasn't an accident that we ran into each other at the market. I'd only planned on spending a couple days in Fiddler's Creek, just long enough to bury my father and hire someone to pack up his shit. But then I saw you walking down Main Street, and everything I'd felt for you back in high school came rushing back. Found out you were single and had bought the Myersons' old house. Since then, I've been busy making plans."

So that's how he'd known where I lived. "What kind of plans?" I asked.

He took a ragged breath. "Plans to move back to Fiddler's Creek. What do you say, Dara? Want to take a chance on me?"

We'd wasted enough time. "Being with you isn't a chance. There's nothing I want more."

Fireworks popped in the distance. *It must be midnight.*

Haydon pressed a soft kiss on my lips. "Happy New Year, Dara."

I smiled, thinking how only a few hours ago, I'd thought I'd be spending the night alone. "Happy New Year, Haydon."

I had a feeling it would be.

INKED ON MY SKIN

Naima Simone

I'm doing this.

I'm about to step out into this arena packed with thousands of people and dozens of cameras, under the unforgiving glare of countless lights. And that's not even counting the millions of people watching on their televisions.

Yet none of that scares me.

Only one thing has my stomach coiled with knots and my heart knocking against my sternum like a hammer. Has me breathing so hard, so fast, the echo of it nearly deafens me.

Seeing Esau Morgan, my brother's former best friend, for the first time in four years.

"Okay, people, it's time," the woman in the '80s hair band T-shirt—god, what was her name again? Jenna? Janice?—announces, clapping her hands to grab my attention as well as that of the other four human canvases standing backstage, ready to have our skin forever inked by the five finalists in *Ink Royalty,* the internationally renowned reality competition TV series. "Meet your person." She turns and waves a hand toward five men and women behind her. "They're going to escort you to your artist and remain on standby just in case you need something like water or a snack. Now remember, you'll get to see the artist's custom design before they tattoo it, but you do not have a say in it. This is their design, and you're the canvas. Again, this is a marathon tattoo session. Three four-hour intervals with a half-hour break in between to eat, use the bathroom, etc. The time starts as soon as you hit the artist's platform. Any questions?"

The others voice their agreement, but I don't speak. I can't. Every bit of me is focused on the other side of that black curtain that separates me from Esau. Part of me wants to push past Jenna/Janice and rush out there to see him face-to-face for the first time since he disappeared from my hospital room with my brother's harsh and so-damn-unfair accusation ringing in my ears.

And the other half? The half that still cringes whenever it remembers the torment and horror that darkened Esau's beautiful gray eyes as he stared at me like I was a broken thing . . . That half braces itself for the rejection and pain that might shatter what Eddie Sutton's attack didn't.

The two women and two men ready to have their skin inked line up in front of me. Of everyone in the group, I'm the most . . . conventional. Nothing on me is shaved, ripped, dyed, pierced, or tatted. Yes, with my tight, black curls, brown, unmarred skin, and a white sundress, I'm the oddball in this crew. But we're all united by one thing.

Our scars.

Yet, I'm still different in that, too. Unlike the others with their mapwork of traumatized flesh that's a result of either surgery, an accident, or burns, my marks are chillingly perfect in execution. A capital *E* carved into my back. A stark and horrifying testimony of a man's attempt to brand me.

Even in this group, I'm looked at with a mixture of horror and pity. You'd think after four years, I would be used to those reactions. And in some ways, I am. But for the most part? I'm not. How can I be? I'm a walking billboard to sadistic violence. Edison "Eddie" Sutton might as well have sliced a *V* for victim in my flesh with his knife that terrifying night in the back room of that frat house. No one sees the survivor.

And that's what I am. A survivor.

Now I just have to make Esau see me. Not as the little sister of the man he called a brother. Not as the girl he believes he failed and left to the twisted attentions of a drunk, vicious asshole who'd been told no.

But as the woman who loves him, heart and soul. And who will do anything to prove to him that I'm his and he's mine.

Including having him ink my skin for the first time.

"It's go time," Jenna/Janice says, and she steps to the side as the curtain slowly opens.

The blinding lights, the deafening applause of the audience—they're almost too overwhelming, and for a second, I freeze. Every doubt, every "What the fuck are you doing?" pile drives into my brain. For four years I wore shirts and dresses designed to hide my back. And now, here I stand, about to willingly expose it and my trauma to the world.

"Your turn, sweetie," the woman at my side whispers. I glance at her, and she smiles patiently. But it's the hint of pity I glimpse in her blue eyes that infuses steel in my spine and gets my ass in gear.

I nod, and she moves ahead of me, leads me down a ramp, and then veers to the right. A smaller stage looms ahead. I easily recognize the equipment occupying the space. A black stool. A chair that looks like it wouldn't be out of place at a spa, with arm and chest pads and an adjustable head support. A chrome workstation and a drafting table. And in the middle of it?

Esau.

Oh, god.

My heart starts a crazy, out-of-rhythm jackhammering against my ribcage as my breath saws in and out of my lungs. My feet become leaden, and I stumble on my platform sandals.

Yes, I've watched him every week on *Ink Royalty* as if the show was my religion and he my deity. But that was through a television screen. Now, he's only several feet away from me. And my body is in the midst of a joyous celebration and a fiery rebellion.

At twenty-seven—four years my senior—he hit his growth spurt long ago, and yet he seems taller to me, bigger. A faded black Henley encases his strong, wide shoulders. Equally faded jeans hang off his lean hips but cling like a stalker to his powerful thighs. Scuffed boots finish off the "I don't give a flying fuck if I'm on TV" outfit. Unable to stall any longer, I lift my way-too-enamored gaze to his face.

He shouldn't be beautiful. Not with those harsh facial bones that jut out like the craggy edges of a mountain. Not with the arrogant slash of a nose and a bit-too-large mouth. A thick, dark red beard can't hide a stubborn, rock hard jaw that screams Beware: Obstinate Man Ahead. But the forbidding features only emphasize the beauty of his densely lashed silver eyes and the indecent lushness of his mouth.

God, I've always wanted to feast on that mouth. Like it was the last pit stop before hell. A place to linger and get my fill until I spend an eternity burning for it.

Esau stills as we near. Tension draws him tighter than a bow notched with an arrow, and his big hands curl into fists beside his thighs. A cold mask drops over his face, and the spotlights trained on him bounce off the metal piercing his left eyebrow and the corner of his mouth.

But as I step onto the stage and stop in front of him, I clearly see the anger swirling in his hooded, molten gaze. No, not anger. Fury.

He isn't happy to see me. At all.

I knew this would be a definite possibility, but shit, having a ring-side seat to that rage, that disdain . . . it hurts.

I blink, battling back the tears, the soul-searing pain. No way in hell am I breaking down in front of millions of people.

He might not want me, but goddamn it, he's going to at least *talk* to me.

And ink me.

"What the fuck is this?" he growls, not speaking to me but to my escort.

The poor girl glances back and forth between us, a frown etching her forehead. But I don't allow her a chance to respond. He needs to get used to addressing me since he's going to have his hands and needles on me for the next twelve hours.

"I'm your human canvas," I say, forcing my lips into a wry smile. "Surprise."

"No." The word is blunt and fierce though his expression doesn't change. "Fuck no."

"Esau," the other woman starts, a tremor in her voice. "I'm not sure what's going on, but—"

"But you have no say in your human canvas just as I have no choice in what you decide to put on my body." His eyes narrow at "on my body," and for a moment, I think I catch a flash of heat. But nope, it's gone in the next instant and was probably a trick of the light. And my wishful thinking. "And yes, I did use my story and our past relationship to get on this show. To get to you. Apparently, the producers thought it would be a real emotion grab for you to help me cover up the scars and pain you were a witness to. How's that for healing and ratings, right?"

For the first time, his expression changes, and my throat constricts as if a hand slowly closes around it. Pain spasms across his face, and his eyes briefly close. When he opens them again, that mask is firmly back in place, his gaze shuttered.

"Is this your idea of payback, then, Tamison?" he rasps. "Fuck me over and cost me a hundred thousand dollars?" Stunned, I shake my head, but he leans forward, pushing his face into mine. "Good. I deserve it."

"Esau—"

"Sit," he orders, turning from me and stalking over to his station.

Hours of viewing this show have taught me how to straddle the seat, my chest facing the rectangular pad. The long skirt of my dress rides up my calves, but I'm not flashing any unsuspecting—or perverted—audience members. Self-conscious, but all my attention laser-focused on Esau, I settle my arms on the rests and watch as he switches out ink bottles on the flat surface of the station and adds more of the tiny caps that hold the liquid.

Under the cotton of his shirt, his muscles flex and dance along his back and biceps. Tattoos sprawl up the tight forearms exposed by the sleeves pushed to just below his elbows, and they crawl up his neck from under his round collar. The requisite skulls and tribal designs. But angels, roses, vines, a portrait of a woman with a haunted, beautiful face too. He's a walking, gorgeous mural; I could study him forever and constantly discover more revelations of him.

When he turns back to me, his dark brown and auburn hair falls into his face, caressing his cheekbones like flirty fingers desperate for a touch. I should glance away, pretend that I'm not staring, but I don't. I can't. Modesty evacuated the building the second I agreed to do this show.

"Lower your top," he says in that deep rumble that strokes over my skin.

I understand what he's telling me, but my body reacts as if he ordered me to strip for him. The dress has a built-in bra, so I'm totally bare underneath, and my nipples already bead in anticipation. I can barely swallow past the lump of nerves and, yes, excitement in my throat as I slowly lower one strap. And then the other. All without breaking our visual warfare.

"Here." He thrusts something at me; I look down and grasp the balled-up material. It's soft, white, and smells like him. Earthy. Woodsy. And all hot male. "Cover up with it."

Nodding, I take the shirt and press it to my breasts before pushing my dress down around my waist.

"Lower," he rasps, and my gaze shoots to his again.

There's no mistaking the heat I see there this time as I push the dress to my hips. It turns his eyes into liquid silver pools. My belly clenches, and an empty ache pulses deep and high inside me. But tainting the desire is despair. No way I can miss the stark pain mingling with the shocking hunger.

I face forward and press my cheek on the head rest, his shirt hiding my breasts from the viewing public. As stunning as it might be to realize Esau could see me as more than his former best friend's little sister, he can't look at me and not see the wounded girl I once was.

Minutes pass, and finally he shifts behind me, his heat brushing over my bare skin. I gasp as a light, almost reverent caress traces the *E* etched into my flesh. Before I can react—hell, *breathe*—his touch is gone and the fine, cool tip of a marker moves over my back in quick, sure strokes. His thighs bracket mine. I don't peek over at the other stages, but I'm pretty damn sure none of the other artists sit so close to their canvases that they're nearly covering them. Embracing them.

But he's not another artist. And I'm not just another canvas.

"You don't have your stencil?" I ask softly.

When he doesn't answer immediately, disappointment twists inside me. The silent treatment. I should be used to it . . .

"What I had planned isn't going to work on you," he says.

It's a little pathetic how elated I am that he's talking to me. God, I've missed him. Like an amputee longing for their discarded limb. I swore I could feel him, but he was never there. I close my eyes and lower my head, savoring that deep, rough rumble.

"Why not?" I press. "I don't care what you tattoo on me. I have zero doubts it would be gorgeous. But drawing an entirely new design would put you behind on your time—"

"You think I haven't seen exactly what I would put on you so many times in my head that I couldn't ink it in my sleep?" he growls.

Holy shit. I don't have an answer. Because I can't speak. Not when he just admitted to thinking about me over the years. To not having forgotten me. By the time I find my voice again, the tattoo machine is buzzing and he's shifting even closer to me.

"Esau." I swallow to moisten my dry mouth. "This is my first time. Getting a tattoo."

"I know that, too, Tamison," he replies. A big hand settles on my hip, and from the way electricity arrows from that spot to my clenching pussy, I've discovered a new erogenous zone. I grit my teeth, trying to hold back a moan. But I'm not successful, because his grip tightens on me. Holding me still. Controlling me. "You promised me once that when you were ready, I would be the first person to ink you. And you were never a liar."

You were never a liar.

The words ring in my ears like an indictment, and they almost drown out the sensation of the needle hitting my skin. Almost.

"Easy, baby," Esau murmurs when I stiffen. "Breathe through it."

His words, his breath, caress my shoulder. I close my eyes, concentrating on that and his broad hands on me instead of the not-quite-painful-but-damn-sure-uncomfortable sting of the needle. After several minutes, I do gradually relax as the sensation switches to irritating but bearable. Eleven hours and approximately thirty more minutes of this. And yet, I can sit through more than that if Esau continues to touch me.

"That's not true," I say, picking our conversation right back up. "I'm a liar. And we both know it."

"Tamison," he starts to interrupt me, but I cut him off.

"No," I hiss, and then I stop, wrangling my emotions back under control. "You walked away in that hospital room and wouldn't let me speak. Now, you're going to listen."

The needle lifts, and I hold my breath. His breaks in harsh puffs against my skin. Finally, he gets back to work, and I exhale.

"I lied to you about having someone else to take me home from that party. I didn't want to see you. And I didn't want you coming there like a big brother swinging by to pick up his little sister from a kid's party. I was tired of you . . . treating me that way. As a little sister. And so I lied. And what happened afterward with Eddie—"

"Don't say his fucking name," he snaps, his rage like a bonfire against my back.

"I have to, Esau," I whisper, staring sightlessly out into the darkened arena. "As long as I do, he holds no power over me. It's like calling the boogeyman out by his name. He no longer controls me."

The needle lifts once more. Longer this time. I can feel his hurt, his anger, his pain beat at me. When he resumes tattooing, I continue talking.

"I never blamed you, Esau."

"You should've," he states flatly. "You were my responsibility. I knew you were lying, but I wanted to give you room, space. But I should've been there to protect you."

"I wasn't your responsibility," I argue. "I was nineteen, not twelve. I made my own choices that night. And neither one of us shoulders the blame for what that animal did. That was on him and he's paying for it."

"Five years isn't enough," he bites out. I jerk in shock, and he hisses a warning. "You can't move like that, Tamison."

"How did you know about his sentence?" I demand, ignoring his warning. "You weren't at court."

"Wasn't I?"

I let that sink in. "I didn't see you."

"I didn't want you to."

I let that sink in, too. "Daniel didn't mean what he said. Let me up." As soon as the needle raises from me, I twist around to stare into his beautiful, tortured eyes. "He was terrified and ashamed because he wasn't there for me. Just like you blamed yourself, so did he. Only he lashed out at you. Almost immediately he regretted it, but you disappeared out of our lives and we couldn't find you." I shake my head. "Not until this show. And I knew if you wouldn't voluntarily see me, I had to make you. I've missed you. I . . ." *Need you.*

Somehow, I manage to keep that in. He doesn't reply, but his gaze roams over my face, and I feel each sweep like the touch of his calloused fingertips.

"Turn around," he says, voice like rough silk. I obey, and he begins inking me again. Just before I abandon all pride and beg him to speak to me, to *hear* me, he murmurs, "I blame myself because I was relieved when you called and told me not to come get you. I didn't want to walk into that frat house and see those preppy motherfuckers with their eyes on you, laughing with you, talking to you, fucking touching you, when I couldn't. You were wrong when you said I saw you as my little sister. I haven't done that since the summer you were sixteen and walked outside in a yellow bikini top and cut-off denim shorts. You wore white earrings, a shell necklace, and blue flip-flops. And your skin, so damn dark and gorgeous, was damn near glowing. That was the first time I considered risking my friendship with your brother to fuck you. To find out if you tasted as sweet as you looked."

Shock pummels me, crashing into me like waves against a rocky shore. Oh, god. Did he . . .? No. Hope and desire have me wishing he'd uttered that confession in his silk-over-gravel voice. Because surely he hadn't just admitted he wanted to fuck me?

"Esau," I breathe.

"Staying away from you was my penance, my punishment. I never stopped wanting you, never stopped fantasizing about getting my mouth on you, my dick in you. It made me a shitty friend to imagine corrupting that innocence, taking it for my own. It made me an even shittier man to dream about it when I'd failed you, didn't deserve you. So I wouldn't let myself have you. Not your pussy, your body, or your friendship."

"Esau, stop," I plead, unable to contain the whimper in my tone.

My chest is an active battlefield. Lust, need, pain, anger, and love war inside me, fighting for ground. Hearing that dark voice wrap around the word "pussy" . . . hearing it describe how he wanted to dirty me for him . . . I'm going up in flames. My breasts swell and sensitize even as my nipples tighten to the point of sensual agony. My sex spasms around air, greedy for the dick he wanted to push inside of me. I want that. Oh, fuck. I want *him*. So damn bad. How I haven't orgasmed right now in front of god and country is a freaking miracle.

But alongside the need dwells the hurt because he's suffered, all self-inflicted due to a burden he has no business bearing. If he hadn't left, if he hadn't run away from my brother, *from me,* we wouldn't have wasted four long years.

"Why are you telling me this now?" I ask, desperate to know.

"Because if you were brave enough to fight your way onto this show just to give me your truth, then I can man the fuck up and do the same."

"And do you . . ." My throat closes around the question as if attempting a last-ditch effort at self-preservation. But I'm determined to dive into the deep end without a lifejacket. I'm willing to drown for him. "And do you still want me?"

"Do I still want to lift this dick tease of a dress and bury my face in that sweet little pussy and see if it tastes like every fucking birthday and Christmas wrapped into one? Do I still want to push you to your knees and watch that pretty, too-smart-for-its-own-good mouth part for my cock? Do I still want to take that throat knowing it makes me an asshole that I hope I'll be the first to do it? Do I still want to push into your pussy, break it until it's shaped for only me? Knows only me?" His voice deepens to a rumble so low it's almost unintelligible. But he could've spoken in tongues, and I would've deciphered it. My heart and my body translate every syllable. "Yeah, baby girl. I do. I've never stopped."

We fall into a silence so thick, so charged, it wraps around us in a cocoon, separating us from the people gathered into the building. Rock groups perform, including the host, who's a front man for a famous band. Former contestants are interviewed and judges offer their opinions on the finalists. Before I know it, my escort appears beside us, announcing the first break.

I replace the top of my dress, stand, and stretch. My back is on fire. So is everything else. My thighs, damp with the evidence of my lust, tremble, and my sex pulses so hard I can barely stand. Behind me, Esau rises and his hand settles on my hip, steadying me.

"Bathroom?" I ask my escort, unable to push another word through my constricted windpipes.

"Sure, this way." She turns, and I don't need to glance behind me to see Esau there. I feel him. His body heat. His presence. His power.

Once we make it into the bowels of the arena, Esau enfolds my hand in his much larger one. "I got her," he informs the other woman with a dip of his chin and a wealth of "don't give me any bullshit" in his voice.

He doesn't wait for her reply but strides forward, and I'm helpless to follow. Moments later, he shoves open a door into what appears to be a small dressing room. A short couch is pushed to one wall and a table with cups, food, and water bottles is set up against another. But that's all I glimpse before hard, long fingers thrust into my hair, tugging my head back, and a firm but so soft mouth crashes against mine.

Oh, god. Our mouths mate as do our tongues. It's our first kiss, but there's no hesitation, no learning curve. He devours me, thrusting inside me, tangling with me, claiming me. This kiss—it's hot, wet, dirty, and perfection.

Clawing at his shoulders, I press onto my toes, begging him with my mouth for more. Maybe he reads minds or maybe he just has a linguistics degree in me, but he understands. Tilting my head to the side, he delves deeper, licking, sucking, eating at me like I'm a forbidden feast he's finally been allowed to take part of. And maybe I am. He is for me.

Without breaking our mouths, he lowers his hands to my shoulders and pushes my dress straps down my arms. I don't try to conceal myself. No, I want him to see me. For so long I've craved that, and as his hooded, silver gaze burns with lust, satisfaction and need slide through my veins, pulling my nipples tight, pooling between my thighs.

"So fucking beautiful," he rasps.

Again, there's no hesitation or uncertainty. He cups me, and from the long, rough groan he releases, he doesn't mind my modest size. Instead, his big hands swallow me, plumping me, squeezing. Ducking his head, he delivers a long, luxurious lick to one nipple, and then closes his mouth around it, drawing so hard I feel the pull in my pussy. Whimpering, I clutch his head to me, gripping the brown and red strands.

"Please," I whisper. "Harder."

He flashes a searing glance up at me, and then puts his teeth to me, grazing me with the edge, and I buck against him at the bite of it. Soothing the sting with his tongue, he gives me one last suck before moving onto the neglected tip, giving it the same sexual torture. That pleasure with the finest edge of pain sizzles through me like flames blazing across gasoline.

Air brushes across my calves, knees, and then thighs. I glance down to see my skirt bunched in his fists, revealing the state of my soaked black thong and my glistening inner thighs.

"For me, baby girl?" he murmurs, staring at how the lace shamelessly clings to my folds. "You're this wet for me, aren't you?"

"Yes." I press my lips to the tip of an angel's wing on his throat. God, every time he calls me his "baby girl" I pant harder, fall deeper. "All for you. It's only ever been you."

"Shut up," he snarls, but the hand that tenderly cups my face belies the harshness of the order. "The first time I come with you isn't going to be in my goddamn jeans. It's going to be inside you. So don't say anything else like that until my cock is so deep in your pussy that I feel those words vibrate around me. We clear?"

I nod, turning my head to press a kiss to his palm.

"Tam," he groans. His lips cover mine, and I'm taken under as he walks me backward. I don't pay attention, trusting him to guide me to his planned destination. When my legs hit the back of something, he mutters, "Turn around and kneel on the couch."

Before I can comply, he's lifting my dress. I sink my teeth into my bottom lip, trapping a moan—of protest or encouragement, I don't know. But then his finger dips underneath the scrap of material shielding my pussy and tunnels through my drenched folds. And I know. Encouragement—and need.

"Esau," I gasp, my head falling back on my shoulders, and then dropping low.

My skirt hides what he's doing from my sight, but god can I *feel*. He nudges my clit, using my own juice to slick a circular path around the sensitive bundle. I jerk against his touch, hissing at the electric shock of pleasure. But a hand at the base of my spine holds me steady and in place as he toys with me, plays me.

And then his tongue replaces his finger.

I scream. Not caring if anyone on the other side of this dressing room door hears. Not when he's sucking at my clit, flicking it, stabbing at it. His groan echoes in my sex as he slides a path through my swollen lips, lapping up my cream as if it's the perfect treat and he's addicted. No part of me is left untouched. Unloved. And when he places two thick fingers against my entrance and presses forward, I arch back into the invasion, craving it.

"So tight," he mutters against my thigh. "So wet and tight. You're going to strangle the hell out of my cock. You're going to leave me bruised, baby girl." Another lick to my clit. Another hard suck that drags me closer to that rapidly crumbling edge. Between his slow, torturous strokes, those wicked fingers curling on every withdrawal, I'm not going to last until he gets inside me. A shiver wracks me from head to toe, and I push back onto his hand, riding it. "You're going to fucking kill me," he mumbles against my sex.

Suddenly, he's gone, and I could cry from the abrupt abandonment. As a matter of fact, I do.

"Esau, don't—"

"Shh." His warm breath bathes my ear before he presses a soothing kiss to my cheek, my shoulder. "I'm not going anywhere."

The crinkle of foil echoes in the room, and seconds later, Esau thrusts his fingers through my hair, his blunt nails scraping over my scalp. With a gentle but firm tug, he jerks my head back.

"Tell me you're with me, Tam," he says into my ear, so I can't miss the plea in his tone. "Tell me you want me inside you as bad as I need to be there."

Despite his hold, I turn my head, meeting his smoldering, desperate gaze. "I want you, Esau Morgan." My breath catches, and I briefly squeeze my eyes closed. Because as I speak, he's slowly tunneling inside me, pushing and branding me. He's almost too big, too thick, and my muscles pulse and flutter around his cock, adjusting to him.

"Keep going, baby girl. Don't stop." He groans as he seats himself fully in my sex, burrowing his face between my neck and shoulder and ever careful of my back. "Tell me."

"Since I realized what need, what desire, what . . . love was, you've been it for me. I want you. I'm yours. I've always been."

"Yeah, you're mine," he growls, his teeth grazing my neck. "And I'm yours."

With one last hard kiss to the back of my head, he clasps my hips and pulls free of my pussy. I press myself against the back of the couch, bracing myself. And he doesn't disappoint. He plunges into me, setting nerve endings on fire, searing me with pleasure and just a bite of pain. He claims me with each stroke, each piston into my body. Each whispered word of praise, of adoration. Each groan that echoes in the room. Each slap of flesh against flesh.

I am consumed as he rides me, gives me no quarter. We've waited years for this . . . this crashing into each other. And he doesn't take it easy on me, working my body, my pussy, molding it to him just as he promised.

Each thrust shoves me closer and closer to the dark but blazing abyss that I want to dive into. But I cling to the edge of reason, not wanting this to end. Savoring every drag of his dick over my walls.

Every strike of his cockhead against that special place inside me that's driving me to an end that terrifies and exhilarates me.

"Give it to me," he grunts, snaking a hand around my waist and between my thighs to flick and rub my clit. "Now, Tam. I want this pussy rippling around me."

With a keening wail, I surrender. I explode. I fly.

Behind me, Esau pounds into me, chasing that same high. One, two, three strokes later he stiffens, and I feel his cock pulse inside my orgasm-tightened walls. Our harsh gasps batter the air, and yet even then, he doesn't wilt against my back, ever mindful of my comfort.

"We need to get back," he murmurs against my hair. "The bathroom's through that door."

Slowly, he pulls free of my pussy, and even though I'm tender, my muscles still grasp at him, as if willing him to never leave. I'm tired, used, but so energized, because . . . Esau.

I make fast work of cleaning myself up and looking presentable in the bathroom and return to the dressing room. He meets me as I cross the floor, grabbing my hand to press a kiss to the back of it. With a jerk of his head, he leads me toward the door.

"Wait." I halt in front of the full-length mirror hanging on the wall. Turning so my back faces it, I peek over my shoulder. "Esau," I breathe.

It's me. Only the outline is done, but it's clearly my face tilted up, eyes closed, wearing a small, peaceful smile. In my thick curls, flowers, fairies, and children dance. It's fanciful, a little haunting, and utterly beautiful. Even with just the outline, the *E* is less vivid, less horrifying. When he's done, it won't be visible at all.

"You're going to win," I rasp, voice thick with emotion.

"Oh, baby girl." He lowers his head and brushes his lips across my collarbone. "I already have."

CHANGE OF SEASON

Leah W. Snow

It is a Saturday in September, and I am standing in the corner next to the television. Except for my collar and an anal plug, I am naked. A Big Ten matchup, Nebraska vs. Ohio State, is playing, which I cannot see and am only partly listening to. My concentration is instead fixed on the ten pennies that I must keep pinned to the wall with my ten fingers or risk punishment. The task focuses my mind to such a degree that I am surprised when the Buckeyes score and my husband shouts, "That's what I'm talking about!" from where he sits on the couch.

I startle at the loud sound and almost lose one of the pennies, but I catch it before it slips too far down the wall. A relief. My fingers are starting to ache, and I am at least glad for that. It distracts me from gloom that has been seeping into me, cell by cell, weighing me down as if the gravity of the earth has my number.

Early that morning at our kitchen table, illuminated by the amber light of autumn streaking through the window, my husband had looked over his coffee cup at me.

"Kitten, you've been far away for weeks. This week especially."

"I know. I'm sorry."

"You're still missing the boys," he stated. He didn't have to ask. We've lived together that long.

I only nodded in return because I couldn't trust myself to speak without tearing up. Again.

The ironic and truly maddening part of my misery was that it had been so unexpected. All summer, I had looked forward to having them both away at college. No longer would I awake to find the kitchen sink—the very one I had cleaned to sparkling at eleven the night before—filled with six cups, two plates, a dessert dish with peanut butter smeared on it, a coffee cup with mold floating at the bottom, and four knives, each with cream cheese plastered to them. With them both out of the house, I would open the refrigerator door and find the leftovers I'd saved for supper the next night. And, best of all, my husband and I would have the house to ourselves for the first time in twenty-one years. We could do whatever we wanted wherever we wanted as often as we wanted without one of them surprising us.

I'd miss the boys, of course, but the perks, I thought, would outweigh any nostalgia.

But I was wrong. As it happened, I was grief-stricken. It wasn't just that they were grown and gone. Watching them become their own men, find their own place in the world, was as much a joy in some ways as bringing them home from the hospital had been. But it was that I was so much older. Sagging. Menopausal. Dried out.

For the first weeks after they'd left, I had kept myself busy. With a vengeance. Working, volunteering, gardening, attending a poetry slam ("You don't even like poetry," I heard my husband say as the door closed behind me), and making near daily trips to the grocery store. Our cabinets were bulging with half-empty boxes and jars of ingredients I'd collected to fill the extra time with cooking.

And that morning as we sat at the table, I hadn't been able to summon the energy to say anything more than "Do you want more coffee?"

My husband put his cup down and reached across the table to take my hand. "I miss them too. But we'll adjust. It hasn't been that long." He squeezed my fingers. "You need a timeout, Kitten. Watch the game with me today."

"But I have so much I need—" I started.

He dropped my hand, looped his index finger through the O-ring on my collar, and tugged, pulling me off balance in the chair. "What did you say?"

I stiffened. It was a rookie mistake, an indication where my mind was these days. Not where it should be. "I'm sorry, Sir, I don't know what I was thinking. Of course I need a timeout." He let go of the collar and cupped his hand on my cheek.

"You're doing too much, Kitten. Ask yourself: is it helping?"

"No, Sir."

"It's only making you miserable, and we're going to fix it. The misery."

"I'm sure you're right, Sir," I said, but in my mind I doubted there was anything to be done.

He turned his attention again to his coffee cup and to his paper. "The game starts at noon. Be downstairs."

Of course, I obeyed. I was sworn to obey him. We'd practiced D/s on the weekends for years, and now with the boys gone, we'd moved to 24/7. And part of me wanted to believe the timeout would help. At least standing still would force me to think deeply about what to do with the rest of my life, now that I was through raising children, finished with the main purpose I'd had for the last twenty-one years. It helped to think of holding pennies to the wall as just a form of meditation.

"Kitten, you still practicing your breathing over there?"

I start again. "Yes, Sir. Thank you for the reminder, Sir." I breathe in again deeply and press the pennies. Still, the gloom is not lifting at all.

"It's the end of the first quarter. You can put the pennies down but keep your hands on the wall."

He stands, and I hear him make that weird elephantine sound he makes when he stretches. "I'm parched. I'm getting a beer. You want something?"

"Water, please, Sir."

"You got it."

He comes up behind me, pulls me to him, and strokes my breasts, then drops one hand to my mound and strokes me there. He nuzzles my neck and my hair, and I snuggle into him. "My Kitten always purrs," he says. He's right. Even after all these years, even at my lowest, he still makes me purr.

He brings me a glass of water with a straw, which he places on a little table at my side. "Take a sip," he says.

This is one of his favorite games. He brings me water when I'm in timeout but doesn't give me permission to use my hands. Instead I must bend from the waist and sip from the straw, which forces my ass back into his waiting hands. He squeezes. "I fucking love when you do that," he says.

He sits himself back down on the sofa and says, "Kitten, bend over. I want to see the sparkle."

"Yes, Sir." I thrust my ass out.

The sparkle he wants to see is the "jewel" at the end of the butt plug. The man likes a good butt plug, and he's bought me several over the years. But this one, silver with a blue crystal on the handle, is his favorite. He rarely chooses another for me to wear.

"I hope to god I never go blind," he says. "Knowing that ass is in the world without being able to see it would be torture." He's sincere about that. I know my ass is not what it once was, but not a single time in the whole of our marriage has he let on that he sees a difference. Maybe he doesn't. I push my ass out toward him a little more.

"That's what I'm talking about," he says.

I stay in the position, except when he gives me permission to take another sip of water, for most of the second quarter.

"Four minutes to halftime," he says. "Come here."

I stand before him, and he gestures for me to lie facedown across his lap.

"How's my girl?" he says, before removing the plug and stroking my ass.

"Better," I lie and wrap my arms around his leg to hold him close. I shift my head so I can smell his scent, which was the first thing I'd noticed about him. It's not cologne. It's just him, like warm wood. I wriggle my body into his and settle down.

He reaches between my legs, nudges them wider with his fingers, and strokes me. "Wet already," he says, his fingers lazily circling my labia, dipping into the slick tunnel and coming out again. "You've still got it, Kitten."

I sigh. Maybe not what I was, but maybe not completely dried out yet either.

"Tell me what's going on in that head of yours," he says, still feeling his way around.

"Nothing really—" I start. And then stop because the tears are welling up again and I can't speak. I sniffle. In a moment his hand is on my hair, petting me gently.

"I haven't seen you this way since you had postpartum so bad."

"I know," I sniffle again. "I'm sorry. It just won't stop."

"Don't apologize." He moves his finger back to my clit and presses gently. I suck in my breath. "Turn over."

I roll over, still on his lap, and he starts caressing my breasts, rolling my nipples between his still-slick fingers.

"It's not good for you to be in your head so much, Kitten." When he pauses, I can feel the breath heave out of his chest as if he has resigned himself. "It's time for the belt. Past time."

My shoulders relax.

"Go get it."

My husband spanks me regularly but always with his hand. I love the feel of his hand on my ass, the sound of the slaps. It makes me wet to hear his breathing grow ragged because I'm bent over his lap, to feel him harden underneath me. He loves watching the redness spread across my cheeks. He even likes leaving the occasional bruise, his secret mark on me. But he doesn't like the welts a belt leaves. There are times, however, and he watches for them, when I need it. When I need external pain to overshadow the pain in my head, a gloom that comes from somewhere I don't understand. I like the belt because there's nothing to understand. It's sharp and immediate, elemental. And if I can stand that pain, if I can prevail over it, well, then I can manage anything.

So with a peacefulness I have not felt since the boys left, I bring my husband the belt—thick and wide and black—and kneel before him. "Thank you, Sir."

"Over the back of the couch."

I lay myself over the couch as he commands. "Spread your legs."

I comply.

"Don't count. Don't thank me," he says. "Just concentrate and take what you want from it. We'll start with five minutes and then see where you are."

"Thank you, Sir."

He lays the cold leather across my ass so I can feel where the first strike will land.

And then he begins, lightly, as is his way.

The leather laps around my cheeks, around my thighs. And then he strikes me sharply up into my vulva, which sends an exquisite flash of pain through my groin and up into my chest. For an instant, a pinpoint within my brain swirls. Part of me wants to let go, howl out. But I'm afraid. What if I start howling and never stop? I pant to hold it in.

My husband stops. "Don't clench," he says. "It's just me. I'm right here."

I lay my head down and take a deep breath.

He starts again, harder this time. I try to relax and give myself over to the pain.

Before I've succeeded, he says, "It's been five minutes, Kitten."

"More. Harder," I gasp.

The next stroke cracks across the tender point where my thighs meet my ass. I moan. The pinpoint in my brain is growing, roiling. My head is spinning, almost like with vertigo. I can hold out. I've held out this long. I can hold it in forever. But do I want to? Is it worth trying to hold onto? Then he strikes me so hard that I rise up off the back of the couch. I cry out, and with it the pressure that has been building in my head bursts. I collapse into sobs, melt into the cushions.

By the end of ten minutes, my ass burns so much I am sure my husband can see heat ripples. I straighten. The hair around my face is sodden and the back of the couch is slick with tears, but the only pain I feel now is the residual sting of the belt, a pain I can manage. The darkness has lifted.

"Talk to me, Kitten." He strokes my back and gently cups my ass. "Better?"

I am silent for a moment, just breathing, relishing the burn, reveling in the touch of the man who still loves me and my menopausal ass. And always will.

"So much better," I say and smile at him. "So much better. Thank you, Sir."

He gathers me onto his lap and kisses my neck. "You go pamper yourself this afternoon. Soak in the tub, and I'll take you out to eat tonight. Then we'll come back home . . . and eat some more." He grins wickedly at me when I look up.

I shake my head and lean back into him. "It's not the end, is it?" I ask him. "Just a new season."

"Brand new." He kisses me. "Brand new and even better than the last."

COOLING OFF

Brit Ingram

The wildfires had been raging for a month. More than two hundred thousand hectares gone already, lost in white-hot flames. Nothing more than embers were left in some areas. This year was looking worse than the last. The entire region was shrouded in banks of smoke, the inductive nature of the topography keeping it trapped in the valleys. The smoke was also drifting south. You could see it from space.

There was some talk of rain in the forecast, but so far there had been nothing. Plus rain often meant lightning, which meant more fires.

About twenty-five firefighters were stationed in this remote town in the backwoods, along with support staff, social services, and a few hundred townspeople. Police were around as well, to enforce evacuation orders and keep the peace.

I wasn't there as a firefighter. I was in emergency ops, so I helped coordinate response to the fires—sourcing supplies, liaising with the press, and coordinating volunteers.

Being there was an adventure at first, but the days were hard.

Ten hours each shift for me this week and no days off yet, although relief was expected in a day or two. It was emotionally draining work. And did I mention how hot it was? Upward of forty degrees Celsius and dry as tinder. The stress and the sweat and the smoke clung to every inch of me. At least that's what it felt like when I signed out of ops and headed toward camp. My hair, tucked away in a ponytail under a ball cap for most of the day, felt dirty as I pulled it free. When I took off my clothes after my shift, I could see a line of grit where the airborne particulate mixed with sweat. It got everywhere. I scrubbed at it with my thumb, knowing that only a long, hot, sudsy shower would make me feel clean again.

I knew I had it easier than the firefighters. Probably easier than the social services volunteers too. I was basically admin staff. And I was surrounded by dozens of hardworking, tough talking, calendar-worthy men.

My friends back home had warned me that firefighters were trouble, so I had expected to fend off all kinds of approaches. But the entire time I had been here—almost two weeks now—there hadn't been even a hint of bad behavior. No innuendos, no jokes, no come-ons . . . I wondered if I should be offended.

No doubt the chief had spread the word—I was hands-off. Considering I was the youngest member of ops, and one of only a handful of women, he was trying to look out for me.

I appreciated the sentiment, but I wouldn't have minded some masculine company. The days were long; I got a little lonely in the evenings. I had a boyfriend back home, but cell service at the camp was patchy and it wasn't like I could have a quiet moment with him on the satellite phone with so many other people around.

Yes, some big, manly hands would be appreciated tonight. Someone to help work the kinks out of my tired muscles.

But there were no helping hands in sight as I made my way to my temporary home.

Home was actually an old hunting resort, made up of a clutch of cabins between the highway and the lake. It was nothing fancy. I shared a one-room cabin with one of the female firefighters, but she worked a totally different shift so I rarely saw her. Today, she was on a flyover with the chief to scope out the perimeter of the fire, so I had the place to myself.

More importantly, I had the outdoor shower to myself.

I had passed some of my coworkers as I walked through the complex, but for the most part the camp was deserted. Everyone was either in their cabins or down at the little restaurant that served as the mess hall/lounge. I approached the outdoor shower with intense anticipation. My little bag of toiletries dangled from my arm, and a nice thick towel hung over my shoulder. I needed a little bit of luxury in the midst of all the smoke and the men and the "roughing it." The early evening was still hot and the air was hazy with smoke. A cool shower would be perfect.

The shower was tucked in behind a utility shed, away from the cabins and the lounge. It was roomy and clean. The original builders must have designed it to capture the best of the scenery because the back was totally open. There was a shower curtain you could pull shut for privacy, but I liked to keep it open. You could shower and get one of the best views in town—the glacier lake, blue-black and still, ringed with trees. The setting sun was lighting up the top of the mountain on the other side of the lake, and I stopped to take in the sight. It was breathtaking.

I stepped into my oasis, shaking my hair free of the ponytail holder. I ran a damp cloth over my arms and up my neck, letting the cool fabric refresh me. Then I stripped, laying my clothes on the little bench off to the side.

I turned the shower on and stepped into the stream of water, letting it caress my body. It felt heavenly.

If I couldn't get one of the firefighters to give me a hand, I could at least have this.

I added soap to my shower puff and started to scrub away at the grit and grime of the day, starting at my neck and working down to my ankles. It felt wonderful to be clean. I was looking forward to nestling in my cot—which wasn't that uncomfortable, considering it was a single—and getting a full eight hours of sleep.

I thought about my boyfriend, Tim, who lived in the southern interior of the province in a small mountain town. It was still early evening. He would just be getting home from work, probably relaxing in the living room or maybe out on a long bike ride. He had big, strong hands, a muscular frame, and a five o'clock shadow that always rubbed me the right way.

After more than two weeks, it was hard being away. Home was a four-hour drive and a bumpy helicopter ride away. I would have to jump him as soon as I got back. Just the idea of being in his arms made my nipples harden. I soaped up my breasts, wishing I was with him.

I couldn't ignore the fact that some of the firefighters were attractive. Okay, I'll admit it—they were hot. Strong, virile, confident, easygoing. Always saving the day, or helping cats and damsels in distress. Their smell, even after a long day, was manly and intoxicating. Their casual banter in the mess hall kept everyone's spirits up. But the way they treated me with the utmost of respect and deference was frustrating. I wanted to be one of the guys. Or one of the girls they took back to their cabins on days off.

A girl could get into a lot of trouble with this crew.

The other night, I was hanging out in the lounge with a few of the guys. It was a subdued night; everyone was tired. The chief was doing paperwork, and some guys were watching TV. I was reading in the corner. Two firefighters—a man and a woman—

were playing chess near the back of the room. I had a great view of their game, and more. I watched them exchange secret glances as he put his hand on her thigh under the table, stroking higher and higher. Her face stayed impassive, but she reached down and pulled his hand farther up, right between her legs. They seemed to stay focused on the game, but before long, she stood up and said she was calling it a night. He didn't wait five minutes longer before doing the same.

My eyes followed him as he not-so-casually exited the lounge—and I met the eyes of another firefighter, who had watched the whole thing too. The chief's nephew, Caleb. Just a little younger than me, and fresh to the site. Handsome as hell. He gazed at me, as if waiting to see my reaction to the little scene.

I flushed and tried to return to my book. When I looked up a moment later, Caleb was still watching me.

Yes, a girl could get into a lot of trouble. Maybe I wanted a little trouble.

The shower was blissfully refreshing. I let myself get lost in the feeling of the water dancing on my skin for a few moments. I hoped it would cool my flame a bit. Tonight, I was literally aching to feel a man's hands stroke my tits, or have him explore my slick pussy with his fingers and use his tongue where his fingers had been. My thoughts turned to Caleb, and I closed my eyes, imagining him being the one to give me what I needed. It made me breathe a little faster. I couldn't resist giving my breasts a hard squeeze with both hands.

I could never cheat on my boyfriend. Not even if it was with Caleb or any other firefighter with a no-strings-attached approach to flings on the job. But that didn't stop me from wondering what sex would be like with him.

My nipples hardened under my hands as I imagined Caleb taking each little nub in his mouth. Would he be gentle and teasing with them? Or would he suck with greed, nibbling the pink peaks and washing my flesh with a voracious tongue? I pinched them lightly, then a little harder, savoring my body's response.

The shower had a great perk—a removable massaging showerhead that I could use to get at every part of my body. Very therapeutic when used on a stiff neck, but I had another application in mind. I changed the setting to an intense pressure and aimed the spray on each of my nipples, letting the water drum onto my skin. I moaned slightly at the feeling. Caleb's mouth would be just as intense. We wouldn't have time to be gentle and exploring. It would be hard, fast, and powerful.

I propped a leg up on the wooden bench and pushed one finger, then another, inside my hot pussy, letting my mind dwell on that thought a bit longer. Caleb's hands still on my breasts. Caleb kissing my belly as he knelt in front of me, dipping his tongue into the very center of my lust. Caleb putting both hands on my ass so he could push his tongue in deeper.

I aimed the shower spray lower, enjoying the feeling of the water massaging my clit while I continued to finger myself. When I had to lean back against the wall to support myself, the cold siding of the shower stall was another sensation for me to enjoy.

My legs were trembling as I plunged my fingers inside, heat starting to radiate through my belly. I pulled my fingers out and lifted them to my mouth, tasting myself. Clean and still a little musky.

But as much as I longed to let the showerhead finish the job, I knew better than to waste water. It was wildfire season, and it was frivolous and stupid to take water away from firefighting efforts. I sighed as I replaced the showerhead and quickly rinsed the conditioner out of my hair.

My precious shower time was short, but I had needed it. I wished I had more time to myself, to continue what I had started with the showerhead. Dinner was only about a half hour away; I could hear voices and laughter over near the cabins. Everyone was probably hanging out in the lounge, joking and bragging after a day in the field. I loved having this time away from them all, indulging in some much-needed and private self-care with no one the wiser. If my roommate was still out in the field, I would have a few minutes of privacy to play with my vibrator before dinner.

I toweled off, and then reached for the body lotion stashed in my kit. This I could take my time with. I could have this one final moment to myself before returning to the guys. One delicious moment to feel like a woman.

I happened to glance out toward the lake as I turned to pick up my towel. There was a picnic table tucked under a stand of birch trees about fifty feet away, a nice private spot overlooking the lake, perfect for a quiet moment.

And there was Caleb. Staring right at me.

I gasped, grabbing my towel for cover. What the hell was he doing there? How long had he been sitting there? From where he sat, he had a clear and unobstructed view right into the shower stall.

The knowledge that anyone taking a walk by the lake might see me had been at the back of my mind, but I hadn't thought it was likely to happen. That was why I left the shower curtain open.

Had Caleb been watching while I played with myself? I felt a flush race over my skin and clutched the towel closer to my chest.

Caleb was seated casually, his back against the table, his elbows propped up behind him. He was watching me intently, but he didn't seem to be in any rush to turn away. He was waiting to see what I would do next.

I hadn't moved since I met his eyes. If it had been anybody else—like the chief or another firefighter—I would have yelled at them to get away and yanked the shower curtain closed in a hurry. I would have laughed off my embarrassment, like one of the crew.

But this was Caleb. The man I had just spent a few delightful minutes fantasizing about. I didn't feel embarrassment. Instead, Caleb's gaze triggered an alertness in my body. I felt a new kind of pleasure from being watched.

Perhaps he sensed my physical need. Maybe he had the same need for a connection. For a release.

Without really thinking about it, I slowly lowered the towel, keeping my eyes on Caleb's. I then turned away, bending slightly to place the towel over the bench. I could practically feel Caleb's eyes running over the curves of my body. I stretched my arms languidly above my head, running my fingers through my wet hair. A thrill ran over my skin, a tingle of awareness.

If he was going to watch, I might as well put some effort into it.

I perched myself on the towel so my butt was at the edge of the bench, and picked up my body lotion. Pumping a generous amount into my hands, I started applying it at my ankles and worked my way up my legs. My knees were together at the start, but as I reached the tops of my thighs, I parted my legs slightly. Just enough to give Caleb a little peek.

I moved on from my lower body and massaged the lotion onto my arms and my shoulders. It smelled like lavender and felt like heaven as I rubbed it into my skin. I pumped some more into my hands and looked up at Caleb as I rubbed it onto my breasts. He had leaned forward and was resting his elbows on his knees as he watched, as if he was trying to get a better look.

He seemed to understand that I was inviting him to watch me luxuriate in a few private moments but he had to do it at a distance.

This was pure decadence. I closed my eyes and let my head fall back.

I had never let anyone watch me play with myself before. Not even Tim. He was no slouch in the sex department, trust me. He was adventurous and giving and always put my pleasure first. But he would much rather be involved in the action than sit back and watch. Caleb, on the other hand, seemed perfectly happy to enjoy whatever I had to share.

So I opened my legs a little wider and ran my hands along my inner thighs. A slight breeze licked at my skin, giving me goosebumps despite the warmth.

With one finger, and the lightest of pressure, I stroked my clit. I wasn't in any hurry. My body was already primed though, and even that slight sensation made me moan. Is this what Caleb wanted to see? Did he walk by the shower by accident, totally innocent? Or did he follow me from my cabin? Did he plan to catch me in a private moment? Whatever his intention, it only turned me on more.

I began to make slow circles on my clit, with more pressure. With my free hand, I pinched first one nipple, then the other, feeling my body start to respond more strongly. My hips began to undulate against the bench.

I propped one foot up on the bench so I could have better access to my pussy. One hand was busy with my clit, so I reached around the back of my thigh to dip two fingers inside my wetness. I looked up and met Caleb's eyes. I hadn't noticed the exact moment he'd unzipped his own jeans, but I could see the outline of his cock as he stroked it. I smiled at him, letting him know I enjoyed the view.

That moment between us felt surprisingly intimate. Knowing that he was watching me and enjoying what I was giving him gave me a thrill, a sense of power. My pussy began to tighten around my fingers, my creamy liquid dripping down to my knuckles.

That tantalizing heat was building up again, along with that tension in my lower belly. But I needed something to take me over the edge. My fingers weren't enough. Caleb's cock looked like it would satisfy the urge I was feeling. The urge—no, the need—to have something big and hard to fill me up, to have something pound deep into me while I rubbed my clit.

I thought longingly of my vibrator, which I had left in my suitcase back in the cabin. But then my eyes fell on my hairbrush, which was peeking out of my toiletry kit. It had a smooth, round wooden handle that flared out at the bottom, about the width of a broomstick. It wasn't the thick cock I craved, but that handle would do in a pinch.

Caleb sat up a bit straighter when he saw me grab the hairbrush. His dick was fully out of his jeans now, and he was pumping his hand faster around his shaft.

I circled the handle of the hairbrush around the entrance to my pussy, feeling the sleek, polished wood as I teased my already plump and wet lips. But the anticipation was too much, my need too strong. I eased the handle in as far as it would go. My pussy tightened around the intrusion with a sensation that made me moan. My head dropped back and I had to pause for a breath.

All of my senses felt heightened in that moment. A trickle of sweat made its way between my shoulder blades. The scent of my musk mixed intoxicatingly with the smell of smoke and pine needles. I opened my eyes to catch the last of the afternoon sun cresting the mountain with orange and pink. Amazingly, a mass of gray clouds had crept up, and a breeze brought the promise of rain.

Slowly, I pulled the brush handle away from the grip of my pussy, almost all the way out, before pushing it in deeply again.

Another pause, another deep shuddering breath.

Caleb was mimicking my pace, taking a pause every time I did. I kept up that slow, leisurely motion, pulling the brush handle out and easing it back in, while using my other hand to keep the pressure on my clit.

The voices back at camp were getting louder and more animated. The dinner bell would be ringing soon. I hoped that no one would walk by the shower and interrupt this moment—but part of me didn't care.

I picked up the pace with the brush, building up to a fast in-and-out, angling it upward slightly so I could hit that one sensitive spot. Again and again, harder and deeper. My hand moved faster and faster on my clit. I kept my eyes on Caleb as he pumped his cock. His mouth was open, and I could see that he was breathing as quickly as I was.

I sensed Caleb's need—and my own couldn't be held off anymore.

My orgasm radiated out across my body, delivering embers of pleasure that made me quiver. My hips bucked in response to waves of heat that swelled and retreated, again and again, finally merging into one powerful crest. All the build-up and tension of the past few days, all the heat and stress and loneliness—it all erupted and vanished in an instant.

It was all I could do to keep my eyes open. But I had to—I wanted to see Caleb as he reached his release. I had to know that it was my pleasure that triggered his own.

It must have been my gasp that sent him over the edge. I heard his grunt in response as his hand stilled and his come spurted to the ground in front of him. I kept the brush handle inside me, the pulsing of my pussy keeping time with Caleb's orgasm, until the waves subsided and I was spent.

After a few moments, Caleb stood and zipped up his jeans, watching me with a smile before heading back toward the cabins. I wondered who he had left behind. A girlfriend back home? A wife? Would we have an interlude like this again? I hoped he had found some relief, however brief.

I lay back on the bench, letting my breath slow and my muscles relax. The wind had kicked up, finally bringing a relief from the heat. I closed my eyes, listening to the evening birdsong and the chatter from the cabins. The crew was gathering near the mess hall, ready to relax after a long, hot day cutting firebreaks and beating back the flames. Tomorrow would be more of the same.

But for me, for tonight, with Caleb, I had my moment of release.

A cheer echoed from camp; I wondered what was happening. Then a drop of rain splashed onto my skin, followed by another, and another.

SPRING FLING

Kyra Valentine

It is a Wednesday morning in late May, and the new green leaves of the trees stir in the warm breeze. The chill of early spring has finally faded away. When Jennie opens the Subaru's sunroof to let the sunshine pour in, the sky above is blue and cloudless. She should be at work, hunched over her laptop with only a window view of this perfect day. Instead, she is flying down the highway, her palms sweaty with nervous anticipation.

When he called late last night, his voice so low on the phone she could barely hear him, he'd said only, "Take the day off tomorrow. We're meeting at 11:30 for lunch."

"What if she doesn't come?" Jennie had whispered back.

"What if she does?" he'd teased, knowing both her secret desire and her anxiety so well.

This morning, he'd texted her the name of the restaurant as she bathed and readied her body. For him. *For them,* she thought, her stomach doing a nervous flip.

She'd taken extra care to ensure her skin was smooth and soft, shaving everywhere and using a sweet vanilla body lotion. Dark denim mini skirt, crisp, white cotton V-neck blouse, sandals with four-inch heels. She'd chosen pale pink lace panties and a matching bra, her hope for a hedonistic afternoon making an outfit of sweet innocence feel like a delicious paradox.

The drive takes her longer than the hour she anticipated, and she arrives at the restaurant a few minutes late, breathless and pink-cheeked. At the door, she feels her phone buzz. She checks it to find a message from him: "I'll be a few minutes late. Charm her."

She smiles, but her palms are still damp and her heart races. He is an extrovert, a skilled conversationalist and storyteller who can make anyone laugh, relax, and open up. This would be so much easier with him by her side. Her phone buzzes again: "You've got this. I'll be there soon." She takes a deep breath and opens the door to the restaurant.

The hostess greets Jennie as she enters and then leads her up a spiral staircase of wrought iron, decorated with leaves and vines. The rooftop deck is filled with flowers overflowing from pots of red clay, with a handful of small, glass-topped tables under crisp white umbrellas. At the far end, a woman sits alone in the shade of the umbrella, watching Jennie as she approaches. She is smiling. She stands and gives Jennie a warm hug.

"I'm Meghan," she says, her voice low and sensual, every bit as sweet as her smile, and Jennie finds herself relaxing despite the surrealism of it all.

"I'm Jennie. It's so good to meet you," she says, taking in the bright colors of Meghan's long silk skirt, her flowing purple blouse, the dark curls of her hair against her pale cheek. Meghan is taller than she, and where Jennie is petite and angular, Meghan has round hips and full breasts. Jennie notices she has a delicate splash of freckles across her cheeks and nose, and beautiful hazel eyes.

They sit, and it isn't nearly as awkward as Jennie fears. They have the rooftop deck to themselves. Meghan orders a glass of wine and Jennie asks the server for a cosmopolitan.

They talk—about the beautiful weather, the delicious drinks, the pleasure of meeting for a sexy lunch date on a Wednesday.

They don't talk about the reason for their lunch, though it hangs in the warm air between them, a naughty, unspoken secret.

The conversation reveals Meghan to possess both an irreverent wit and a keen sense of observation. They chat easily, but Jennie is still relieved when she sees Ewan's tall figure appear at the edge of the rooftop deck, shading his eyes from the sun with his hand. Ewan's blue shirt is the color of his eyes, and she can see that he must have gotten his sandy-colored hair cut for the occasion. He is at the table before they can stand to greet him, leaning down to kiss first Jennie and then Meghan on the cheek. His hand rests briefly on Jennie's shoulder; that quick touch is enough for her to feel his pent-up energy. She shivers as the thrill travels down to her toes.

Jennie and Ewan rarely meet in such public places, for he is her secret, and she is his. Both married, they enjoy the freedom of technical permission from their spouses, granted with the understanding that their trysts must not ripple through other parts of their lives, disturbing either social standing or professional reputations. It's an arrangement that suits Jennie and Ewan both; in fact, they rather like that despite modern sensibilities, an open marriage still remains a touch scandalous, a dirty secret that hasn't quite earned respectability or traded transgression for the dullness of convention.

Here, in the bright sunshine of the open restaurant, their transgression is magnified; Jennie knows the very posture of their bodies in this public place exposes the forbidden craving they have for each other more plainly than any spoken confession. She can feel Meghan watching them both, their secret exposed, her verdict unrendered. A few days earlier, they had told Meghan the truth—that they were married to others, and that inviting anyone else to share their bed pushed the boundaries of their agreement to keep their liaison in the shadows—while crossing their fingers that she would not flinch. She had replied only that she was open-minded.

Now, as he takes his seat at the table, Ewan is in his element, his charm and intensity on full display. "You're both a drink ahead of me," he teases. He orders a bottle of wine for them to share. They order sandwiches. As he pours the wine he proposes that they play truth or dare, his smile full of mischief; Jennie and Meghan quickly agree.

He leans over to whisper to Meghan. "Isn't she beautiful?" he says, nodding toward Jennie. "Have you been thinking about kissing her?"

Meghan looks at Jennie, a smile playing on her lips. "Naturally," she says.

"Maybe I should tell you what it's like," he replies. "Just to help you imagine." He takes Meghan's wrist and slowly strokes the inside with his thumb.

"When you kiss her, her whole body relaxes into you. She becomes so sweetly . . . compliant," he says, his voice soft, his thumb pressing just a bit. A tiny sound escapes Meghan's lips. Jennie flushes, feeling Meghan's eyes on her.

"Truth or dare, Ewan?" Meghan says to him, playfully reminding him of the game, her eyes still on Jennie.

"I'll save the dares until we've had more of the wine," he laughs. "Truth."

"Which of the two of you first proposed this?"

"Well, lunch was my idea . . ." he replies.

"Not lunch," says Meghan, her voice sultry. "You know what I'm asking."

"Jennie then," he says. "Don't let her sweet innocence fool you. Even now, she can barely contain herself. She's soaking wet, I guarantee it. She cannot wait to please us both. She's very good at it." Jennie meets his gaze and smiles.

"We'll see," says Meghan teasingly. "Your turn."

"Truth or dare?" Ewan says to Jennie, his eyes meeting hers as the server brings their food and pretends not to listen. Jennie's reply is almost inaudible. "Dare, please, sir," she says, a small smile playing on her lips.

"I'd like Meghan's panties in my pocket," he says briskly. "Now."

Meghan's eyes widen, but she shifts her body so that her posture is more open and her body easily accessible. She nods ever so slightly at Jennie. The server has left the table, though his reluctance to descend the stairs suggests he has overheard. Ewan had deliberately not lowered his voice in making his demand.

Jennie hesitates.

"I said now."

The server casts a sidelong glance their way as he finally descends the spiral staircase, but then he is gone. With the litheness of a kitten, Jennie is on her knees, sliding her hands up Meghan's smooth, white legs beneath her skirt. She feels a bit of satisfaction as Ewan clears his throat, knowing that he does so when he struggles to maintain his composure. She tugs Meghan's panties from her hips, then leans forward and kisses Meghan's inner thigh, tasting her sweetness. Meghan inhales sharply and shoots Ewan a look, still holding her breath. He only smiles at her. Jennie can feel the heat of Meghan's body in the warm fabric, scarlet red with lace. Slipping them down Meghan's legs and over her ballet flats, Jennie holds them out to Ewan.

"My pocket," he says smoothly, and as Jennie leans in to tuck the panties away, he kisses her lips lightly. "Good girl," he whispers. "Now it's your turn."

"Truth or dare?" Jennie asks impishly, and Meghan takes a long moment to reply.

"Truth," she says at last.

Jennie considers for a moment, and then asks with genuine curiosity, "Have your partners been mostly men or mostly women?"

"Women," replies Meghan promptly, her hazel eyes sparkling with amusement. "I haven't been with a man in eight years."

"Well, at least there isn't recent history for me to compete with," Ewan says with a grin.

They have emptied the first bottle of wine, so he orders another. The game gives way to his usual tendency to ask endless questions, which Jennie gently blunts as needed, knowing his curiosity is matched only by his disregard for boundaries. Remarkably, Meghan does not find his questions intrusive or uncomfortable. In fact, she is intrigued, drawn in by the chemistry between Jennie and Ewan.

She had expected from them the feverish but superficial energy of a newly consummated love affair, the kind that blooms between two people who are chasing the thrill of novelty that masquerades as love. Instead, Ewan and Jennie are remarkably in sync, so at ease with each other that they wordlessly trade plates halfway through the meal because he notices her wistfully eyeing his meal. Though they are sitting across from one another, not quite close enough to easily touch, the deep affection between them is obvious. Meghan realizes with pleasure that she has stumbled into a circumstance more sublime that she anticipated.

Ewan pours the last of the wine into their glasses and leans back. Their chatter has slowed into lazy, ambling conversation, the sun warm on their backs. They trade funny stories, exploiting every opportunity for sexual innuendo. Jennie's quiet sweetness turns sly as Ewan becomes bolder; she clearly knows just how to tease him.

"Well, ladies," Ewan says at last. "I have had such a good time." He drains his wineglass and looks at them both earnestly. "I think there are three choices now."

"Tell us," says Meghan. Her cheeks are flushed from the wine and the flirting.

"Number one," he replies, "we finish up, pay the bill, and go on our way, having enjoyed a really nice meal with excellent company."

He's silent a moment before continuing. "Number two, we order dessert, enjoy each other's company a bit longer, pay the bill, maybe kiss goodbye, and go on our way, similarly satisfied."

Again he pauses.

"And number three?" asks Jennie playfully, knowing he's waiting to be prompted.

"Number three, Meghan takes us home with her."

The beat of silence that follows is short, but feels long to Jennie. Ewan's blue eyes study Jennie, who is watching Meghan and holding her breath nervously.

Meghan flashes a smile at them both. "Door number three, of course," she says, as if there were never any question. Ewan catches Jennie's eye and cannot hide his astonishment; for all his boldness, he was unsure of their chances. They have never quite been able to make this happen before. Jennie can read it in his face: oh, my god, we did it. He is quick to pay the bill.

At the top of the iron stairs, he waits for Meghan to get a few steps ahead, and then places a hand on Jennie's lower back.

"Do you want this?" he whispers to her.

"Yes," she replies, squeezing his hand. "This is perfect."

Outside on the sidewalk, Meghan tells them she lives only two blocks away. So they walk, the wine flowing in their veins, the afternoon sunshine on their faces. Three days of rain have made the air smell of earth, and the spring colors shimmer in the sunlight. They are giggly and flirty, and when Ewan runs his fingers slowly down Meghan's spine as they walk, Jennie starts imagining: Ewan pushing Meghan's thighs apart with the weight of his body, their mouths hungry and roaming. Meghan's salty wetness on Jennie's fingertips, on her lips, on her tongue.

She remembers the smoothness of Meghan's skin under her shaking hands when she slid her panties off.

Meghan leads them to a small townhouse at the end of a row, unlocks the door, and invites them in. The foyer is small and shadowy; there is a white cat sitting in the doorframe to the next room, flicking its tail and watching them warily.

As the door closes behind them, Ewan gently pulls Meghan close and kisses her deeply, his hands sliding to her ass as she sighs with relief. She meets his hunger with her own, her hands roaming his chest, one arm sliding behind his neck. She presses her full body against his, hard, and he gasps. Jennie is standing close, hardly daring to breathe as she watches them, their kiss so achingly beautiful. Ewan slips an arm around Jennie's waist, his lips still tasting Meghan.

Meghan breaks the silence: "Doesn't she know when to get on her knees?" she says to him.

He smiles wickedly. "Just tell her."

Meghan kisses him again, slow and deep, and then says with a note of sternness, "On your knees, my sweet."

When Jennie kneels beside them, Meghan turns her body a bit to give her room. His mouth still on hers, Ewan pulls Meghan's skirt up slowly. Jennie kisses Meghan's inner thigh, slowly working her way up her body. Meghan lets out a soft moan. Her skin is slick beneath Jennie's lips; Ewan still carries her panties in his pocket. Ewan reaches down to stroke Jennie's hair as she tastes Meghan, close to her swollen pussy but not quite there. Softly, still kissing, Jennie traces the edge of Meghan's pink pussy lips with one finger. Meghan shudders at her touch. She and Ewan are still kissing as if they will consume each other, pausing only to catch their breath, though Jennie can tell that her light touch is distracting Meghan from him. Her finger slick with Meghan's wetness, Jennie slowly slides it inside her, just a little at a time. She revels in the electric, trembling heat of Meghan's body, stroking her until she squirms with pleasure.

"Oh, my god. We need to go upstairs," insists Meghan breathlessly.

Ewan releases Meghan's skirt and Jennie stands. For a moment, the three of them survey each other's disheveled clothing and hair, and giggle. Then Meghan takes their hands and pulls them both upstairs.

To the left of the top of the stairway, there is a set of double doors from the hallway, which Meghan slides open to reveal a large, airy bedroom full of the afternoon sunshine. The walls are the color of beach sand. The floor is bamboo, with a white jute rug. Japanese art hangs on the walls. The only furniture in the room is a queen-sized bed, neatly made, with white sheets and a thin blue blanket. The spare, clean lines of the room seem to throw their flushed skin and barely controlled desire into sharp relief. Meghan is frantically unbuttoning Ewan's shirt while he strips off his jeans. He murmurs to her, just loudly enough for Jennie to hear, "I want Jennie to undress you for me."

Ewan reclines on the bed, alone, and nods at Jennie. She has stepped out of her heels but is otherwise fully dressed. Ewan notices the way the sunlight catches her deep red hair, a rainbow of colors in every strand. Her movements are so familiar to him, his lover of almost a decade. Her white blouse hugs her small breasts, and he imagines their softness in his hands, the way she moves against him when he slides a thumb over her hardened nipples, how she utters his name like she is summoning some kind of dark magic from him and from the perfect union of their bodies.

In that brief moment in Meghan's bedroom, he studies the graceful curve of Jennie's neck, the feel and taste of her skin flooding his mind, the memory of the familiar earthy scent of her hair making his cock stir.

Jennie lifts Meghan's purple top over her head, then unbuttons the single button that secures her skirt at her waist. Rather than letting it fall to Meghan's feet, Jennie kneels and lowers the skirt, which Meghan steps neatly out of. Jennie stands and moves behind Meghan, where she shyly unclasps her bra and removes it, slipping the straps over Meghan's arms.

"You may touch her," Ewan says to Jennie, for he can read Jennie's desire in her every movement. Meghan turns around to face her. Slowly, Jennie draws her fingers across Meghan's breasts, ever so lightly circling her nipples with her fingertips. Meghan reaches to caress her cheek, and then kisses her mouth, Jennie's fingers still shyly exploring her body. Ewan is watching them, transfixed, barely breathing.

But it is Jennie Meghan wishes to tantalize. "Shall we make her watch?" she asks Ewan carelessly, casting a glance at him and pulling away from Jennie.

Ewan searches Jennie's expression for a moment. "Would you like that, pet?" he asks her, though he has already heard the quickening of her breath and knows exactly what she craves.

"Yes, sir. Very much."

"As you wish," Ewan replies, and extends his hand to Meghan, who joins him on the bed.

Meghan stretches out beside him, on her back with her head resting on his arm, and relaxes into his kisses. His free hand slowly works its way down her body as they kiss, stroking her cheek, sliding to her neck, caressing her breast. She bends her knees and parts her thighs for him, arching her back and inviting him in. But he is slow, teasing her body first, twisting her nipple between his strong fingers until she gasps, and then sliding down to pull it into his mouth. Jennie is mesmerized, watching them. Meghan tips her head back, the whiteness of her throat exposed. Ewan's hands and mouth are everywhere but where Meghan so clearly needs them. Jennie's own cunt aches at the sight of Meghan's swollen pussy lips, slick with her desire.

Meghan whimpers and shifts her body, practically begging him though she speaks no words, but still he resists, again simply running his hands slowly over the curves of her torso, tasting her skin, gently grazing her with his teeth. His cock is hard and pressed against her side so that she can feel how much he wants to be inside her. He returns his mouth to hers and, in that same moment, slides two fingers just barely into the wet, open folds of her cunt, moving them while she writhes in his arms. He then withdraws his fingers and gives her clit a quick stroke, taunting her with the lightest touch.

Meghan lifts her hips in frustration. "Ewan," she says, her voice thick with desire. "Ewan, please. Please."

At last he gives in, his own need making the wait too hard to bear. He pushes two fingers deep inside her again, his thumb brushing across her clit. She squirms and cries out, moving against him.

"Not yet," he says to her. "Not yet." He is kissing her, inhaling the scent of her skin.

"We need to taste you," he says softly. His fingers pump inside her with a steady rhythm.

Meghan's eyes are closed and she gasps with every thrust of his hand.

Jennie is watching them, still as a statue, trying to etch every moment into her memory.

Seeing him like this, both his desire and his restraint on full display, is the most sensual thing she has ever seen. She wants them both beyond expression.

"Jennie," Ewan says, "undress now. Bra and panties only." He slows his rhythm and Meghan again moves in frustration. Jennie pulls off the denim skirt and white top, but leaves on her pink lace bra and panties, the latter of which she can feel are soaked through. He nods at her approvingly, and she crawls onto the bed beside him, taking his place beside Meghan. Jennie kisses her mouth, her neck, the perfect crevice at the base of her throat. Ewan moves farther down Meghan's body, pushing her thighs apart. He parts her pussy lips gently with his fingers and inhales her, making her wait. At last, he leans in and kisses her cunt, a slow, deep kiss.

"Oh, god, please, please," Meghan begs before Jennie quiets her with kisses. Jennie knows exactly how talented Ewan is with his tongue. He teases Meghan with a few soft strokes along her swollen lips, even penetrates her for just a moment with his tongue. But he knows what she really wants. Slowly at first, and then a bit faster, he flicks his tongue over her clit, and her string of words and pleas dissolves into sighs and other unintelligible noises.

When he can see that Meghan is nearing the edge, he whispers to Jennie, "My love, my love. She is divine. Come and taste." Jennie has never performed oral sex on a woman before, never felt an aching clit swell beneath her tongue, never tasted the tangy sweetness of a woman brought to orgasm. She moves to Ewan's side and watches for a moment, absorbing the rhythm of his movements. She can imagine exactly how every stroke feels to Meghan. At last, Ewan withdraws, presses his lips to Jennie's, and moves aside for her.

For a moment, Jennie cannot recreate the rhythm. Then she feels the pulse of Meghan's body under her mouth and lets that guide her. Meghan's cunt is slicker and sweeter than she had expected, and figuring out the pattern that makes her gasp and squirm is easy. Knowing how she herself likes it, Jennie makes the vibrations of her tongue as soft as she can manage.

"Oh, sweet Jesus yes just like that," Meghan cries, her voice letting Jennie know Meghan is barely present with them. She has entered that transcendent space where the rational mind is fully conquered by the wild unleashing of carnal pleasure. In that place, there exists only the physical body as it yields to the relentless waves of fierce sensation that overwhelm all coherent thought.

Ewan has positioned Meghan so that her head is at the edge of the bed, and after those words leave her lips, he slides his cock into her open mouth. Meghan has one hand wrapped in Jennie's red hair; she raises the other to touch Ewan as he fucks her mouth. The sight of Jennie's head between Meghan's open, shaking thighs is almost too much for him. He cannot hold back, though he wants Meghan to peak first.

And she does, letting out a long, piercing cry and clenching Jennie's hair tightly in her fist. Her body shudders beneath him, and then he orgasms too, pulling his cock from her mouth so that he leaves a hot ribbon of come across Meghan's body, from her lower lip to her hips. It glistens across her breasts. Jennie watches, relishing the sight on Meghan's pale skin. She crawls over Meghan on hands and knees, leaning down to gently kiss her and lick the cream from her lower lip.

"May I?" she whispers, and Meghan murmurs, "Yes, please."

Slowly, Jennie works her way down Meghan's body, using her tongue to clean every trace of him. She loves that she can taste them both at once. Ewan watches for a moment but is too fatigued to remain standing. Instead, he climbs onto the bed next to Meghan and closes his eyes, his fingers laced through Jennie's. Meghan shivers beneath Jennie, suddenly aware of the coolness of the room. Wordlessly, Jennie lowers her body to Meghan's, her head just under Meghan's chin, their legs a comfortable tangle of limbs. For a few long moments, they all three sleep.

Meghan stirs first. The light has shifted in the room; it is late afternoon, and the brightness of the sunshine has softened, suffusing the room in golden light. She gently slides out from under Jennie. Naked, she walks to the window and peers outside. She stands there for a long, pensive moment. Ewan awakens while she is standing there, but her back is to them and she does not see him. Gently, Ewan strokes Jennie's cheek.

"Your turn," he whispers to her.

Jennie slides beneath him, and he kisses her long and deep, as if they are long-separated lovers reunited at last. He extends his arms, pushing himself up so that he can look into her green eyes. She arches her back and opens her legs wordlessly, and then he is inside her, never breaking his gaze. He fucks her with a steady rhythm, one that she clearly knows, and she wraps her legs around him and holds him tight, her lips parted, her eyes on his.

The golden light is slowly fading around them as Meghan, who has turned, watches in reverent silence.

She has never watched anyone make love, not in real life but also not on TV or in movies.

Actors are always conscious of the camera, of their roles, of the audience, and porn is all about exaggerated performance, the titillation of the show.

There is no show here. Jennie and Ewan appear to have forgotten they are not alone.

Their complete surrender to one another, to the deep connectedness that suffuses their every interaction, is laid bare. They say no words. The room is almost silent. His breathing quickens to match hers as he thrusts deep inside her again and again, their eyes locked.

All at once, he tears a raw, piercing cry from her throat as she finally closes her eyes and lifts her chin, her back arched, her knees shaking, her fists clenched, tears flowing down her cheeks. The sound is at once wrenching and beautiful. Meghan can see that Jennie has held nothing back from him. She has never seen anything so acutely private become so utterly exposed.

Jennie's sudden climax breaks over him like a storm, its energy heightening his own. He thrusts deep inside her, his body shaking, his hand now wrapped in her hair. Abruptly, his gaze shifts, his eyes meeting Meghan's as he comes hard, her name on his lips: "Meghan, oh, Meghan," he groans, and he smiles that wicked smile. Meghan cannot look away; they are three again. Then Jennie giggles, and the spell is broken.

As the sun sinks low in the sky, they kiss goodbye on the doorstep. Meghan kisses Ewan with warm enthusiasm, her arms thrown around his neck. She kisses Jennie more tenderly, lingering on her lips for a long moment. Then Meghan watches them walk away, into the spring night. The season feels thick with promise.

THE EIGHTH WONDER OF THE WORLD

Mia Hopkins

Sophie races to the front of the boat and leans over the rail. My sister pulls her back.

"Be careful," Jen says.

"But the water is only five feet deep," Sophie says, repeating what she learned from the Internet this morning at breakfast. "They color it blue to hide the tracks and ugly stuff."

"You know you can drown in two inches of water, right?" Jen says.

I take a seat next to the captain's wheel. Is it real?

Sophie leans over the rail again. Jen grabs hold of her T-shirt and catches her new pink baseball cap before it falls into the dark water.

"Hey, cut it out, Soph," I say in a quiet but stern voice.

She sits down and I give her a nod. For the millionth time, I wonder where she gets this daredevil streak. Her dad is a square. When I was her age, I would've rather curled up and died than broken any rules.

As the boat fills up, I settle into my seat. The July heat makes my mind wander. This last year has been hard, particularly on Sophie. I suppose I wanted to celebrate the end of the divorce with something out of the ordinary. Before I could second-guess the expense, I booked a room in the largest and most expensive hotel the park had to offer, bought three-day passes, and took a long weekend off at work. I even got my fun-loving sister to accompany us. Sophie adores her.

I'm not trying to bribe my daughter, am I?

I look at Sophie's glittery pink princess hat and the remains of a six-dollar churro dusted over the front of her T-shirt.

Okay, maybe I *am* trying to bribe her.

The skipper—cast member? Ride operator?—starts the engine, and the boat chugs loudly over the water.

He speaks into a handset with one hand and controls the steering wheel with the other. He's young, maybe a college student on summer break. The passengers on the boat giggle and groan at his puns. His easy smile is natural in this most unnatural of situations. He delivers his spiel confidently as we take an imaginary voyage over the rivers of the world and pass animatronic animals splashing in the rapids.

"Take a look at these elephants up here," Skip says. "You may think that's water coming out of their trunks. But it's snot."

Drowsy, I study Skip. He's dressed in a khaki shirt, shorts, and a wide-brimmed hat. His name tag says Tyler. I can smell him from where I sit, laundry detergent and sunscreen, a touch of sweat. He's tall and lean, with a sharp jaw and the hint of a Boston accent. I wonder what's brought him here, to this place and this moment.

"Watch out for these rocks up here," he says. "They're limestone, but a lot of people take them for granite."

Between puns, he catches me staring at him.

Shit.

I try to look away, but his eyes hook mine like barbs. They're an uncertain shade of green, like oxidized pennies. I think of fountains, wishing wells, and secret desires that won't come true if you say them aloud.

He holds my gaze for half a second and like a dart to my gut, I feel it.

Heat.

Desire.

Or do I?

It's been a long, long time. Years.

The spark catches inside me. But after everything that's happened, how can I trust myself to recognize what's real and what's imaginary?

I blink and he looks away at last, leaving me blazing in my seat. I glance at my sister, but she's preoccupied snapping photos of Sophie. I look at the other passengers. No one seems to have noticed the exchange between me and the skipper.

Like some shy schoolgirl, I look at my hands folded in my lap. My fingers tingle. All of me tingles. I should be embarrassed but I can't deny how good it feels to flirt with a stranger, if this can even be called flirting.

The boat passes under an overhang. A big waterfall crashes down, enclosing us like a curtain. A fine mist of chemical-laden water bathes our faces. The spray smells like chlorine and grass clippings, strangely familiar, as if my body is dredging up sensory memories I'd buried a long time ago.

Skip announces, "And here it is, folks, the eighth wonder of the world. The backside of water." He looks straight at me. "Isn't it beautiful?"

And then—he winks.

Winks?

What the fuck?

I stifle my smile and look away, trying to be cool.

As if to bring me back to reality, Sophie chooses this moment to get up and sit in my lap. "It's hot," she murmurs.

Automatically, I put my dumb flirtation on ice and go into mommy mode. I give Sophie a drink from my water bottle, take off her cap, and comb her damp hair through my fingers.

Skip continues, selling each corny joke. The boat follows its preordained route, and I second-guess myself. How many times does he do this a day? How many lonely older women does he wink at every shift?

"And now we come to the most dangerous part of our journey, folks," Skip says, "the return to civilization."

As he pulls the boat up to the dock, the passengers give him a polite smattering of applause. Sophie jumps out of my lap, takes Jen's hand, and together they hop off the boat. I stand up. As I wait for the other passengers to leave, I see Skip's back as he chats with another employee. He takes off his hat. His dirty blond hair is reddish in the bright sun.

Sophie's pink ball cap is in my hand. As I look at it, I realize something.

I don't want to return to civilization.

When no one is looking, I drop the hat on the bench. I get off the boat without looking Skip's way again.

I'm almost to the exit when I hear someone's footsteps behind me.

"Excuse me."

I turn around.

Skip is tall. I tip my head back. His hat's still off, so I get a better look at him. Up close, pale freckles dapple the bridge of his nose. When he smiles, faint creases appear around the corners of his eyes and I realize he's not as young as I thought. He's definitely not as young as the energy he sends out.

He holds up Sophie's hat. "I think you dropped this," he says.

I resist the urge to snatch the cap up, thank him quickly, and scurry away like a mouse. Visitors bottleneck around us on their way to the next amusement. But I force myself to stand still. I look at him for a moment as he holds the hat frozen in the air between us.

No, I think. *No, I'm not ready to return to civilization at all.*

"What time do you get off?" I say softly. My voice sounds like someone else's voice. I am shaking all over and trying desperately not to show it.

Skip's copper eyes widen a millimeter. His manufactured smile freezes in place. He looks dumbstruck for a moment. I didn't think a man who slings puns all day long could ever be dumbstruck.

After a beat, his voice drops. "Four thirty."

In this moment I am no more real to myself than a rhino with a robotic head or a fiberglass hippo rising out a five-foot-deep facsimile of the Mekong River. "Meet me," I say.

His eyes narrow. "What's your name?"

I don't answer. "Room 1338."

He doesn't say yes, but he says, "The big hotel?"

I've got a chance. I take the hat.

"Yes," I say. "The big one."

I've read stories of park visitors propositioning pirates or princes. But me? No. That's not my style. The river boat skipper—that's my style.

Still trembling, I follow Sophie and Jen as they visit the third gift shop of the day. My heart is beating hard, circulating adrenaline, blood, and what I imagine to be dark water, filling my veins from some deep well inside me.

So.

This is what it feels like to step outside of yourself.

Correction: this is what it feels like to *choose* to step outside of yourself.

The divorce was my ex's idea. He chose this new life for all of us. At first I was angry, and then I was ashamed, and then I felt guilty about letting my marriage fail.

Over time, I came to understand our relationship was never destined to succeed, no matter what I did or didn't do. Soon, stepping outside of my comfort zone became easier. I could go back to full-time work. I could find a place to live where Sophie could stay during her weeks with me. I could go to the Social Security office and change my name back. When I signed a receipt for our first breakfast here, my old signature spilled easily out of the tip of the pen. Muscle memory had stored it in my hand, safe and sound.

I could imagine the life that I wanted. I could will it into reality.

Only one thing has remained elusive for me.

My ex-husband was my first. My only.

Over the years, I learned how to take care of myself. But there were things I longed for in my marriage I couldn't ask for, things I thought I'd never be free to pursue. These yearnings I placed firmly in the world of fantasy—until today.

"Jen," I say.

My sister looks up from a display of magnets.

"I have a really bad headache. Would it be all right if I returned to the hotel while you and Sophie enjoy the rest of the day here?"

"Of course," my sister says, and once again I feel grateful for her open heart.

Sophie hugs me from behind. "Can I watch the parade?"

"If your Auntie Jenny says yes."

"Can I watch the fireworks?"

I told her no last night—too far past her bedtime. But today I say, "Sure, if your Auntie Jenny says yes."

Satisfied, Sophie cheers and skips away to the back of the store.

Jen studies my face. She knows me better than anyone, but she doesn't know this side of me. Not even *I* know this side of me.

"Are you okay?" she asks. "You look kind of pale."

I wince as if in pain. "I think the heat got to me during the last ride. I'm going to lie down, take a nap, maybe get some room service. Text me when you're on your way back, okay?"

"Okay." She gives me a half-hug. "Feel better."

After a quick pit stop at the drugstore, I return to the hotel room. Housekeeping has made up both queen-size beds with fresh sheets. I shower, shave, and dry my hair. I put on just enough makeup to feel right. I slip on one of the thick, white bathrobes hanging in the closet and stash all of Sophie's toys and books in the closet. Last, I hang the Do Not Disturb sign outside on the doorknob and secure the deadbolt.

I check the time. Four o'clock.

I throw the curtains wide open and lie down on the bed closest to the big windows.

One deep breath, in and out.

Who am I? Who does this kind of thing?

I close my eyes and imagine this person into being.

A woman, not old, not young.

Newly single.

Her own name, her own time.

Her own body to do with as she wishes.

Her own mind.

Gently, I place one hand flat against my chest above the *V* of the bathrobe. With my thumb and forefinger, I trace the hard wings of my collarbones and press the tip of my middle finger into the hollow at the base of my throat. I imagine Skip on top of me, solid, strong. I imagine him kissing me there, the hot tip of his tongue tasting the empty space.

"Beautiful," he whispers.

* * *

There's a quiet knock at the door.

I open my eyes, stand up, and retie the robe. On tiptoes, I look out of the peephole. Skip stands in the hallway. I take a moment to study him. He's wearing jeans, worn-out boots, and an olive green T-shirt. The strap of a backpack is slung over his shoulder. His hair is dented where the band of his work hat pressed into it. He's looking down at the doorknob with a faint smile, as if he knows I'm staring at him and wants to give me privacy to survey him as I please.

The confidence I had ten seconds ago falters.

What am I doing?

Who do I think I am?

He knocks again. His voice is muffled through the thick wood. "Hello?"

He calls me back. I open the door.

He steps inside without a word. The door automatically locks when I close it, but I close the deadbolt to be sure. He puts his backpack down on the couch, stretches, and smiles. "Hey."

"Hey," I echo back to him. I sound overly casual, as if we aren't complete strangers. "I didn't think you'd come."

He shrugs and looks around, still smiling. "This is nice. I've never been in one of the rooms."

"We're enjoying it."

"You're staying here with your family?" he asks.

"They're still at the park," I say. "They'll be gone until closing."

He nods and looks at the big lemon tree etched into the wall above the beds. I notice he doesn't ask if I have a husband or boyfriend.

"Do you want a drink?" I say.

"Sure."

In the bathroom I've stashed a six-pack in some ice. I pull one out and pop it open for him. Such a simple move, but my mind goes back to the hundreds of times I did this for my ex. I blink and push that thought away. Annoyed, I take a deep drink of the open beer, pull a new can out, and toss it to Skip where he sits on one of the beds. He opens it himself and takes a swig, his eyes on me the entire time. When he speaks, the punster is completely gone. His deep, soft voice is devoid of antics.

"So, what do you like?"

I've never been asked this question. I put my beer down on the nightstand next to the strip of condoms from the drugstore. My hand shakes. My voice shakes. My body pulls taut at the prospect of relief. "I like to be told what to do."

His strange eyes glitter at me. A man who pleases others for a living would probably enjoy the inverse behind closed doors. "Do you like it rough?"

My voice was not welcome in my marriage. It definitely was not welcome in the bedroom. But my voice is welcome here, and I use it. "Not at first. But rough at the end . . . that's good."

"I think I understand." He takes another drink. "Should we begin?"

I nod.

"Okay," he says. "Go stand by the windows."

My feet pad softly on the thick carpet. I turn to face him again.

"Take off the robe," he says.

I untie the robe and drop it. Cool air kisses my skin. Skip stares at me, beer in one hand, his other hand rubbing the thick bulge in his jeans. We're behind one-way glass, but I feel like my nakedness is on display for everyone below.

In silence, he continues to stare, face relaxed, lips parted slightly. His gaze travels from my face to my breasts, my stomach, my thighs, and my legs.

The body parts I'm most insecure about begin to tingle, activating my self-doubt. Stretch marks corrugate the skin around my navel. My C-section scar has faded, but it is far from invisible. I grit my teeth, trying to stay in the moment and not let my insecurities get the better of me. I watch Skip as he rubs himself with the heel of his hand, slow, lazy downward strokes along his fly and down the inside of his thigh. What hides there is thick and getting thicker—a perfect distraction from my anxieties.

He tips his head toward one of the armchairs. "Pull it to the window. Put the robe on it. Then sit down."

Watching me, he takes a long drink as I follow his instructions.

"Open your legs," he says.

My heart beating hard, I lean back on my hands. Eyes on him, I slowly spread my knees apart. Cool air touches the insides of my thighs.

"Wider," Skip grunts.

I arch my back, pushing my pussy to the edge of the seat where he can see everything. Skip hisses when the lips of my pussy open. The hot gaze of his strange green eyes makes my skin feel raw, like I've been sunburned in a place that never sees sunlight.

He takes another drink. I watch his Adam's apple move, and I find myself wanting to take a bite.

"Touch yourself," he says.

I have never, ever done this in front of another person. Just the thought makes me so wet, a trickle of warmth runs down the inside of my thigh, showing Skip how much I'm enjoying this.

We both watch as I run the pad of my middle finger gently up one outer lip of my cunt and down the other, barely missing my aching, swollen clit. I repeat the movement. I take my time. I have always liked touching myself, but to be able to do it without shame, in front of a witness, heightens the familiar sensations and makes them new. I go a little faster. I use two fingers. The muscles in my pussy and my ass tighten with anticipation.

In a daze, I barely register that Skip has gotten up from the bed. I look up at him. He stands in front of me and strokes my face with one hand. Resting his other hand lightly on my neck, he then closes his fingers slowly until he is holding my throat. His grip is neither hard nor gentle. When he kisses me, my body jerks with pent-up delight. His lips are cold and beer-bitter, but his tongue is hot and sweet. When its tip goes into my mouth, I press two fingers inside me and squeeze them with my pussy. An orgasm trembles deep in my core, but I hold it in place.

Skip kisses me hard before he leans back. He takes my hand and pulls it slowly away from my body. Looking into my eyes, he gets to his knees. With a smooth movement, he cradles my hips in his hands, pushes me back against the glass, and puts his mouth to my pussy.

"Yes," I whimper.

Greedy, he goes right for my neglected clit. As he licks it without mercy, I grip his shoulders. The overload of sensations makes me clench hard, barely reining in my growing orgasm. He feels me fighting him and doubles down, pressing one thick finger inside me. He finds my spot with ease and begins to stroke it with the same rhythm as his tongue. Chased from two directions, I can't hold back. Skip shakes my climax loose and I come—I come all over his face with a deep, shameless moan. He doesn't stop until the final waves have passed and I've collapsed into the chair, trying to catch my breath.

"Good?" he says with a smile, even though he knows damn well it was.

Still on his knees, he takes my tits in his hands and gives each of my tender nipples a sweet little suck. "You're fucking delicious, by the way," he murmurs.

I watch as he stands up. His big, sexy hands unbuckle his belt and lower his fly. He slides down his jeans just enough to take out his cock. It's hard as hell, almost purple, and mesmerizing in the way that thick, straight dicks are mesmerizing. There, jutting out from his lean hips, his cock looks too big for his body, as if there was a mix-up while they were putting him together and somewhere out there is a giant muscleman walking around with a skinny dick.

Skip says something.

"What?" I ask.

"I said, what are you thinking about?" He smirks.

Instead of answering his question, I smile and open wide. When I take him deep, he closes his eyes and throws his head back with a groan. My mouth waters as I go down on him. Everything about him is new, and as if he can sense my eagerness, he reaches down and runs his fingers through my hair. My scalp ripples with pleasure. I take him even deeper.

"I bet you have a wild imagination," he whispers.

I don't say anything because I can't.

"I bet the inside of your head is a fucking playground."

He has no idea.

I strum the underside of his dick with the smooth edge of my tongue. I alternate between soft and hard pressure and feel him thickening as his desire grows fiercer. He grabs the roots of my hair and pulls gently. In response, I swallow, squeezing him hard.

"Ah, god. Wait, wait," he says.

Eyes on fire, he grabs my arms and pulls me upright. With his big hands, he grabs my tits and presses his cock between them. He thrusts as I look down, mesmerized by the sight of his slick head fucking my cleavage. I cover his hands with mine and push down, increasing the pressure. He groans and thrusts again, thumbing my nipples, now slick with spit and precome. "I've always wanted to try this," he says, breathless.

"Is it what you'd hoped?"

"It's better."

He smiles and happily fucks my tits until his own imagination is satisfied. When he lets go, he grabs my wrists and pulls me to standing. His grip hard, he flings me to the nearest bed, grabs my hips, and bends me over the high mattress. He kicks my legs wide apart, and I hear the clinking buckle of his belt. Hazy, I realize he's still dressed. With my bare feet, I stand on the tips of his leather boots and arch my back, offering him everything. He groans again and runs his thick fingers up and down my wet pussy. The sound makes me even wetter.

"Ready?" he asks.

"Yes."

He gets the condom on. With one hand, he holds me down. With the other, he guides the hot head of his cock inside me. I close my eyes and hold my breath. Slowly—achingly slowly—he thrusts, then pulls out. He does this three times, going deeper each time. The pain I feel at first swirls, shifts, and transforms itself until I can't exactly call it pain. When he is inside me as far as he can go, he freezes. We each take a deep breath. Now my pain is nothing but hunger—insatiable, unimaginable hunger.

"So good," he whispers.

All of his caution is gone. His grip on my hips is like steel. When he fucks me, my teeth rattle and click with the force of his thrusts. I grip the duvet in my fists and try to get my balance. From this position, I can't see him, but I can hear him. He's panting, his belt buckle bangs against the bed frame, and his worn jeans rustle softly against the backs of my legs. I can smell his sweat and the ghost of his sunscreen. The taste of his cock still lingers in my mouth—bitter, salty, mildly sweet.

He leans forward and flexes his whole body, adjusting his angle until he finds my sweet spot. Like a heat-seeking missile, he hits it, again and again. When I open my eyes, I'm standing in the machinery of my own imagination. Thunderheads gather, threaded with lightning. Dark water threatens to flood the room, drowning us both.

My fantasies welcome him in, and I realize two things: first, I've momentarily forgotten his name, and second, his name doesn't matter. His is the first of many dicks. This is the first of many joyful fucks, here in my new life where there's no point in separating what is real from what is fantasy.

Another loud moan escapes my chest, and before I realize it, I'm coming a second time, hard and wet and messy. The contractions are powerful, steady as a drumbeat. Soon, my orgasm cascades into his. His whole body goes rigid and his grip gets even tighter. His arms give out. His weight crushes me against the bed, and with each desperate thrust I hear him whispering in my ear, not my name, but the word *Fuck* again and again. As I drift down from my climax into a dark river of sleep, I remember I still haven't told him my name.

Hours pass. Somewhere between sleep and waking, we fuck twice more. Naked at last, he lies above me in bed, the length of his strange body touching the length of mine. He's younger than me. Indefatigable, his cock is as eager to go the third time as it was the first.

And me?

I enjoy him, my treat for stepping out of my comfort zone, for diving into the dark water and letting myself get mangled on the tracks.

My phone buzzes. Groggy, I check the text. It's Jen, on her way back with Sophie. I turn on the lamp and look around. The room is pristine. No beer cans, no condom wrappers. Definitely no Skip. Good. I throw on a tank top and pajama pants and close the drapes.

Jen walks in with Sophie passed out in her arms. We change the exhausted little girl into her nightgown and tuck her into the clean bed.

"Have you had dinner?" Jen whispers.

"No."

"Me neither."

We order a pizza and have it delivered. Giggling like teenagers, we sit on the floor of the hallway to eat it. Jen tells me about her adventures with Sophie as we scarf down our slices.

We're a bit sad to be returning home tomorrow. But how can I tell my sister, how can I tell anyone, there's no going back from this?

"I'm so glad you planned this trip," Jen says.

"I think Sophie enjoyed herself," I reply.

My sister looks at me sideways. "But how about you? Did you enjoy it?"

I think about pennies in wishing wells and the profound ache between my legs. I take another hot bite of pizza and burn my tongue. But I don't care—it tastes too good to stop now.

"Yes," I say, my mouth full. "I did."

CALYX

Margot Pierce

My hand shakes as I slide the keycard into the reader. The light flashes red, the door doesn't unlock. I curse under my breath as I wipe the card on my skirt and try again, eager to get inside before anyone sees me. Nobody local stays at this hotel unless they're having an affair, and people in this town already find me suspicious enough as it is. I teach art at the high school, and if I'm seen here, everyone's going to think I'm trying to steal somebody's husband—and that's the *best*-case scenario. The worst-case scenario? Someone discovers the truth.

When the door finally unlocks, I breathe a sigh of relief and hurry inside, shutting it quickly behind me. The hotel room is large and tastefully done in a neutral, modern aesthetic, which is pretty on-brand for Cleardale, a bland suburb dotted with business parks and gated communities. I always thought I'd move back to the city after I got divorced, but here I am, firmly in my forties, and I still haven't left.

I set my bag on the dresser and open it up to dig out the box of condoms I picked up on the way. I have no idea what will happen tonight, but I like to be prepared.

"Matteo is *such* a great guy," Violet had said, tucking a swathe of white-blonde hair behind her ear. "I'd take him in a heartbeat, but he's looking for someone closer to his age. And I know you don't do this sort of thing, Claire, but seriously—you'd be perfect for him."

Violet and I met last year at a summer arts program. We hit it off as friends immediately, even though she's much younger. She reminds me of how I used to be—bold, adventurous, unconcerned by what other people think. You wouldn't know it, but I was fearless like that once. I used to shave my head and line my eyes with kohl like war paint, and to make my art, I never thought twice about breaking the law. Then I got married and everything changed. That's why I accepted Violet's proposal. I wanted to go back to how I used to be, if only for one night.

"But isn't it illegal?" I asked, lowering my voice so nobody would hear. "If I get caught—"

Violet clucked her tongue with disapproval. "Vice laws are just vestiges of a puritanical system designed to criminalize sexual agency and control women's bodies, but if you're really worried about it, just let him pay for the hotel room and see how it goes. It's only illegal if he pays you for the service."

I step into the bathroom to check my hair in the mirror. I'm wearing my sexiest pair of strappy heels and a halter dress that ties behind my neck to show off my shapely arms. My hair is as wild as it always is, a controlled chaos of curls that flare from my scalp in tight ringlets—chestnut brown with streaks of gold. My makeup is minimal with just a touch of color to complement my freckled olive skin and green eyes. All that's left from my aggressive street-punk years is my nose ring, a diamond so small you can only see it when it catches the light.

A loud knock jolts my heart into a panic. I smooth out my dress as I hurry to the door and check through the peephole. Standing in the hall is a man in a dark suit, his back turned as he wipes his palms on the front of his jacket. I open the door and quickly usher him inside before anyone sees us. Then, once we're both safe from prying eyes, I turn.

He's more attractive than I expected him to be. Tall, with thick, dark hair and even darker almond-shaped eyes. High cheekbones, strong jaw. He wears his age well, with just a little gray at the temples and a few charming creases at the corners of his eyes. I take in the full sight of his lean body in a beautifully tailored suit, a nice departure from the golf shirts and khakis I usually see in this town. My mouth is suddenly dry.

"Jesus, you're *gorgeous*," he finally says, rubbing the back of his neck as he stands at a respectful distance. "Violet didn't tell me much. I wasn't sure what to expect."

My cheeks heat at the compliment. "You look pretty great yourself."

"Matteo." He starts to offer his hand, then retracts it. "Is that too formal? Should I kiss you on the cheek?" He offers his hand anyway, and I laugh as I shake it.

"Claire." I release his hand and guide him into the room. "How was the drive up?"

"Not bad. Lots of traffic getting out of the city, but after that the roads were clear."

"Good." I decide to take a seat on the edge of the bed. He removes his suit jacket and loosens his tie as he takes a seat in the armchair across from me.

We sit in silence. I chew on my lip, wondering if I'm supposed to be the one who brings it up. Violet never explained how these things actually work.

I sweep a wild flare of curls from my eyes. "So, Violet mentioned you wanted someone older."

"I did. I do. You're perfect. Ageless."

The corner of my mouth turns up. "I'm forty-three."

He lifts a hand. "Forty-five. And nervous. Obviously."

I suppress a smile as I slide off the bed to search the minibar for a bottle of water. I crack it open and hand it to him before grabbing one for myself. "Have you done anything like this before?"

"A few times in the city." He takes a pull from the bottle and sits back. "But they all seemed so young and, I don't know—the situation's weird enough as it is. Are you sure I can't pay you? I feel like I should be paying you for your time."

"No, it's fine." I take a sip as I return to my seat on the edge of the bed. "I'm not sure I'm ready to cross that line yet."

"Understood." He pulls his tie free from his collar and unfastens the top button. "I'm a lawyer, by the way. Divorced. Nobody would ever guess that I'm . . ." He takes another sip of water and clears his throat. "So, Violet says you're an artist?"

"Used to be." I straighten my posture. "I teach art at the high school."

"Used to be? You gave it up?"

I sigh at the question, reluctant to get into it. "I always thought I'd go back to it, but . . ." I pause, uncomfortable with the reminder of how much I've changed over the years. "Anyway, it's too late now."

"It's never too late, is it?" He sits forward as he begins rolling up his sleeves. "What kind of art?"

"I was a painter. There's still some of my old stuff online. When I was a street artist, I went by the name Calyx."

He looks up. "No shit? You're Calyx?"

My lips part with surprise. It's been twenty years since I've used that name. "You've heard of me?"

"I used to live around the corner from that mural you painted on West Broadway. Didn't you get arrested for vandalism or something?"

I laugh and run a hand through my wild hair. I feel giddy, suddenly flooded with memories of those exhilarating years when I snuck out at night and scaled buildings with a backpack full of paint, my heart pumping with adrenaline. "They dropped the charges. The one they got me for was the billboard—"

He snaps his fingers at me. "At Times Square. You were on the news."

I laugh, my cheeks heating with embarrassment. "I still can't believe I thought I could pull it off."

"See, but that's why you were my hero. I was an uptight law student, and there you were, this mysterious badass sneaking out at night to cover the city with some of the most beautiful murals I'd ever seen. You're the reason I got interested in art."

I raise a skeptical brow. "Really?"

"Dead serious. I started going to galleries because of you. I still make time to go to a museum once a month." He lifts his hand. "Swear to god, I'm not bullshitting you right now."

Our eyes lock and my heart stutters. I lick my lips to speak. "I wish I'd met you back then."

His chest jumps with a laugh. "I wasn't nearly cool enough for you—trust me. I wore polo shirts and khakis and spent all my time in the law library. I fantasized about running into you, though. All the time."

I catch my bottom lip between my teeth, then release it with a smile. "Yeah?"

"I used to fantasize that I'd catch you painting a wall and—" He laughs as he strokes his jaw. "And I'd, um—"

"Blackmail me into performing sexual favors?"

"The opposite, actually. You'd—" He suppresses a smile. "You'd rough me up a little and make me get you off."

A fire ignites beneath my skin. "Where? Like, in an alley?"

He nods slowly. "You'd make me get down on my knees,

and . . ." His cheeks turn red as he stifles a laugh. "I can't believe I'm actually telling you this."

"No, keep going."

He shakes his head and takes another sip of water. When I laugh, he suppresses a smile as he swallows. "It was just a phase."

My smile falls with disappointment. "Oh."

He starts to speak, then stops himself, studying me for a moment before finishing off the bottle.

It's time. He needs me to start the session. That's why he's here, after all. That's why he paid for this room and drove two and a half hours to meet me here in Cleardale. I take a sip of water, then screw the cap and set the bottle aside. I look down at my perfectly polished toenails in my strappy heels. I wasn't sure which color he'd like so I went with a deep, dark red to match my fingernails. When I look up, I notice he's staring at the empty bottle in his hands. I wonder if he needs my permission.

"You can look at them if you want."

He clears his throat and sets the bottle aside, then glances at my knees before looking away. He tries again, this time stealing a glimpse of my calves. The moment his gaze lands at my feet, his breath quickens and he averts his eyes. He grips the armrests, steadying his breath before looking again.

Violet warned me about this part. She calls it "kink paralysis." Some fetishists keep their kinks so deeply buried that when they finally have permission to experience them, it takes them a few minutes to adjust. Which means I need to be patient. And gentle.

"Take your time," I say calmly.

He rubs the back of his neck as he bows his head, then looks up, like he's trying to steal a peek without getting caught.

"Sorry," he murmurs. "It takes me a minute."

"Take your time."

He nods and takes a deep breath, before slowly lifting his gaze.

This time he stares. I cross my legs and watch his eyelids flutter in response. The rush of power sends a titillating thrill down the center of my body.

"Come closer," I say quietly.

Without hesitation, he pushes out of the chair and approaches, unfastening a button on his shirt to reveal a glimpse of dark hair on his chest. When he kneels on the floor in front of me, the sight sends another shiver of excitement through my body. My skin feels hot.

I offer my foot.

He touches it with a shaking hand, lifting his dark eyes to meet mine. "May I?"

"Please."

With great reverence, he unbuckles the tiny strap and gently removes the shoe, placing it to the side. He wipes his palms on his thighs, then gets to work on the other, carefully picking at the strap until the tiny buckle comes loose. Once both of my bare feet dangle over the edge of the bed, he goes still.

"Touch them."

He releases a shaky breath as he lifts a hand to gently caress my instep. I fight the urge to run the ball of my foot over his erection, visibly hard against his thigh, and remind myself to stick to Violet's list of suggestions. I want to do this right.

"Do you know how to give a foot massage?"

"Yes, of course," he says breathlessly. He eagerly takes my left foot and brings it to his chest, working his thumbs into my arch.

I lie back against the bed and close my eyes to focus on enjoying the firm pressure as he works his way to the ball of my foot. According to Violet, this is about as far as I should expect the first session to go. He's a foot fetishist and this is all he needs from me: the freedom to indulge his kink in a safe, nonjudgmental environment. But I want more. I want to stroke his cock while I look into his eyes, and I want to wrestle him to the ground and ride him for my own gratification, and I want to tie him up and own him and use him and tease him until he screams my name.

Matteo isn't the only one who's learned to hide their kinks.

I remember when I told Andrew, my ex-husband. While I lay there unsatisfied after sex, my mind humming with unfulfilled desires, I told him about how, when I was a teenager, I flirted with boys by wrestling them to the ground until they begged for mercy. Andrew laughed, thinking it was just a funny story, so I kept going. I told him about the time in college when I marked a guy with my nails and claimed him as property, and that I still fantasize about tying men up and using them for my gratification. And I said that every once in a while during sex, I wanted to do that to him too.

"Jesus Christ, Claire," he spat, recoiling from my touch. "You hate men."

I didn't. I don't. I tried to explain that it wasn't like that.

"You need to see someone," he said. "That's not normal. There's something wrong with you."

Matteo strokes my calf with a soothing touch and begins massaging my ankle. "What are your limits?"

I open my eyes to look up at the ceiling. "My limits?"

"I'm happy to just massage your feet and legs." He clears his throat. "But I'd love to kiss them."

"Oh." I smile to myself. "Yeah, that's fine."

"And"—he breathes deeply—"worship them."

I'm not sure what he means by that but it sounds nice. "Sure. Go ahead."

After he lifts my foot to rest on his shoulder, I feel a soft kiss on my ankle as he caresses the top of my foot. It's nice. He takes my foot in his hands and kisses the arch as he slowly glides a hand up my calf, his fingertips trailing sparks up the back of my leg. The sensation is erotic, subtle.

"This okay?"

I nod, closing my eyes. "Feels good."

He kisses my big toe, then runs his tongue across the pad before grazing it with his teeth, sending a bolt of pleasure straight to my clit. My eyes flick open as I suck in a breath, startled by how arousing it is.

He stops. "Too far?"

I shake my head. "No, it's good. Keep going."

He goes back to massaging my heel, one hand working my ankle as his tongue licks and swirls around a smaller toe. He sucks gently, then grazes the pad, and I'm hit with another electric zing. My clit pulses, heat building beneath the surface as he moves from one toe to the next, worshipping every sensitive surface with an expert tongue. I had no idea having my toes sucked could be so erotic. When he returns to my big toe, I feel it everywhere. The nape of my neck, my fingertips, my inner thighs. My clit pulses with frustration.

My fingers curl into the skirt of my dress. "Don't stop."

He groans as he moves to the other foot, one hand still firmly massaging the first, and when I feel his teeth, a new rush of sparks races up my inner thighs and explodes deep inside me. A slow, sensual heat builds and throbs in the center of my body.

I need to touch myself. I reach down and gather my skirt in my hands, pulling it up enough to slip my hand into my panties.

"Oh, fuck, Claire."

I lick the tips of my fingers before slipping my fingers beneath the silk to find my swollen clit. When he releases my feet, I jerk my hand away, suddenly panicked that I've screwed up.

"What's wrong?" I ask, my heart racing as I push myself up on my elbows.

He starts to speak, then stops himself as he rubs the back of his neck. "That fantasy I told you about . . . it wasn't just a phase."

My senses sharpen. "Is that what you like? Being controlled?"

He goes quiet but I can see it in his eyes, a plea for me to understand that the answer is yes. He's still kneeling on the floor, the bulge of his erection visible through his trousers. I sit up and touch my toes to his knee, my gaze locked on his as I slowly slide the ball of my foot up his leg. When I brush against his cock, his eyes roll closed.

I stroke him slowly with my foot as I study his reaction, watching as his head tilts back and his fingers curl into his palms in ecstasy. It's the sexiest thing I've ever seen, both the intense vulnerability of his arousal and his body quivering with restraint. When I pull my foot away, his head bows forward with a breathless gasp.

"I like being in control," I say cautiously.

"I could sense it." His voice is a dry rasp.

"But that doesn't mean I hate men."

"I know." He blinks slowly as he lifts his eyes to meet mine. "I want to submit to you. That doesn't mean I'm weak."

I stare at him in wonder. "I know."

"I'm yours, Claire."

I swallow dryly, my pulse racing with a surge of adrenaline. "Then stand up and take off your shirt."

He rises to his feet to tower over me as he unbuttons, shrugging it from his shoulders to reveal a surprisingly athletic torso. Dark hair flecked with silver dusts his chest and trails down the center of his abs.

"Pants, too."

He toes off his shoes and unbuckles his belt, unzipping his fly before pushing his trousers down his hips. Once he kicks them off, he straightens, his athletic body on full display for my hungry gaze. When I notice a large wet spot of precome on his dark gray boxer briefs, my breath catches in my throat.

I slide off the bed and approach him. Without my heels, I'm only eye level with his chest. I inhale the scent of his clean cologne and watch the rise and fall of his shallow breath, then look up at him as I lick my palm.

"Yes," he whispers.

I slip my hand beneath the waistband to wrap my fingers around the hard shaft of his cock. His body tenses as I slowly stroke, precome slicking my grip.

"You want to be mine?" I ask, studying his eyes.

"More than anything," he breathes.

"Did you ever jerk off thinking about Calyx?"

"All the time."

"Did you think about me wrestling you to the ground and sitting on your face?"

"Oh. Fuck." His eyes roll closed as I pick up my pace.

"What did you think about while you jerked off?"

"Being consumed by you, overwhelmed, trampled, smothered, drained, used."

Those words hit me like a drug—I close my eyes and press my forehead to his chest, my arm flexing as I work his cock in my grip. He grunts with restraint, his abs taut, his head bowed, his breath warming my cheek, and I release a shuddering breath at the exquisite erotic tension in his body. My panties are soaked.

"I'll do anything you want," he whispers, his breath coming in rapid gasps.

I squeeze the base of his cock, feeling it pulse in my grip, then release as I step back. "Underwear, too," I say, turning to climb onto the bed. "I want you naked."

He hooks his thumbs into the waistband and pushes them down his hips, his thick, strong cock springing free. I hike up my skirt and tear off my panties, before scooting back on the bed to prop myself up against the throw pillows. "Come here."

He approaches from the foot of the bed and climbs up to kneel between my feet. He immediately brings my foot up to kiss it, lifting his gaze to watch as I pull up my skirt and tease my frustrated clit with my fingers.

"Fuck." His voice rasps with need as he kisses my instep, watching as I sink my fingers inside myself. When he bows to kiss my toes, I run my free foot through his hair. He shudders as he presses his forehead to the bed.

"You want to be mine?"

"Fuck. Yes. So much." He keeps his head down as he slides his hands up my legs.

I gather the hem of my skirt in my hands, lifting it up to my hips. "Then prove it."

He lifts his head, his gaze hooded as he slides up my body and hooks my legs over his strong shoulders. As I run my fingers through his thick hair, I'm transfixed by his dark, expressive eyes, full of intelligence and strength and naked vulnerability. *You're mine,* I think as I admire the flecks of gray at his hairline, the high cheekbones, and straight, dark brows. My body's throbbing with anticipation as he looks up at me, parting my folds with a slow, sensual lick, then closes his lips around my clit.

My head falls back as he teases me with the most sensual suction, the tip of his tongue working perfect magic. The pleasure builds in delicious waves. I think about his fresh-faced twenty-something self in khakis, kneeling in a dirty alley as I grind my pussy against his eager mouth, my skirt hiked around my hips, his fingers digging into the backs of my bare thighs. If only we'd met back then, maybe I wouldn't have married Andrew, or given up my art, or tried to change who I was to fit into a life that was never my size. Then I open my eyes to see this beautiful grown man between my legs, his forehead creased as he focuses on my pleasure, and I think that maybe it doesn't matter. Maybe he's right—maybe I never would have noticed him back then, when I was young and wild and fickle. But now, as a grown woman who's lived and learned, I do.

He reaches for my feet, holding them in his hands as my toes curl and my back arches, my eyes rolling closed with the growing need for release.

"Yes," I rasp, my knees raised, my hips circling and grinding against his eager mouth.

He releases a foot and shifts his position to slip two fingers inside me, curling them upward to coax me to the edge.

"Yes," I gasp, rocking my hips as he draws my clit between his lips and trills his tongue with delicious precision.

He groans, his own hips rocking against the bed, his fingers stroking the upper wall with perfect pressure. I hold my breath as he draws me to the edge of release, my thighs taut, my toes curled, my shoulders lifting from the bed, and then it hits, the pressure shattering in an exquisite, blinding release as I fall back, crying out as I grip his shoulders. My body shudders and shakes as the waves crash and ebb, the orgasm gradually fading to a tingling, frayed whisper.

Breathless, I open my eyes a crack to see him looking up at me with heated adoration as he wipes his mouth with his hand. I lick my lips as the last traces of my orgasm shimmer across the surface of my skin. "Open the nightstand."

He slowly pushes up and reaches across my body to pull the drawer. He goes still for a moment, then grabs a condom and sits back on his heels as he tears it open, his breathing urgent as he rolls the condom down the length of his cock. He positions his body over mine, resting his weight on his forearms. I look up into his dark, soulful eyes and reach down to guide the head of his cock between my slick, swollen folds. He pushes gently to ease the tip inside me, his head bowed, his lips lightly brushing my cheek. I turn my head to kiss him softly as he sinks in an inch, pausing to let me accommodate his thickness.

"I'm yours," he whispers. His dark lashes flutter as he pulls back and pushes again, inching deep enough to make me gasp. I dig my nails into his hips and feel the way I did when I was still racing through the city, claiming bare walls with my art and marking my territory.

"Say it again," I whisper.

"I'm yours."

"That's right." I dig my fingernails hard enough to leave a mark. "You're mine."

His eyes roll closed as he pushes deeper, then slowly open. "Oh, god, Claire. This is—"

"You've always been mine."

"Always." He kisses me deeply as he pushes in. I wrap my legs around his hips and pull him deeper, holding him inside to feel his cock throb. Our lips locked, I roll on top of him and sit back to ride his cock, still wearing my dress, my heart bursting with something deeper and stronger than lust. It's gratitude for the gift of his vulnerability and for the adoration in his eyes and for making me feel like myself again. And as I use his gorgeous cock for my own sexual pleasure, its thickness stretching me to reach places that haven't been touched in years, there's a silent understanding that this is exactly what we both want and need—he needs to be owned and I need to be in control. We fit, filling each other's aches and absences, his cock swelling inside me with each urgent rock of my hips, his hands cupping my heels. When I look down into his dark, beautiful eyes, it's as if I've known him my whole life. He reaches for my hands, and I lace our fingers to show him that I feel it too. I bend forward to pin them beside his head as I drive my hips to take his cock with the raw, primal hunger of twenty frustrating fucking years, because now, finally, my hips have found their home.

"You're fucking mine," I rasp, nipping at his lip with my teeth, the pleasure building to an unstoppable crescendo. Stars light up behind my eyelids and I cry out; he wraps me up in his arms, anchoring me against his body as he thrusts up. With a few powerful strokes, he jerks inside me, grunting into my hair as his cock releases in beating waves. And then, as we pulse and twitch in each other's arms, there's nothing but the sound of our breath.

He strokes my back and kisses my shoulder. I'm euphoric, drunk on pleasure, and light as air. It's as if a huge burden has been lifted from my shoulders.

"So, can I take you to dinner sometime?" He glides his fingertips down my bare arm.

"I'd love that."

"There's a place in the city I want to take you. Maybe we can go to a gallery or something."

The thought makes me smile. "I miss the city."

"The city misses you." He kisses my hand and brings it to his heart. "I think I've been looking for you my whole life, Claire."

I smile, closing my eyes. As I drift in a drowsy haze, it's as if everything Andrew's said to me over the years has suddenly lost its power. I feel like myself again. Free. "I'm glad we finally found each other."

CABINET OF CURIOSITIES

Olivia Waite

The glasshouse at Ruche Abbey was a jewel box and a prism. Sunlight touched the angled windows and shattered, splashing slivers of rainbow everywhere.

Mrs. Phoebe Attleborough held her striped gray skirts behind her and stalked into the artificial jungle, looking for the tiger at its heart.

She'd heard stories of the great house, its lushness and luxury, but she still wasn't prepared for the sheer scale of it all: great sweeps of lawn, gardens botanical and ornamental, ponds for the fish and the waterfowl, woodlands for pheasants and peacocks and hares. Harriet Kenwick, seventh Countess of Moth, famously hoped to collect every species of creature in the world. By all accounts she was off to a grand start, and half the naturalists and explorers in England brought her offerings from their voyages around the globe.

Phoebe stopped for a long moment to stare as one window revealed a water buffalo, ambling happily across the lawn between the glasshouse and the aviary.

The buffalo paused and turned its horned head to stare back.

Phoebe waved a little, so as not to seem rude.

Mollified, the water buffalo returned to its walk, shuffling into a nearby pond and taking great mouthfuls of the weeds along the bank. The ducks complained loudly at being displaced.

Phoebe adventured on, past broad-leaved tropicals and delicate hanging orchids. Finally she found her quarry, beneath the great central arches of iron and glass.

The countess wore black, her gold hair pinned up plainly, sleeves shoved back to the elbow, fingers plunging confidently into the dark loam at the root of a rosebush. Everything around her was roses. English, French, Italian—every variety Phoebe could name, and then some. The scent was thick and sweet, and Phoebe gasped a little for air.

The seventh Countess of Moth looked up at the sound, and smiled.

Phoebe gasped again as that smile pierced her through.

She'd always been painfully susceptible to smiles from Harriet Kenwick. Even now, looking at her, she could see the lovely, laughing Lady Harriet from when they'd first met. She saw the memories since, all the weddings and births and funerals, and could so easily imagine forward into the future, as gold hair became silver and the lady's skin folded itself demurely with old age.

Phoebe ought never to have come.

Too late—the countess was already striding forward, wiping her hands with a handkerchief. "My dear Mrs. Attleborough," she said, holding out her hands. "Welcome to Ruche Abbey."

"Thank you, my lady," Phoebe replied, taking the countess's hands. They were warm and slightly damp from the soil, and they sat so naturally in Phoebe's own.

As Lady Moth leaned in, her lips graced Phoebe's cheek. Her

skin seemed to have absorbed the essence of the roses around her: so soft and so sweetly scented.

Phoebe went dizzy with it. Heat and self-consciousness climbed up her neck like a strangling vine.

The countess was still smiling, which didn't help Phoebe's dizziness any. "My dear Mrs. Attleborough, it has been far too long," Lady Moth said. "There must be something very particular that brings you all the way up from London."

"There is," Phoebe confirmed. She cooled a little at the thought of it. Thoughts of Lawrence could ice over anyone's ardor.

The countess peered at her a moment—the steel of her gaze held Phoebe in place like a pin—and then nodded. "Come," she said. "Let me show you the aviary."

What else could Phoebe say but yes?

Lady Moth's black gown looked starker in the sunlight, a shadow that blotted the emerald of the lawn. Her widowhood was two years old—long enough to have gotten over the loss of an ordinary kind of husband, but not nearly long enough to recover from either the best or the worst. Phoebe knew all about widowhood. She had lost Felix Attleborough five years since; the ache of it was a dear, familiar part of her now, no more easily put aside than her left or right hand.

Lawrence Attleborough, her late husband's brother, was the perpetual thorn in her side. Three days ago he had marched out of his study, brandishing his niece's latest letter and shouting demands that Phoebe make a visit to her friend's estate.

To have one's comfort be dependent upon the goodwill of such a man had begun to chafe long before Phoebe had set aside her widow's weeds.

The countess led Phoebe on a skirting path around the pond (the water buffalo snuffling happily in the shallows) and toward a fantastical cottage with accents of red and gold in the Chinese style. The walls weren't glass, but wire mesh, the better to keep in the clouds of songbirds. Phoebe spotted finches, nightingales, and waxbills among all the brown- and bright-colored species she had no names for. Other birds fluttered in individual cages, their wings bright flashes and their cries piercing.

And there, at a delicate table in the center, a young gentleman bent over his sketchbook. The subject of his drawing sat in a chair across from him: a laughing young woman with chestnut hair and rosy cheeks, a jonquil parrot preening and showing off on her finger.

The young lady lit up even brighter when the two women entered. "Aunt Attleborough!"

"Matilda," Phoebe replied, and accepted her niece's enthusiastic kiss.

Matilda was even more enthusiastic about the young gentleman, whom she introduced as Mr. Alexander Selborne. "He is one of the foremost ornithologists in England," she said glowingly, as Mr. Selborne beamed and blushed in equal measure.

Phoebe, who'd seen how elegantly his pencil had captured the tilt of Matilda's smile as well as the lines of the parrot's plumage, only quirked an eyebrow. "Tell me about your family, Mr. Selborne . . ."

He was a second son, she learned: heir to a comfortable estate on his mother's side. He was intelligent, well-spoken, a little shy—and quite plainly in love with Miss Matilda Attleborough. Who just as plainly returned the sentiment.

In Lawrence's eyes this match was a disaster.

Matilda turned anxious eyes to her uncle's widow. "Are you staying with us long, Aunt Attleborough?"

"Your aunt's plans are not yet fixed," the countess put in smoothly, "though I hope a tour of the grounds will persuade her." She turned back to Phoebe, her smile warm, her eyes sparkling. "Will you walk, madam?"

Phoebe had heard eyes compared to jewels for their brightness. People forgot that diamonds and emeralds and such were stones, hard things with edges that could cut. The countess's eyes at present were two sapphires, glittering above the pearly curves of her cheeks.

They spoke of a battle to come.

"Lead on, Lady Moth," Phoebe replied.

The countess murmured farewell to Matilda and Mr. Selborne, and led Phoebe out of the aviary, away from the house. They walked along the lawn, which sloped up, then more sharply, and terminated in a small hill: Phoebe followed the countess around the base of the hill and found herself in an artificial grotto, cleverly concealed. Three small arches were carved into the earth, their mouths facing the stream and the solemn thickets of the wood beyond. It was a secret place, hidden from the sight of anyone watching from the windows of the great house.

Anything could happen here.

A small bench was placed beneath the central arch. Phoebe took a seat, folded her hands in her lap, and waited.

The countess spun on her heel and raised her chin. Her smile was gone now, but her eyes still glittered. Her blonde hair looked darker here in the shade, like buried gold. "Lawrence Attleborough sent you."

Phoebe nodded. "He did."

"To stop his niece from marrying Mr. Selborne."

Phoebe clutched her hands together. "That's right."

The countess pursed her lips as though she'd bitten a rotten apple. "He sent you because we are old friends, and he thought you might have some influence with me."

"And because it was easier than coming himself," Phoebe went on. The facts were very plain: she listed them plainly. "He is the head of the family and controls both my income and hers. He will cut her off without remorse if she marries against his will, and he will do the same to me if I fail to prevent the match."

The countess's rosebud lip curled more with every word out of Phoebe's mouth. "So you've invited yourself to my home, to interfere in the happiness of my guests. You've come to ensure Miss Attleborough and Mr. Selborne do not marry."

"Ah," Phoebe said, sighing. "You misunderstand. I have come to make absolutely certain that they *do*."

The countess's sapphire eyes went wide.

"I know what it is to live with a husband one loves," Phoebe went on. "And I know what it's like to live beneath Lawrence Attleborough's authority. The difference is not a question of preference: it is a matter of survival." The countess was still staring, eyes even wider, rosebud lips parted in shock. Phoebe wrapped shaking arms around her own waist. "Do you know anything unsavory of Mr. Selborne?"

The countess snapped her mouth shut, seizing on the question like a hawk diving after prey. "No," she said. "He's as kind as he has appeared to you today."

"He has money enough to support Matilda?"

"She will be more than comfortable."

"Will his family treat her well?" Phoebe took another breath. This question was the most vital. "Will they accept her even if her uncle disdains her?"

"I believe so." Lady Moth's eyes flashed. "But if they will not protect her, then I will."

To doubt her was impossible. Phoebe felt the tension melt out of her, leaving only hollow bones behind. She wanted to laugh, or weep with relief.

She wanted to fling her arms around the countess and kiss her.

But it wouldn't be for gratitude, if Phoebe did that.

She slumped on the bench, a moment of weakness, before her spine went straight again. "Thank you," she said. Thankful that her clasped hands hid how they were shaking. "How quickly do you think we can get them wed?"

The countess waved a hand. "Reverend Porcher is coming to dinner tonight," she said. "We can arrange everything with him at very little trouble, if it suits them."

It suited them very well indeed, as it turned out. Matilda's face bore an angel's ecstasy. Mr. Selborne's joy was quieter, almost holy. He sat at her side holding his wineglass like a chalice, as she arranged all the matrimonial details to her pleasure. His eyes met Phoebe's once, and he raised his glass in a silent toast.

Phoebe flushed and dropped her eyes.

She ought to let herself enjoy this evening: it was probably the last comfortable one she was likely to have for some time. Lawrence was bound to be furious, and now his rage had only one possible target. So she threw herself into activity when the company retired to the breakfast room to sort shells after dinner.

One of the countess's collectors had brought her a wealth of marine shell specimens, and it was habitual at Ruche Abbey for guests to lend a hand with the science of sorting out one species from another. All manner of plates, platters, sieves, and serving-ware had been filled with shells and set out wherever they would fit; the salt-sodden taste of them pickled the air and lingered on the back of the tongue. Phoebe assisted the countess's young daughter Catherine, a quiet girl of ten who had her mother's gold hair and an eye for the boldest shapes and colors. The countess herself moved from group to group, offering morsels of knowledge like caramels, her hands shuffling through the array of whelks and snails and mussels and oysters.

Phoebe's dread returned in full force once darkness fell. After hours of restlessly turning from one side of the bed to the other, she gave up the struggle and went down to find something distracting in the library.

Instead, she found the countess in the breakfast room. Lady Moth was certainly a distraction, though: her hair let down in long swoops and waves, her rose silk dressing gown loosely tied at the waist, lace fountains at her elbows, the linen of her bed gown split down the long, pale line of her neck.

Phoebe's mouth went dry. She pulled her eyes away, to the countess's lovely hands.

Lady Moth was sorting shells. Not leisurely, as if it were a round of cards, the way her guests had played it. But methodically, precisely, as if she were assembling the pieces of some great puzzle. Gray beside gray, white against white, the soft clicks of shell against silver rattling like the claws of some great stalking beast.

She turned her head when the light of Phoebe's candle joined hers. "So now there are two restless souls out of bed," she murmured.

Phoebe stepped forward, setting the candle aside. "Are you looking for something in particular?"

"Always." Lady Moth fingered an oyster, and then slipped it into a pile with the others. "All of these are ordinary, already known—I am looking for something new. Something special." One corner of her mouth rose, as her hands plucked a snail shell from the throng. She turned it over, and then rejected it, putting it aside. "I had something special once, and I want to find it again. Or something like it." She shook her head, amusement and resignation mingling in her face.

"I can see one problem with that," Phoebe replied.

The countess cocked her head, challenge lighting her face. "What's that?"

Phoebe moved forward. "You're looking for one thing. One

thing on its own can never be a collection. But look . . ." Her hand dove into the pile of oyster shells, fanning them out. "What's special is when things come together." She arranged the shells to form a rose, just on the verge of blooming, and then added a few spiky whelks in a line like thorns running down the length of a stem. "You could set all of these in the grotto where we spoke today—they'd be beautiful in pattern, catching the light coming off the waves."

Lady Moth's hands fluttered over the shape, coming near but never touching it. She looked up at Phoebe, an admiring light in her eyes. "You may have something there, Mrs. Attleborough." She smiled. "Some of the best ideas come in the middle of a restless night, don't you find?"

Sympathy turned over in Phoebe's breast. She wanted to help, if she could. "What else do you do, when you're restless?"

"I used to fuck William."

Sympathy died, murdered on the spot by the bolt of pure shock that ran through Phoebe. Sizzling heat followed after, rumbling through her like thunder.

"My late husband," Lady Moth went on, almost dreamily, "was everything polite, reserved, and gentle—until his blood was up and his clothes came off. There's not a room, not a surface in this house he considered off-limits, when the appetite was on him. We had one another bent over chairs, spread out on tables, pressed up against the walls."

She touched one finger to the back of the desk in front of her. Phoebe had a sudden vision of Lady Moth there, on her back, skirts flung up, her breasts bare and gilded by candlelight . . .

Phoebe clutched her free hand on the doorframe, feeling the wood bite into the pads of her fingers.

Lady Moth went on: "Since losing him, it feels like I've barely made contact with anything. He died, but I'm the ghost. So I walk the halls at night, unhappy and ravenous. Desperate for someone to make the blood rush through my veins like it used to." She fixed Phoebe with that skewering glance again and took a deliberate step closer. "Do you think there's anyone else around who would do?"

Phoebe must have misheard that. Lust and longing were whispering in her ear.

But Lady Moth stepped forward again, and again. She was an arm's reach away. Her hem whispered against Phoebe's on the bare floor of the threshold. Her eyes flickered down Phoebe's figure, then up again, the hunger in them shining brighter than the moon outside or the candle at Phoebe's hand.

Lady Moth licked her lips, a quick darting flash of her tongue, and Phoebe was lost.

How easy it was to fist her hands in that fall of silk and linen, to make the countess gasp. Phoebe pulled the other woman closer by inches, and watched the flush spread over the countess's neck and collarbone. She wanted to bend her head and trace it with her mouth, learn its temperature, see if her tongue and her breath could make goosebumps rise. Oh, to have Harriet Kenwick shivering beneath her . . .

She looked up. Lady Moth's sapphire eyes were as tender as Phoebe'd ever seen them. The countess topped Phoebe by several inches, yet she didn't lower her head to close the distance between their mouths.

So Phoebe did it for her. Stretched up on her toes, pressing herself against the taller woman's body, slanting her lips against the rose of the countess's mouth. Lady Moth was everything soft and stubborn: her lips parted, yielding to the insistent stroke of Phoebe's tongue, even as her spine stayed straight and braced against the pressure of Phoebe's weight. She'd said she was desperate, and Phoebe could feel it, her body tense and tight as a harp string.

In need of another's hands to make the music.

This was something Phoebe's own desires eagerly seized on. She broke the kiss, settling back on her heels with a thump.

The countess blinked, looking deliciously muddled.

"Your bed?" Phoebe asked. "Or should I lay you out in this room, like one of your treasures?" She cupped the underside of the countess's high breast, almost but not quite brushing her thumb against the nipple just visible beneath the thin cloth.

Lady Moth made a strangled, needy sound in her long throat.

Phoebe's smile was feral with intent. "You spend so much energy observing the world as it's brought to you—but I wonder, has anyone ever properly cataloged you?" Her hand gently tugged at the neckline of Lady Moth's bed gown, which slipped obligingly sideways to bare one breast to Phoebe's hot gaze. It curved with the same perfection as any shell. "Pearl and coral," Phoebe murmured approvingly, and pinched the countess's nipple sharply between two fingertips.

The countess squeaked. The sound arrowed straight to the heat between Phoebe's legs. She dropped her head and sucked that nipple, still pinched, into her mouth.

Lady Moth shuddered from head to heel, twisting against her own clothing, still bunched in Phoebe's other fist. Phoebe let her tongue flick sharply against that delectable peak once—twice. The countess's hands fluttered everywhere: Phoebe's shoulders, then her hair, then gripping her wrist, all while Phoebe held her by a morsel of fragile flesh.

Phoebe wanted those hands on her skin.

But eager as she was, and much as she wished to gratify Lady Moth's neediness, there simply wasn't *room* where they were. Any attempt to fling the countess to the floor or against a wall or onto one of the well-upholstered sofas would send a score of plates or platters crashing down with a noise that would be sure to wake half the house.

Phoebe was too jealous to want the countess's charms displayed for anyone but herself.

She let her mouth move from Lady Moth's breast to the hollow of her neck, where the traces of a hundred roses blent now with the sharpness of salt and sweat. "Come with me," she whispered in one shell-like ear, as gold curls trembled. She took Lady Moth by the hand and together they rescued their candles and crept up the stairs.

Phoebe made straight for her own room, with its tossed-about bed and view of the back garden—but the countess resisted, pulling Phoebe into her own, much grander suite across the hall: sitting room first, with a lavish bedroom beyond. She pulled the curtains wide and let the moonlight flood in. From here the bulk of the estate presented itself for viewing: glasshouse, aviary, lawn, and wood, with the ripples of the pond and the rambling river beyond.

All for the woman who turned away from the window, watching Phoebe, her breath still coming fast and that stubborn look coming back into her eyes. The collector's gleam, Phoebe realized—and it was fixed upon her.

"You said you miss being fucked, my lady," Phoebe said, desire putting the rasp in her voice. "I would dearly love to fuck you. But not to hurt—are there rules you would like to set, for what I can and cannot do to you?"

"Harriet," said Lady Moth.

Phoebe blinked. "Pardon?"

"I wish you would call me Harriet," Lady Moth—*Harriet* went on. Her head tilted to the side consideringly. "I understand it can be thrilling to be fucked on account of one's rank—there's a sort of game to making a countess beg for it, I've heard—but I've always preferred to imagine I could shed the title with the clothing." Her eyes flashed. "I do enjoy being made to beg, though, if you need a suggestion for how to begin."

It could have been a joke, except it wasn't: Phoebe didn't miss the wistful note in the way Harriet's tongue lingered on the word *beg*. But the woman had been holding herself together for so long, it would be difficult for her to let go now.

She needed to be surprised, before she could be pleased.

There was one way to do it: Phoebe slipped at once out of her dressing gown.

Harriet's eyes went wide and her bosom heaved.

Phoebe tugged her shift over her head and tossed it aside. She'd been cold when she first crept out of her restless bed; she was the furthest thing from cold now. Her heart burned like a fallen sun in her chest.

Phoebe was going to do what she'd yearned to do for fully twenty years: she was going to fuck Harriet Kenwick.

Without a stitch of clothing, she strode forward toward Harriet, who smiled eagerly—and with a certain charming smugness—as Phoebe approached. To the left the vast bed waited, spread with tempting quilts and plumping pillows.

Phoebe ignored it, grasped Harriet by the waist, and pushed her back—hard, but not too hard—against the cool expanse of the window behind her. Harriet's shiver was swallowed whole as Phoebe kissed her, a deep, demanding thrust of tongues. Harriet's dressing gown was tugged rudely down her shoulders to puddle on the floor, leaving her in only a shift that gaped wide at the neck and which was so thin the moonlight was enough to turn it nearly transparent as glass.

Phoebe let her gaze linger over the silhouette of Harriet's hips. A sweeter curve had never been seen in nature, she was sure.

Then she was rucking up the hem to Harriet's waist, slipping both hands beneath and up and clasping them over the swells of Harriet's breasts.

The woman's head dropped back and she arched her bosom forward, patience cast aside. Phoebe pinched both her nipples at once, beneath the linen, and rejoiced as Harriet cursed in a choked, wondering voice. One of Phoebe's thighs had slipped between Harriet's legs, and Phoebe pushed gently up against the heat and the wet she found there.

Harriet's hands clutched at Phoebe's shoulders, and she began to ride Phoebe's thigh. "Faster," Phoebe demanded, and then pinched again, took a nipple in her mouth, licked—then scraped it with her teeth.

Harriet cried out, hips jerking, her rhythm stuttering as pleasure sent her reeling.

It was a start, but Phoebe wanted to give her more. She made sure her feet were braced solidly and pulled Harriet's leg up, hooking the knee around Phoebe's hip, leaving her spread open right where Phoebe's hungry hand could reach her. A quick suckle on her own two fingers and then Phoebe was pressing them into the hot pulse of Harriet's cunt. Harriet's own hands scrabbled at Phoebe's shoulders, her hips still working, her lips whispering hoarse pleas in broken tones.

Phoebe slid her other arm up along Harriet's back, the better to anchor her in place. Harder and harder her fingers thrust, wetness coating her hand to the wrist, slippery flesh surrounding her and making Phoebe's whole body throb in answering echo. Harriet's nipples were hard points against Phoebe's chest, her throat a column of pearl and salt beneath Phoebe's tongue. Her mouth drifted up again to Harriet's ear, gold curls haloed in moonlight. "Is this when I should make you beg?"

Harriet whimpered. Her curls bounced as she nodded, teeth

digging into her lip, hips arching against Phoebe's hand. "Please," she said, the word slipping out on a moan that sent flames running down every one of Phoebe's nerves.

Phoebe clucked her tongue. "Oh, no," she said, not bothering to hide the smile in her voice, "that was far too easy. The idea is to *make* you beg, is it not?" She sucked on Harriet's earlobe and gave a particularly deep twist to her fingers.

Harriet cried out, clapping one hand to her treacherous mouth and biting against the heel of her hand.

Phoebe kept talking while she thrust, her breath hot, her tone a teasing purr. "What should I make you beg *for,* that's another question. 'Please may I come' is so unspecific. 'Please, don't stop,' that's a little better. 'Please, don't stop fucking me' . . . 'Please, Phoebe, go deeper' . . . 'Please, a little harder' . . ."

Harriet was whimpering against her own hand, but dropped it now. Her eyes were wild, the whites gleaming like moons. Her voice was clear as a bell: "Please, Phoebe, for the love of god, take those lovely fingers of yours and fuck me as hard as you possibly can."

Dear lord.

It took several swallows before Phoebe could clear the dryness from her throat. She'd nearly come herself, just from hearing that. "Say it again," she demanded hoarsely.

"Please, Phoebe—" Harriet began, rather breathlessly, but then the words became a high, keening wail as Phoebe began driving her hand as powerfully hard as she could, as deep as it would go, fingers plunging into the slick, sliding muscle and the ball of her hand grinding into the pulsing pearl of flesh just above. Harriet exploded, gasping for air, muscles shaking, her one thigh clenching tight against Phoebe's hip. Phoebe felt Harriet's nails biting like claws into the bare skin of her shoulders, and buried her face in the delectable curve of her lover's throat.

At last Harriet's hand reached down and gripped Phoebe's hand to stop her. They slipped apart, both panting, the air suddenly cool against overheated skin. Harriet's leg slipped down from Phoebe's hip, and already Phoebe missed the pull and the weight of it.

She smiled, though there was sadness in it. If she were to have only this night, before returning to the prison that was home, she felt she'd made the most of it.

Harriet raised wondering hands to Phoebe's temples, brushing back her hair. "Stay with me," she whispered. "Not just tonight. Come and live with me here."

Phoebe gaped. "What?"

Harriet was entirely serious. "Why should you go back to London to be miserable with Lawrence? I have more room here than I know what to do with. We've been friends for twenty years, Phoebe—and lovers for only one night. Don't you want more time? Don't you deserve to be rescued, as you rescued your niece today?" Her lips curved in a smile far too shy for what they'd been doing. "Will you make me beg for this, too?"

Phoebe shook her head, wordless and overwhelmed. She'd been offered a choice between a feast and a slow starvation of the soul. It was too much to comprehend just yet, too big a feeling to clothe in mere words—but Harriet was still waiting for a reply. "Are you sure?" Phoebe asked.

Harriet's smile burst over her like a sunrise. "I'm certain," she said, as her hands slipped around Phoebe's bare waist. "What was it you said? 'What's special is when things come together.'"

Phoebe's laugh was half strangled. "We haven't quite managed that yet."

Harriet's lips curved wickedly, and her arms pulled Phoebe closer. "Then allow me to rectify the error."

It was dawn before Phoebe slipped back into her own room,

tousled and trembling and thoroughly sated. Later she wrote a very enjoyably defiant letter to Lawrence, and sent it along with the servant Harriet dispatched to retrieve her things from London. His reply was curt: "May you enjoy being part of Lady Moth's collection of oddities," he'd written.

"I will," Phoebe promised with a grin, and tossed the letter into the fire.

BLUES

Amy Glances

It's not like I don't know what everyone is saying: "It must be so hard to be her sister!" What? With her beautiful singing voice, gorgeous auburn locks, and a tail that goes on for days, who wouldn't wonder what it would be like to grow up in her shadow? And look at what she did with it! She married that boring prince, and now she's stuck at home raising his three little brats. No, thanks.

Anyone can take a little trip down to see the sea witch and wheel and deal for some legs. Some of us just know how to use 'em a little better than my sister. I knew exactly what I was going to do with my pair. I knew the moment I saw him.

It was late afternoon, and I was sunning myself on a rock. I like to have the tannest tits in the group. It gives me exotic appeal next to all those girls who avoid the shallow waters like they would a school full of jellyfish. While my breasts were out soaking up the sun (don't believe any of that seashell-bra bullshit), I must have dozed off, because a noise startled me so much I almost jumped out of my scales. That's when I saw him.

He didn't notice me at first. He had fallen asleep on the sand.

He stood up slowly and headed toward me when he realized I was there. I recognized what kind of human he was right away, with his sunburnt skin, unkempt clothes, mariner boots, and, more noticeably, his seaman swagger. I had seen his kind many times before on big vessels brandishing flags with skulls and crossbones. I was terrified.

Growing up, my father had told us stories about how cruel humans can be. Especially pirates. There were tales about pirates catching mermaids and keeping them in aquariums below deck or in nets they dragged behind their ships. Pirates were ruthless, dangerous, and to be avoided at all costs.

Which, of course, only made me more curious. I often snuck out late at night just to catch the sounds of a pirate ship sailing through. They threw parties on their boats, and you could hear the music, merry shouts, and delighted squeals well into the night. I was always so jealous of the lucky ladies on board, who sounded like they were having the time of their lives. The best sound by far that came from these ships, though, was the laughter. You could hear it for miles. The sound carried over the waves and into the lucky creatures of the sea, filling them with wonderment and a little jealousy. I was way too scared to actually try to meet these jovial land dwellers, though. What if my dad was right? What if they were cruel to us? I couldn't risk it.

But that day on the beach, when he started walking toward me, I was frozen into place. There was something magnetic about him. He reminded me of that laughter, and I wanted to get as close to that sound as I could.

"Miss," he called to me, "miss, you shouldn't sit so close to the water. You might get swept away with the tide."

With my tail conveniently hidden below the waves, and never being one to shy away from the attention of a male, I couldn't help but challenge him.

"Would that be such a bad thing?" I asked as he made his way slowly to me.

"Then, how would I learn your name?" he asked.

I could see him better now, his sandy blond hair, bleached lighter by the sun, and his muscled arms, from years of hoisting sails.

"Why would you need to know my name?" I asked, just to let him know I wasn't scared off that easily.

"I'm a decent fellow; I'd at least like to call you by name when I kick you out of my bed tomorrow morning."

I couldn't help but laugh. Sure, I love handsome men (mermen up until this point), and I'm a bit of a glutton for the ones with big egos—which he clearly had—but funny men have always been my biggest weakness.

I searched in vain for a quick comeback, and he continued coming close. As he came closer, I could see his eyes for the first time. They were the most incredible shade of blue I had ever seen, which is a bold statement. Believe me: when you come from where I do, you see a lot of blues.

He plopped down beside me and somehow managed not to break the jug of rum he was carrying.

"Would you like a drink, miss?" he asked.

"I'd hate to see you drink alone," I responded.

He passed me the jug. I took a healthy swig and handed it back to him.

"We're celebrating," he explained.

"It looks like you're celebrating alone." I pointed out the obvious.

"Oh, no, me and the other captain," he responded.

"And where is he?" I asked.

"Right here. Meet Captain Morgan," he said and passed me the jug again. At this I couldn't help but giggle. So hard, in fact, that my long, blonde locks slipped from the places they were concealing my bare chest.

My breasts were revealed not only to the quickly sinking sun but also to my new companion, who took the opportunity to steal a glance. If I were more modest I suppose I would have shifted so at least my nipples were covered once again with my locks, but there was something about having his eyes trained on me that made me feel powerful. I arched my back ever so slightly to improve his view.

He caught himself staring and looked up to meet my eyes. That's when I was hooked. Those eyes were like the brightest part of the water when the sun reaches new depths in the middle of the day—only bluer.

He had been tipsy when he walked over, but the moment our eyes locked there seemed to be a moment of clarity, or vulnerability maybe, undiluted by the strength of the spirits. I was mesmerized. Caught. He leaned forward to kiss me, and I didn't—couldn't—pull away.

His lips were much warmer than the mermen's lips I had kissed before. They tasted faintly salty. I leaned in closer, wanting to take in his earthy smell. I could taste the rum when he grazed my tongue with his. He began kissing slowly down my neck and brushed my hair off my shoulders. The air had gotten chiller, but his kisses warmed my skin. My tail was still safely below the water, and since it had gotten darker, it was no longer visible. His tongue trailed my collarbone. I didn't want it to end, but I knew this encounter had a definite limit.

There was one thing I was really curious about, now that I had a living, breathing human man who was close enough to touch. I'd heard stories about what humans were like where there wasn't a tail. My girlfriends said these creatures were furry. We all giggled about that one! What would anyone need a patch of fur down there for? What *I* really wanted to know was what their dicks were like. I could only guess. I was this close—I wanted to find out. I also wanted these kisses to last as long as possible.

His tongue worked its way down my breasts, his breath leaving its warmth on my skin. I wanted his whole body close to mine, but I knew that wasn't possible. I'm brave, but I'm not an idiot. Still, I had to feel him. When he took my nipple into his mouth, I made my move.

I slipped my hand under his waistband. His lips cupped my breast, and his tongue softly circled my erect nipple. My fingers slipped down, stroking his soft hair. The tales were true! As I weaved my fingers into the strands, I discovered his erection. I was so shocked at how big it was that I almost pulled my hand out of his pants. But as the tips of my fingers reached the hard shaft covered in soft skin, he bit down on my nipple, and the sensation felt so good I wrapped my fingers around him, making him groan in pleasure.

I finally got to be part of all that excitement I had listened to going on above the waves on so many nights. He was much more expressive than the guys I grew up around. I forgot all about myself for a moment as he teased my nipple with his teeth. I stroked him slowly and firmly. It wasn't until I felt his fingers drag across my stomach that I remembered the part of me that he had probably only heard tales about, and slipped into the water. I could hear him calling after me as I swam slowly back home.

Days went by. I couldn't stop thinking about him. I wanted to know what it would feel like to have his hard shaft inside me. Sure, I'd had plenty of sexual encounters, but none with a human, and certainly none with eyes like those. I was spending all my time lounging on rocks near where I met him, hoping to see him again. Every now and then I would hear a voice from afar that I was sure belonged to him, but each time, when I found the ship and swam close enough to see who was on board, I was disappointed. After a few weeks of being completely unable to think about anything else, I knew I had to take action.

I decided to visit my friend the sea witch. She's in such demand these days I had to make an appointment. When I got to her sea cave office, she greeted me warmly with a hug and a smile. (I know what you might be thinking, and no, she's nothing like what you've heard. Let's just say my sister can be a bit of an exaggerator. I'm sure they swam in different crowds in school, and my sis probably just didn't like the premium rate she was being charged so she started a little rumor to hurt the witch's business.)

As I explained my conundrum, she listened intently. When I finished, she said it sounded like I was in need of her bestselling potion: the one for human legs. She even had some premixed product on hand, and I could have it free of charge if I promised not to tell anyone. (Turns out my sister's storytelling had actually helped her business. Now everyone was happy walking out of her office with any rate lower than a payment plan that lasted an eternity.)

The instructions for the potion were easy enough. I just drank it when I wanted legs, and I would have a pair of gorgeous gams instantly. I'd get my tail back ten minutes after I had an orgasm, making for an easy exit strategy if this pirate wasn't very skilled in that department—though something told me he was.

I tried to imagine all the infinite possibilities a pair of legs would give me. I was thinking of the positions that would be available to me now, especially what it would be like to have sex standing up. More importantly, I just wanted to see those blue eyes again and feel his warm skin on mine.

Next I had to find him. For the next few weeks, I spent my days swimming as far as I could and searching for any boat flying the

Jolly Roger. I chased a few ships for miles, but there were no signs of him on board.

Then, early one evening when the ocean was remarkably still, I heard the sound of his laughter. It was faint, but it was definitely him. I swam in the direction of the sound and spotted his ship heading for a small island. The ship was dark, and it looked like they were planning to pillage the place.

I hadn't planned on bothering him while he was working, but I thought this might be my only chance. I swam as fast as I could to where his ship was anchored. There weren't any voices coming from it, but I could hear the sounds of oars hitting the water. They were quietly taking the dinghies ashore under the cover of darkness.

I swam ahead until I reached the rocky beach. I guzzled down the potion in one shot and had my new legs instantly, as promised. There weren't even any growing pains. Walking was surprisingly easy; I wondered why I hadn't tried this years ago. The only immediate issue was my stark nakedness. I had to find something to cover up with quickly.

As I approached the village, I could hear screaming. The pirates had been spotted. An alarm sounded; people were running out of their houses. Finding some clothes was going to be easier than I anticipated.

I thought homeowners who had the biggest houses might try to stay and protect their homesteads, so I found a humble abode and shimmied through a window. As I had guessed, the place was empty. I found the bedroom and opened the closet. There weren't a lot of clothes left behind, but I was able to find a flimsy sleeping gown to slip into. That's when I heard a familiar tone.

"Hey, who's there?" he yelled.

I recognized his voice instantly.

"Please don't hurt me, sir," I yelled back.

"Of course I'm not going to hurt you, miss, unless you want me to," he said and let out a hearty laugh.

I tried to stifle my giggle as he entered the bedroom where I was standing. He paused in the doorway and took in my figure. I watched his crystal-blue eyes follow the curves of my breasts under the gown, and then, down my bare legs. I could tell he was pleased, but I wasn't sure if he recognized me.

"Why would I want you to hurt me?" I asked coyly.

He walked closer, and I backed up until I was against the wall.

"Because you might just like it," he said, putting his hands under the hem of my gown and onto my new legs. I bent forward, eager for his calloused touch.

He took advantage of my compliant state and grabbed both my arms, pinning them over my head against the wall. He held me like that with just one hand, while the other hand felt my breasts through my gown. A moan from deep inside was the only sound I could make in response to this glorious sensation.

He spread my legs with his free hand and dipped a finger inside me. I had never been so wet outside of the ocean before, and his finger glided in me. I moaned even louder as he explored my depths, bringing with each new touch an incredible, never-felt-before feeling.

His strokes quickened, and so did my breathing. I was so turned on, already craving climax. He felt so amazing I didn't want it to end, especially since I had such an intense curfew and probably wouldn't be able to see him again for a very, very long time, if ever.

Suddenly, he released his hold on my arms and swung me around so I was facing the wall. He wrapped one of his arms around my neck. I could still breathe, but it was more difficult. He unfastened his belt, and his pants crashed to the floor. My heart raced. He pulled up the hem of my gown, and that's when I felt it.

He was shoving that hard-as-coral shaft of his inside me. I briefly felt his soft skin against my wet lips and then gasped as he thrust himself deep inside me. He moaned loudly. It felt impossibly big. I had never been so filled by someone in my life. He lingered deep inside me.

When he pulled almost completely out of me, I whimpered. He thrust into me, much harder than before, and I yelped. He did it again. This time my noises were pure pleasure. He thrust into me again and again, harder and faster each time. I was no longer thinking about how bittersweet this climax was going to be, just how badly I wanted it. He must have wanted it just as badly. He was grunting loudly now, in sync with my moans. The sounds of his arousal were pushing me over the edge. When I started to climax, he thrust himself deep inside me and exploded. My entire body clenched his, until his warm fluid spilled inside me.

He held me, and I wanted desperately to stay in his arms, but I knew I only had those ten precious minutes before my newfound legs would be replaced with my faithful but slippery appendage. With a heavy heart, I tore myself from his grasp and headed for the door. As I looked back to catch one last memory of those devastating blues, he called after me: “I like you better with the tail.”

THE CONFERENCE

Anuja Varghese

"If you'll turn your attention to Figure 6.2, you'll note that the trend of mid-level donor fatigue, as reported in the 2018 survey results documented on page ninety-three of your handbook, continues throughout those campaigns utilizing a segmented data approach as well as those utilizing . . ."

Shalini's eyes glazed over as the numbers projected on the screen at the front of Ballroom A all started to blur together. It was only the second presentation of the day, but already her brain felt numb. The navy suit jacket she dusted off for job interviews and industry conferences like these felt too heavy for mid-June, and she shifted uncomfortably in the hard-backed chair. She had only come to put in the necessary appearances, as she herself was giving a presentation the next day on "engaging diverse millennials." It was a cringeworthy topic that somehow seemed to pop up at every conference she went to. Shalini had no delusions that it was either her master's degree or her years of experience that kept her on conference presenter lists. She was simply a thirty-five-year-old woman with brown skin who photographed well and could keep a room awake for an hour, and that seemed to check off all the right boxes. Token or not, she always felt guilty turning the frazzled conference committee members down whenever they asked her to participate, but now, as the expert at the podium clicked to his sixty-seventh slide, she sincerely wished that this time, she had just said no.

When the lights finally came on, Shalini applauded with everyone else, then, snatching her purse from the floor, made a beeline for the ballroom doors, hoping to make a quick escape before she could be cornered into conference small talk. According to the schedule, lunch would be served in Ballroom B—soup and salad and sandwiches, weak coffee, probably some kind of dry, fruit-filled cake for dessert. Conferences in movies were always in the coolest places, Shalini grumbled in her head, like Las Vegas or Hawaii, and something crazy always happened. No such luck here. Going to a conference in the city where she already lived was convenient at least, if not very much fun.

Shalini sighed and began making her way past the convention center's main doors, following the signs to Ballroom B. A group came in from the busy street outside, bringing with them a warm breeze and a smell that stopped Shalini in her tracks. That was a smell she would know anywhere. She looked for a moment down the long hallway ahead and thought of the egg salad sandwiches that lay in wait, the wilted lettuce, the slimy slices of Swiss cheese, then turned on the heel of a blue pump and walked out into the sunshine.

To the side of the doors, three girls (college students, Shalini guessed) stood behind a folding table, selling samosas out of large tinfoil trays. They were fat and greasy, stuffed with peas and cubed potatoes, drawing a small crowd with the wafting aroma of cumin, chili, and deep-fried dough.

"Two for a dollar!" the girls chorused. "Help us raise funds to send kids to summer camp!"

Shalini got in line and pulled a five-dollar bill from her wallet. "I'll take four please," she told the girls. "But keep the change."

"You followed the smell too, huh?"

With her brown paper bag of samosas in hand, Shalini turned to the voice next to her and, for a split second, wondered if it was a real man or some conference-induced hallucination that had spoken to her. In dark jeans and a black V-neck T-shirt, he looked like he could have stepped out of a Calvin Klein ad or a Bollywood movie. Even in her heels, Shalini didn't quite come up to his shoulder, and she took a step back as he literally towered over her to reach for his own grease-stained brown bag.

"I guess I did," Shalini replied.

He grinned, revealing dimples that softened the sharp lines of high cheekbones. "Should we sit?" he asked. Shalini heard the trace of an accent, but one she couldn't place. She followed his gaze to a bench a little farther down the street.

"Um . . ." Shalini wasn't sure what to say. Was he gorgeous? Definitely. Was he hitting on her? Maybe. Was he very likely just a kid and she too old and sensible for this kind of meet-cute when she had a whole afternoon of conference panels and presentations ahead? Well . . . "Sure," she said.

They walked together to the bench and sat down side by side. Shalini expected him to keep talking, but he seemed content to eat in silence, watching the cars and people pass by. It felt strange at first, but as she ate her samosas next to him, Shalini realized that she felt oddly comfortable sitting with this complete stranger, not saying a word. Eventually, Shalini ran a reluctant hand through her dark waves, warmed now by the sun, and said, "I guess I should be getting back to the conference."

"Yeah, me too," he replied, although the way he leaned back on the bench with ankles crossed did not suggest he was in any hurry.

Shalini raised an eyebrow at him. "Are you here for this conference too?" Clearly he had missed the memo that everyone was supposed to wear their best professional costumes today.

"I am," he said, and then, "or my boss is anyway. I'm kind of just along for the ride."

"Ah. Well, it was nice to meet—"

"You know, I've never been to Toronto before. Growing up, my parents worked for NGOs, doing a lot of fieldwork, disaster relief, refugee aid, that kind of thing. So they moved around all the time and I moved with them. But anywhere we went around the world, the Canadians we met were always the friendliest people. I thought Toronto must be the coolest city; I always wanted to see it. And now . . ." He smiled and stretched out his hands, palms up. "Here I am."

Big hands, Shalini caught herself thinking. Broad shoulders, bright eyes, stubbled chin, and full lips. She really should get back. *How old are you?* she wanted to ask him. *Where are your parents now? When do you leave? Would you like to kiss me?* "What's your name?" she asked.

"Kailash," he said. "But everyone calls me Kai."

"I was born here," Shalini said. "Just down the street at St. Mike's actually. Toronto seems pretty boring to me most of the time, but I guess it's got to be somebody's Hawaii."

He looked at her quizzically. "Somebody's what?"

"Never mind," she said, shaking her head. She thought one more time about going back into the convention center, but then she looked at Kai, who was looking back at her, a small smile turning up the corners of his mouth, as if he had known all along they were destined for an adventure together. The idea of returning to the conference suddenly seemed laughably bad. "What if we skipped the rest of the conference today?" Kai cocked his head at her and she quickly continued: "I mean, look, you're not really seeing the city if all you get to see of it is the convention center. Maybe I could . . . show you around?"

He didn't say anything, and Shalini was suddenly gripped by the panic of an oncoming awkward moment. He probably already had plans in place or friends to meet or, no doubt, could walk into any bar along King Street and have no trouble at all finding far more attractive tour guides than her. She bent down and plucked her phone and a business card from the side pocket of her purse. "Or, you know, whatever," she added, as she scrolled through her texts, pretending to read new messages, of which there were none. "Here's my card," she said, holding it out. Then with a little laugh, "See? We're networking. That's all these conferences are really for anyway."

Kai took the card from Shalini's hand and looked at it. "Shalini," he said, drawing out the first syllable a bit, letting her name melt in his mouth like butter. He looked back at her. "I'm happy to meet you, Shalini," he said. "And I accept your offer."

Shalini felt her stomach flutter, which was ridiculous because she was neither a giddy teenager nor a character in a Jane Austen novel. "Okay, then," she said. "What do you want to see first?" Kai paused and then turned around and looked up. Of course. Shalini stood and shrugged out of her suit jacket, folding it over one arm. She pulled her sunglasses out of her purse, slipped them on, and then said to Kai, "Let's go."

The CN Tower was Toronto's most recognizable landmark. It dominated the city skyline and was packed with tourists year-round. For Shalini, it had always been a fixture in the background, a place she passed every day on her way to work but had never once considered visiting herself. Now she waited in line with Kai behind her, to get into the Tower and take the elevator up to the viewing deck. Enclosed by floor-to-ceiling windows all the way around, the view from the top of the tower was spectacular. Shalini pointed out buildings and streets and places with funny stories attached to them. She surprised herself with how much of the city's history she had at her fingertips without ever realizing it was there.

Kai took it all in, snapped pictures, asked questions, laughed easily along with her. If he was conscious of the way he drew the gaze of women and men alike as he followed the glass walls in a full circle, until he came to revolving doors, he made no sign of it. Shalini followed him outside onto the balcony, which was surrounded by high railings and protective wire mesh. The view from indoors through the glass was much better, but it left the balcony almost entirely free of other people, and when Shalini went to stand beside him behind the iron rail, they found themselves quite alone.

"So, what do you think?" she asked.

"I think it's a hell of a way to start the tour," he said.

She smiled and gave him a sidelong glance. She saw the kiss in his eyes before it traveled to his lips. He wasn't hiding it, wasn't trying to take her by surprise. She had time, only a few seconds perhaps, but time enough, if she wanted, to back out of the moment. Instead, Shalini leaned in and let the kiss take hold. There was a gentleness to it, an unhurried parting of her lips with his, the tip of his tongue making only the briefest inquiry, making no demands.

He drew back, leaving her mouth tingling, her skin hot to the touch. Shalini took a steadying breath, and then said, "Where to next?"

"I heard you have a museum made of crystal?"

Shalini laughed. "Not quite," she replied. "But I know what you mean."

They left the tower together and hopped onto a streetcar.

Somewhere along the way, Kai took Shalini's hand and held it, so that they arrived at the museum with fingers intertwined, at ease with one another as if they were old friends or lovers, not strangers who had met not two hours ago.

The Royal Ontario Museum was a sprawling institution with several school busses parked out front and groups of rowdy kids on field trips rushing from one exhibit to the next. Over a decade ago, the museum's main entrance and ground floor had been rebuilt, taking the shape of a massive, multifaceted crystal formed out of glass, aluminum, and steel. Most people thought it was an eyesore, but Shalini liked it, liked the audacity of it, the way it reflected light differently than any other building in the world.

Shalini and Kai spent the afternoon exploring the museum from end to end. Shalini hadn't been inside since she was a kid, and she felt like she was seeing everything for the first time, just as Kai was. They saw dinosaur bones and ancient civilizations, birds' nests and bat caves, so many wonders of nature, history, and art. At every turn, they found ways to make casual contact—the brush of her arm against his in the elevator, his hand on her bare shoulder as they both leaned down to read about the helmet-crested corythosaurus. By the time they wandered together into the softly lit Ancient Egypt exhibit, the museum was near closing, the crowds had thinned, and a tension had built between them that began to demand release.

"Hey, look at this," Shalini said, as she came upon a low, stone arch built right into the wall.

"What is it?" Kai asked, coming up behind her.

Shalini read from the plaque mounted beside the strange doorway. "It's a replica of the Tomb of Kitines from the second century AD."

"Should we go in?" His voice was so close. If Shalini had taken a half-step backward, she would have been pressed against him. She walked forward into the enclosed space of the reconstructed tomb and, ducking his head to get through the arch, Kai followed.

The interior was dim, the cool, gray stone of the walls engraved with hieroglyphs from top to bottom. "I'm not sure if we're supposed to touch," Shalini said, even as she ran her fingertips across the markings in the stone.

"I think it's allowed," Kai replied softly, and with a slight shiver, Shalini realized he wasn't talking about the walls. "In fact," he said, pushing her hair aside to touch his lips to the back of her neck, "I'd say it's encouraged."

Shalini dropped her purse, turned around, and reached up to pull his face to hers. His arm was already encircling her waist, drawing her in, the kiss between them no longer a question but a command. *More,* it said. Shalini swept his mouth with her tongue and felt a breathless rush of excitement as he deepened the kiss in response, backing her into the stone with the force of it. He was fumbling with her belt, too distracted by her lips and her scent and the way her hands had crept up beneath his shirt to focus on getting it undone. Once he had it, he pulled back to look down at her as he deliberately unbuttoned and unzipped her pants, then slipped his hand inside.

Shalini caught his wrist. This was crazy. She should have waxed. She should have worn sexier underwear. She should have gone back to the conference like a responsible adult. "Kai . . ." she whispered. She was already so wet. "Somebody could come in."

He was stroking her through the fabric of her panties. "Somebody could," he agreed, his face set in mock seriousness.

"We'd get kicked out," Shalini said, but her eyes were closing as his fingers met bare flesh, her breath coming in shallow gasps as his thumb found her clit and began to work it in tight circles.

"We probably would," he said, one finger slipping inside.

Shalini dug her nails into his wrist, the other hand pressed to the wall behind her. *Don't scream. Do. Not. Scream.* Two fingers now, moving, curling, the thumb still circling, faster, his mouth against her neck, then her cheek, then her ear, to murmur, "But it would be worth it . . . to see you come."

So she came, her cheek pressed against a hieroglyph, legs shaking, the announcement that the museum was closing barely registering as it played over the speakers outside of the tomb.

Kai took a step back and watched as Shalini turned to face the wall, retucked her camisole, rebuttoned and rebuckled, and tried to regain a bit of composure. "You okay?" he asked, when she leaned her forehead on the stone.

"Yeah," Shalini replied. "Can you wait for me out front? I just need a minute."

With Kai gone, Shalini took a deep breath. *What am I doing?* She was the kind of woman who dated nice men who took her to nice restaurants, lawyers or software engineers, teachers or regional sales managers. They met all her listed criteria and she met theirs. She was not the kind of woman who blew off conferences to play tour guide to a stranger. And she was definitely not the kind of woman who had orgasms in public places, who even now was thinking about the hardness of the stranger's body, what he would look like naked in her bed. She ran her fingers through her hair, reapplied her lip gloss, and checked her reflection in her phone's camera. She was not the kind of woman things like this—men like this—happened to. Except that maybe, just for today, she was.

Shalini made her way out of the museum and found Kai standing in the shadow of the crystal. "Hey," she said. "Thanks for waiting. Do you want to grab a drink somewhere?"

"Sure," he replied. Shalini turned to start walking, and Kai fell into step beside her.

The museum was in Yorkville, one of Toronto's ritziest neighborhoods. Shalini came to window-shop sometimes but, for the most part, steered clear of the high-end boutiques. The clothes in the artfully arranged windows they passed were for long-legged, willowy women, with narrow hips and unobtrusive breasts. Shalini's proportions seemed to confound the salesgirls of Yorkville; she had quickly learned to seek out other options that were kinder to her wallet and her pride alike.

A bit of bling against a black backdrop caught Shalini's eye. It was lingerie but was displayed in a gilded frame rather than on a mannequin. She seemed to be looking at what amounted to three scraps of delicate white lace, two that formed a top piece and one that formed a bottom, all connected by several strands of glittering gemstones.

"Good choice."

"What?" Shalini made a noise that was half laugh, half snort in response to Kai's comment. "I don't think so," she said.

"Why not?"

"Because it's ridiculous?"

Kai paused, looking intently at the lingerie in the frame, and then said, "I think it's beautiful." He shifted his focus to her. "I think you're beautiful."

Shalini felt heat creeping into her face and tried to laugh it off. "It might be beautiful on someone else, like, say, a Victoria's Secret model, so I'll let you know if I find any of those." She turned and kept walking, Kai a few paces behind.

After a few minutes of silence, Kai said, "Models are fantasy. I've come across a few here and there . . ." *I bet you have,* Shalini thought. "And it's their job to sell a fantasy, to be a fantasy woman." He stopped and took her hand, forcing her to stop too. "I think when it comes down to it, most men prefer something real."

As he brushed the hair back from her face, there was such earnestness in his expression that Shalini had to laugh. "Who *are* you?" she asked, but let him bend his head to kiss her, and now, knowing that his fingers had been inside her, the memory of that pleasure still fresh in her mind and in her body, Shalini felt something more intimate in the pressing of his lips to hers.

They walked together a little farther, and she led him down a cobblestone alleyway, where the steady buzz of music and chatter floated down from a rooftop patio. He stopped to read the sign above the door. "Hemingway's?"

"Restaurants come and go all the time," Shalini said. "But Hemingway's has been here forever." They made their way up the stairs and were lucky to snag a table overlooking the street. Shalini watched him over the top of her menu as he skimmed the drink list. "You are of legal drinking age, aren't you?" she asked, only half joking.

He gave her a half smile and said, "I'm twenty-five."

"Okay," she replied and waited for the inevitable question. He didn't say anything. Finally she asked, "Do you want to know how old I am?"

Kai looked at her. "Does it matter?"

It mattered online. It mattered to her parents. It mattered when she looked in the mirror and wondered when she had stopped being young. But it didn't matter here, not tonight, not with him. "No," Shalini said. "No, it doesn't."

One drink turned into three drinks turned into five drinks turned into dinner, and before Shalini knew it, the sky was dark and Kai was asking for the bill. They took the subway to Yonge-Dundas Square, which was full of people waiting for a concert to start. Screens flashed on all sides, a man held up a sign proclaiming that the apocalypse was near, a group of kids were breakdancing in a wide circle, and a pulsing Latin beat surged through the growing crowd as the opening act took the stage. To Shalini, it all felt a bit chaotic, but Kai was delighted.

"It's your own Times Square!" he shouted over the music. "It's beautiful!"

Shalini laughed. "You're drunk!" she shouted back. She was a little drunk herself.

Kai grabbed her hands and tried to get her to dance. He moved with an easy, fluid grace, comfortable in his clothes and in his skin, the screen above them casting him in an otherworldly blue glow. "You're beautiful!" he said, trying to spin her around.

Shalini, still holding her purse and blazer, wearing shoes she hadn't intended to wear for this long, rolled her eyes at him. "You think everything is beautiful!" she retorted, but doubted he could hear her over all the noise. As the music slowed, he pulled her in and they simply swayed together.

With his arms around her and his head right above hers, Kai said, "Maybe when you've seen as many people and places at their worst for as long as I have, you start to look for the beauty in everything."

Shalini rested her head against his chest and closed her eyes, and for a few minutes, the whole world that wasn't his heartbeat in her ear faded away.

"Come on," Kai said, breaking the spell and striding out of the square with Shalini in tow.

"Where are we going?" she asked him, when it finally registered they were heading north on foot.

"I'm gonna buy you that . . . that lace thing in the frame!" Kai proclaimed.

"I don't want it!" Shalini protested, and then, "I'm sure it costs a thousand dollars," and finally, "The store's probably closed!" But Kai was undeterred.

"Wait!" Shalini called. "Maybe you can buy me something else."

"Like what?"

Shalini grabbed Kai's hand and before she could lose her nerve, pulled him into sliding doors under a flashing neon sign that read "Seduction Love Boutique." The store spanned three levels, with magazines and DVDs in the basement, toys and other novelties on the ground floor, and trashy lingerie, BDSM gear, and fetishwear upstairs. They made a cursory tour of the store before heading to the second floor.

"Latex?" Kai asked, holding up a box with a woman in a skin-tight catsuit on the cover.

"No," Shalini said.

"Leather?" he suggested, picking a red leather corset off a rack and holding it up for her to see.

"No."

Then he put a package in her hands. Shalini looked at the contents and then looked at Kai, the desire crackling between them suddenly sharp and bright as lightning, cutting through the alcohol, cutting off any thoughts she might have had of extending their adventure on the city streets any further into the night. There was only one place left to go now.

"Lace," he said. And this time, he wasn't asking.

They went to his hotel room, the plastic package in an unmarked red bag. With the door locked behind them, Kai slipped out of his sneakers and pulled his shirt over his head. He stretched long arms and pulled back the curtains to look down at the street below. Shalini put down her things and picked up the bag from the edge of the bed where Kai had left it. She took it into the bathroom, closed the door, and looked at her reflection in the mirror. Was she really doing this? She had planned for a quiet evening at home, maybe a glass of wine, enough time to go over the notes for her presentation the next day. She hadn't planned for any of this. She hadn't planned for Kai. She ripped open the package.

The matching thong and teddy were made of cheap, white lace, the jewels embedded in the fabric obviously plastic. She put the pieces on anyway; immediately, they made her feel like someone else. She spilled out of the garments' confines in the wrong places. They did nothing to hide the areas she usually worked so hard to flatter, conceal, or contain, but tonight, she just didn't care.

From outside, she heard knocking and Kai's voice, then silence again. Her heart was beating so fast, but the strip of lace wedging itself between her pussy lips was already damp. She walked into the room. They were really doing this. An ice cream sundae in a silver bowl sat on the round table by the window. Shalini looked at it, and then looked at Kai sitting in the chair beside the table in nothing but a pair of black briefs. "We didn't have dessert," he said, his eyes moving over her body. "So I ordered some."

Shalini licked her lips and gave the lace a slight tug. "It doesn't fit exactly right," she said. Why was her voice shaking?

"Come here," he told her, so she did, stopping between his spread legs. He ran his hands over the lace, along her sides, caressing the curve of her hip, cupping her full ass. On the edge of the chair, he buried his face between her thighs, inhaling her, licking her, tasting her wetness.

"That's not fair," Shalini breathed. "I already had my turn today."

"Who says we're taking turns?" Kai replied, making her cry out as he nibbled lightly on the flesh of her inner thigh.

"I do," Shalini said, and climbed astride him in the chair. He was hard beneath her and she wanted him so badly, but she wasn't going to let it be over that quickly. She rubbed her pussy along his shaft through the briefs, and he groaned, gathering up her breasts, feeling the dark nipples harden against his palms. Shalini reached over and scooped up a spoonful of ice cream. She brought it to Kai's lips. "Thanks for dessert," she said. He took the ice cream offered and then, with one hand on the back of Shalini's neck, guided her mouth down onto his. She kissed him deeply, lapped the sweetness from his tongue, and felt his kiss become more urgent. "More?" she asked and reached for the bowl again, but he beat her to it. He tipped it onto her chest, making her gasp at the coldness of it, seeping through the lace. The material tore easily when he wrenched it apart to set her breasts free so he could eat the ice cream right off her hot skin.

All this time, Shalini hadn't stopped grinding her pussy into him; the sensation was too much to control any longer. He took her face in his hands and said, "Shalini, I really want to fuck you."

"That's good, Kai," Shalini replied, hair wild, breasts sticky and sweet, cunt soaking wet. "Because I really want to be fucked."

She slid off of him and caught her breath, retrieving a condom from her purse on the floor. She dropped the thong, he lost the briefs, and with the rubber in place, Shalini positioned herself above him, legs splayed wide, hands on his shoulders for balance, and then slowly took the full length of him inside her. She touched her forehead to his, eyes locked together, as she started to rock her hips, finding a rhythm that set them both on fire. Holding her in place, Kai met her rolling hips with his own deep thrusts, and when he knew he had her on the edge, he reached down to stroke her clit with two thick, wet fingers until she screamed and collapsed in a heap on his chest. With a hand in her hair, Kai asked her, "Can I come inside you?"

"Yes, do it," she said, flicking her tongue over one nipple, then the other. He came with a stifled cry, his lean body rigid in release. After a shared hot shower, Shalini got dressed and took a cab home, seeing the beautiful city around her with brand new eyes.

Back at the conference the next day, Shalini looked for Kai but didn't see him. She gave her presentation, drank her weak coffee, exchanged the usual pleasantries, and left at the end of the day satisfied that she had made up for yesterday's disappearing act. Outside the convention center, the girls had packed up their samosa table, but just a little way down the street, Shalini noticed a man sitting on a bench, just watching the cars and people go by.

"Mind if I join you?" she asked, sitting down beside him.

"Not at all," he replied.

"New to the city?"

He grinned a familiar grin, dimples flashing. "Yeah, but I had an amazing tour guide." He looked at her then, all mischief and warmth and wanting. "Maybe I could . . . show you around."

Shalini laughed out loud. He was still gorgeous, still hitting on her, but this time, she had no hesitation whatsoever. "I accept your offer," she said. "Let's go."

THE INSTRUCTION MANUAL

Alexis Wilder

Trying desperately to concentrate on the instruction manual, Bree fidgets with her ring at her new standing desk. Nick had special-ordered an extra tall model to accommodate her; they'd assembled it together last weekend. She pictures his face as they'd screwed it together, his sandy blond hair falling over his brow in front of his crystal blue eyes. Very distracting. The fact that she removed her underwear before cracking open the manual—*specific applications for this I/O circuit are detailed in later chapters. Chapter 7 uses the 8255 PPI circuit*—and the anticipation of what's about to go down, here in their home office, make it increasingly difficult to visualize the workflow as described. She knows she has to focus on precisely how to wire the components together—*that ground and 5+ volt connections also have to be made to each transistor array and relay (Figure 6.6). The +5 volts is connected to pin 2 of each*—or else she'll just have to reread the whole thing. That might still serve his purpose, but she doesn't want to waste time.

Nick enters the room and immediately undoes his tie. He walks slowly, stripping his suit from his perfectly sculpted body, and she inwardly chides herself for noticing. Naked and breathtakingly beautiful, he takes the time to arrange all his clothes, hanging his suit on the rack behind the door. It is maddening to her. The goal here was for Bree to not acknowledge Nick's presence, and here she is, hyperaware of his every movement. Dying for him to get on with it and reach for her body, she consciously loosens her jaw and breathes deeply to make herself relax.

Bree does such a good job of refocusing on the instruction manual—*two drive motors can be mounted back to back as a single unit as shown in Figure 4.5. The four 8-32 tap through holes*—that it comes as a surprise when he finally goes down on his knees and crawls toward her under the desk, touching her hip lightly.

She knows she's not supposed to notice how warm his hand is over the fabric of her dress. His breath on her wrist. How his arm is trembling slightly as he caresses her hip and slides his hand back to cup her ass. Bree has read all about people who can completely turn off the sensations of their body, and she tries as hard as she can to sink into that mind-set. She controls her breathing—*maximum distance to the outer edges of the wheels should be 15¾ cm so that the assembly fits within the base dimensions. After the wheels are*—but can't help but feel as he sinks all the way down between her feet on the floor, sliding his hot hands up the backs of her thighs.

She moves her bookmark up to the previous section and starts rereading about the intricate wiring she would need to do to complete this section of the circuitry. She doesn't precisely feel it as he pulls her skirt up, but she sees it in the corner of her mind almost as if it is happening to another person. In the forefront of her thoughts is the component's wiring, and she wishes it was on the desk in front of her so she could go over the panel while reading about it. She realizes it's a good idea for next time, if she doesn't totally screw this up and there is a next time.

This makes Bree reflect back on that night a few weeks ago when Nick had first expressed to her that he wanted to explore what he called his detachment kink. It had been their tenth anniversary; one of her friends had recommended that they get a hotel room to mark the occasion and get away from the kids for the night. They were having a candlelit dinner in the hotel's attached restaurant and decided to tell each other new fantasies in an effort to keep things fresh between them. She went first and divulged that she would love a thousand times more oral sex from him.

"I'm constantly aware of how I might taste to you at any moment. Always wishing you would want to go down on me without me having to ask for it." Bree tucked her hair behind her ear, surprised she could still feel nervous speaking to her husband of ten years.

"I hadn't realized I wasn't doing enough for you on that front," Nick said, shifting in his seat. "It's only that I usually can't wait to fill you up. But this is good—I love that we can talk like this. It's good to know these things. I'll do better. I love how it feels when you gush all over my tongue."

Bree was wet just from his words, and her excitement to hear what new fantasy he wanted to try instantly tripled. She knew he wouldn't be rushed, though, so she didn't question him.

"God, Nick. Keep talking like that and there won't be any time at all for foreplay."

"We could join the bathroom stall club now before we eat, then head up after and take things slow."

"Tempting." Bree gestured toward their approaching waiter. "I think that's our food coming out, though."

"Then you're saved, for now. But I do reserve the right to drag you to an unattended bathroom at a time to be named later."

"Deal."

After they'd finished their meal, Nick ordered some sweet brandy drinks off the place's cocktail menu and slid close to her in the booth. The waiter smiled at them and took a few moments to rearrange the few items on the table to better suit their new positions before placing their fluted glasses carefully.

"That's better," Nick said once the man was gone, sliding a hand to cover her leg just over her knee. "Do you know what first drew me to you?"

"I've always assumed it was my devastating beauty." Bree said it with the tiniest hint of sarcasm. She knew Nick hated it when she was self-depreciating but didn't usually mind it when she was just pointing out the obvious. Objectively, he was the more beautiful of the two of them—by far, in her estimation—and she found ways to remind them both of the fact fairly often.

"Close, but no. It was actually that you didn't find me all that special."

Bree quirked an eyebrow at him.

Nick raised both hands in placation. "No, really. Specifically, you didn't give one shit about my presence."

"Not true."

"You didn't. I came in and you were in the middle of a discussion with Alise and Will. They both greeted me while you stood there expectantly, waiting for all that to be over so the three of you could return to your discussion. You barely even glanced at me. It made a big impression."

"I don't remember that. I remember you teasing me and being an ass all through dinner. I didn't even realize you were flirting until you insisted on walking me home even though I obviously needed no help on that score from you."

"Of course, because you're so tough. Anyway, at that point I'd had every woman I ever pursued wrapped around my finger in short order. Yet there you were, not even batting an eyelash in my direction. I had a hard-on all through that dinner."

"You did not."

He nodded. "It's true, and now I want to try and get that feeling back."

"Well, we do have two children together so it might be a bit late to play hard to get."

He leaned in closer and whispered the rest breathily into her ear. "What I want is for you to otherwise engage your mind while I commit lascivious acts upon your body. I want you there and consenting, but completely occupied with other matters while I fuck you. Impervious to my ministrations. I want you to tolerate my copulation but totally ignore me."

"I'll try," she said out loud, thinking that what he asked was impossible. How could she ignore the best thing that had ever happened to her?

She snaps back to the now as his tongue crosses roughly over her clit. She feels her hips jerk her pelvis closer to his jaw involuntarily and places both forearms on either side of the material to dive back into her reading. They had discussed this element of their play in advance, but feeling his mouth on her now, she realizes how foolish she's been, thinking she could withstand this stimulation from him without a reaction. Intellectually, Bree knows that Nick needs to get her wet enough to accept his cock, but as he continues to lap at her pussy, she's getting very sure she won't be able to hold onto her feigned disinterest for much longer.

The harder she focuses on the words in front of her—*one end of each to an IC pin circuit foil as listed in Figure 6.2 and pictured in Figure 6.1. After the wires are soldered, push them flat against the board*—the further and further his actions on her flesh recede from her mind. She knows he's there beneath her, licking, sucking, and fingering her, but it's as if it is happening to another person.

The nuts and bolts of the directions are actually quite engrossing, and she's getting excited to do the build after this. Bree is feeling so detached that she allows her mind's eye to clinically observe that Nick's fingers are working at a particularly sensitive place within her. He chuckles deep in his throat when a gush of her juices pours out to cover his hand.

She remembers him arriving home from work just a few short hours ago. She'd asked about his day and he was halfway through a story about his boss before he even asked why it was so quiet.

"Where are the kids?"

"Sleepover at your mother's."

"Oh." He finished his story about his boss and got around to asking about her day.

"It came."

Bree pulled the robot kit they'd ordered out from behind the counter. His jaw dropped open, understanding all too well what that meant for their evening.

"I need to read all about the circuitry. It's a very long instruction manual. Probably take me an hour to get through it." She pulled the instruction manual out of the box and flipped idly through the pages, watching out of the corner of her eye for his reaction to her announcement. "Maybe more."

Bree falls out of her memory and back into the moment when Nick pushes her legs away from his shoulders. She can sense rather than feel him moving around under the desk, touching himself, obviously readying his cock for the adventure ahead. Her pussy clenches at the thought of him pressing in until she has to stifle a moan. Nick's cock could not be a more perfect fit for her. The feel of the thick crown of his cockhead rubbing past the rim of her opening is a sensation so sweet the memory of it alone has her weak. A dangerous path for her mind to take.

Nick bends up and out from the far side of her desk, and as he rounds it, coming toward her, she can see the purple handle of the plug he's worked into his own ass. Bree catches herself breathing harder from watching him and she immediately reorients herself to the manual—*statement for the ZX81/TS1000/TS1500 as described in Chapter 3 and as you did for the software. If you are plugging an RX81 board directly into the TS2068, then start the*—He pinches her nipple and uses it to pull her breast up and out from her chest. Bree is very proud that she only notices it peripherally. *Two will operate within a voltage range of 9.5 to 18 VDC. The maximum current draw is 800 mA. The motor steps 7.5 degrees per pulse.* She is more than able to drown the sensations of her body out this time, just with deep thought.

Nick walks over to stand behind her, bumping his erection against her ass. He grips her hip in one hand and uses his feet to push hers farther apart on the floor. She nudges back against him and makes him take a step back so she can walk her feet back and lean down lower onto her elbows, face still pressed into the manual, reading away.

This was the point where she lost it, their first time trying this. Nick had finished explaining the fantasy pretty thoroughly to Bree while finishing their drinks in the restaurant. They went upstairs and things got started perfectly. She read a new science fiction novel while he got them both ready to fuck without her involvement. It had felt unusual to Bree, but considering that was the point, and he was getting so into it, she settled into her book and tried to tune it all out. Then he'd slid his dick in, and she lost it utterly. The act of penetration had never made her come so fast. She'd had to bite her own lip shut in order not to vocalize through her intense, long-lasting orgasm. There was no pretending for her to do. She knew he could feel her muscles gripping and pulling at his cock for his release. He'd told her repeatedly that it was okay, that she'd done well, but he had not nutted or wanted to mess around anymore that night. Bree was left so disappointed that she hadn't been able to give him his cherished fantasy just how he wanted it.

Bree remotely feels his thick cock slide easily into her, but rather than dwell on that, she reads on—*driver board (Figure 7.2) has enough room for at least three more motor drive outputs if one is not sufficient. All you have to add in the way of hardware is an SAA 1027 for*—and she notes that she is truly detached from the workout Nick's cock is giving her pussy. He slides all the way out and then back into her, groaning, pushing, and pulling against her body in his solo attempt to get off. His cock fills her cunt up deliciously, but that is where she allows the feeling to end. Usually, he stays mostly inside her and uses short, rapid thrusts to work himself closer without overstimulating her entrance. Now he seems totally fixated on chasing his own pleasure without worrying about the timing of her orgasm. His drawn-out movements, dragging his rock-hard prick in and out of her so slowly, speak of an attempt to delay his gratification. But his strangled grunts and moans give away that he isn't going to last much longer. Bree hasn't heard him so worked up in years.

Bree rereads the section on the verbal command modem in an effort to better understand how the mechanism will respond to them—*prepared the 8255 I/O circuit as described, you are ready to proceed with the connection of the digitalker board 8255, but not the expansion*—and understand what they tell it.

Nick's momentum picks up and the skin of his cock feels like satin over steel, so Bree flips ahead into the conclusionary section. Nick looks over her shoulder and says, "You're at the conclusion already? The conclusion, oh, god, the conclusion, read it out loud. Please, Bree. Fuck."

She reads it out loud to him, proud of how steady her voice remains. ". . . Prevent interference with the motor control, bumper switch, and voice recognition machine code routines already in the robot software. The BASIC routines include avoidance software."

He pulls all the way out of her and removes the flexible cock ring he's had firmly gripping his erection. Reaching for the remote on the corner of the desk, he triggers the vibration function of the plug in his ass and groans as the buzz settles into him.

Bree continues to read as he pushes into her body again. ". . . See from the different applications suggested in the software presented here, there are endless numbers of uses—" In some other space and time she feels the vibration of the plug through his body and cock straight into the walls of her vagina. It shakes her overtaxed nerves even further into shock.

She feels herself pulling and clenching around him so she begins to assemble the mechanism in her mind in great detail as she reads the final few elements of the build. It works. In Bree's mind, the robot she's just completed assembling whirs to life just as Nick finally reaches his bursting point. He moans and groans through a long, loud orgasm just as she reads the last sentence of the conclusion blandly.

"The addresses for the USR statements in the 13k listing (Table 5.10) already reflect these new address locations."

He sighs deeply as she finishes reading, his chest resting on her back, while his legs shake with his post-orgasm twitches. Bree flips through the diagrams, further examining the connections. After Nick comes down, he pulls out but still cuddles her from behind, stroking her hair and telling her what a great job she did. Bree is surprised at how tired doing nothing has made her.

He must have lit candles here and in their room before joining her in the office earlier; she smiles to think that he had prepared so carefully for her aftercare. He removes the dress she still has on, and then pulls her into their gigantic standing shower. She watches with interest as he washes himself briskly first and then takes care of soaping and rinsing every inch of her skin.

"Thank you, thank you, Bree. That was one of the best orgasms of my life. Next time, I'm going to make you come while you're still ignoring me. I'm going to outlast your body and force your orgasm while you're still detached from sensation. Next time."

She just laughs at him.

Nick dries her, leads her to their bed, and carefully lays her down. He pulls a pillow from along the headboard and slides it under her hips to cant her body up in the right direction. Watching her with fevered eyes, he pushes a button on the stereo to turn on a classical piano solo. It fills the room with quiet romance, and Bree thinks her heart might burst with love for him. He quickly settles down to lie between her spread, lovely long legs and proceeds to plant open-mouthed kisses up and down them for what seems like forever, heightening her anticipation to a fever pitch. Finally, he brings his lips to her ready sex and slowly takes her apart with his sucking and stroking, making her come around his gifted tongue, twice—no instruction manual required.

EASY RIDE

Katrina Jackson

I signed my divorce papers 402 days ago. My therapist says I'll stop counting the days eventually. I don't know that I believe her, but I've only been seeing her for ninety days, so I'm trying to remain optimistic. Besides, I just need someone to talk to, now that I'm alone.

When I applied to be the new associate dean of liberal arts at East Bay Community College, I only wanted to get away from my ex-husband and his new wife, my former best friend. I wanted to be somewhere where no one had ever known me as Mrs. Neil Kent.

That's how people used to introduce me at the boring society dinners where Neil hung me from his arm, in clothes he'd chosen for me, a hairstyle he'd criticized me into adjusting, and makeup he didn't like but assured me I needed. I wasted years of my life at events he'd never have taken Carla to, because she was too loud, her clothes too garish, and her personality just too much. At least that's how he'd always described her to me.

I used to be too much. When Neil and I first met, I had passions.

I used to blare my music at four in the morning and dance while I cleaned my kitchen in my underwear. I loved wearing prints and bright colors. I laughed loudly and incessantly. I don't want to sound arrogant—although my therapist says self-esteem isn't arrogance—but I used to be great.

Then Neil got a job at a prestigious investment firm and everything changed. I became a husk of myself, a pretty mannequin for him to show off. I didn't recognize what had happened to me until I was running barefoot down our quiet street after walking in on my husband and best friend fucking in my bed.

That was 476 days ago. And even though I now live 2,769 miles away, sometimes I still wake up in the middle of the night in a cold sweat, haunted by the sound of their laughter and moans. I've mostly scrubbed the images from my brain, but I can't seem to exorcise the sounds.

So I see my therapist twice a week, hoping that she's right and one day I will move on. One day I'll laugh loudly again. One day I won't stand in front of the mirror and hear Neil's voice in my head saying, "You're wearing *that?*" I won't remember Carla laughing at me: "Of course Neil's not cheating on you." One day I'll like who I am again. But it's only been 402 days since I stopped being Tysha Kent and started trying to figure out who Tysha Freeman has become. I haven't been her since I was twenty-two and she feels like a stranger.

I remember that twenty-two-year-old Tysha was delightfully impulsive. She'd definitely have snatched a flyer from the campus community events board for a "community fundraiser and get together" at the Oakland Footmen's motorcycle clubhouse. She'd have put on something tight and short and gone to the party because "why not?" But I'm not that girl anymore. I can rattle off all the reasons why not without thinking. Still, I keep that flyer in my purse; it's a leaden reminder of who I used to be.

On Friday night I leave campus at exactly five o'clock. I drive home certain that tonight will be like most nights since I left Neil. I'll have a frozen pizza, a glass of wine, and a good cry on the couch. But when I drop my purse on the table by the door, it topples over and the Footmen logo—a tiny motorcyclist under a raised fist—stares up at me like a challenge.

I decide to take it.

Instead of going to the kitchen and opening the freezer, I carry that flyer to my bedroom and throw my closet open. I have to dig to unearth a sparkly rose-gold cocktail dress I bought four years ago but never wore. Neil thought it was too loud, too tight, too short. I slip it on and find that he was right. It's perfect. Then I pull every shoebox from my closet until I find the brand new pair of Perspex peep-toe heels, a post-divorce gift from my cousin because she knew Neil would've hated them.

I sit down at my vanity to do my makeup. I look at myself and know that I want more, because Neil always wanted less. Less foundation, less eyeshadow, nude lipstick, less me. I fight through that conditioning with shaking hands as I brush and blend the creams and powders over my skin. It takes me three tries to lay down the thick line of winged eyeliner I used to love. I put on more coats of mascara than layers of clothes on my body, and I swipe a matte, dark plum lipstick on my lips that accentuates their full curves. It's not as much or as perfect as twenty-two-year-old Tysha preferred, but it's far more than Tysha Kent had been allowed.

I call an Uber and sit on my front porch lest I change my mind while I wait. I clutch my purse in my lap as the driver takes me to the "wrong" side of town. The side of town that hasn't been gentrified yet, where there are still trash-filled lots stalked by feral cats. The side of town my well-meaning white colleagues suggested I avoid when house-hunting.

I stand in front of a warehouse surrounded by a tall chain-link fence, take a deep breath, and then rush forward as I push the air from my lungs. I hand over the twenty-dollar donation entrance fee and let the bouncer stamp my hand with the Footmen insignia, flinching not at his touch but at the tangible proof that I'm here, that I did this. And then I step into a room full of as much leather as those society events had been draped with silk.

I expected a motorcycle clubhouse to smell like stale beer, cigarette smoke, and engine oil, and I'm almost right. The beer at least smells fresh, and the smoke drifting into the rafters isn't from cigarettes. The backlit bar illuminates the low, round tables in front of me, while soft spotlights make the dance floor across the room seem mysterious and sexy. Al Green plays over the speakers, his gentle rasp a sharp contrast to the bar full of men covered in leather and jeans.

"You look lost," someone says, and I jump. The voice isn't too deep or too high-pitched, but it is smooth. And playful. I think that's what catches me off guard.

Neil had always been so serious; he'd critiqued every ounce of silly from me.

"I might be," I say in a shaky voice, wondering at this impulsive decision as I look up at this stranger.

Even in my heels he towers over me, with broad shoulders and a smirk and dark, intense eyes. I should shrink from him. But I don't. When he invades my personal space, I swear I can feel his warmth touching all the bare skin I've left exposed. I lean into it.

His face is half-covered in a dark beard that makes him look dangerous. But when he smiles, I see a toothpick between his teeth. My sex clenches. Facial hair isn't usually my thing. Or more accurately, Neil had always been clean-shaven and I'd never known anything else.

I can't help but catalogue all the ways he's unlike Neil. My therapist assures me I'll stop doing this too—but not yet.

"Someone invite you?" he asks, his eyes lewdly assessing me from head to toe.

"I-I saw a flyer on campus."

He squints at me and frowns. "They card you when you get here? You don't look like a student."

It's only when he says that that I realize I could run into one of my students, and I'm terrified at the possibility. "I shouldn't have come," I splutter and I try to turn.

"Whoa, whoa, hold on now," he says, grabbing me around the middle. His big palm slides around my hip, holding me still. "I didn't mean that in a bad way at all." He says the last two words to my cleavage, his hand flexing on my waist.

"I'm not a student," I whisper.

"Good. I'm not into jailbait." And then his eyes shift to mine. "Lemme give you a tour."

"Um . . ."

He smiles mischievously, that toothpick bobbing. "I'm the club's social chair," he says. "It's my job to welcome new people. But this would be my pleasure."

The way he says that last word is dirty. There's no other way to describe it, because he's not trying to hide his lust. And that, more than the toothpick or his hand on me, keeps me from running away. Because Neil never looked at me with such hunger.

His hand slides to the small of my back as he turns me toward the room. He walks me around the bar, nodding at people absent-mindedly as we pass, his arm almost possessive around my waist and his hungry gaze locked on mine.

"So you haven't been to one of our get-togethers before?"

I shake my head.

"What made you come tonight?"

"I-I don't know actually. I just moved to California," I admit.

"Where from?"

"North Carolina."

His feral smile widens, and his fingers gently dig into my hip. My breath hitches.

"That's where you got that sexy-ass accent?" he asks with a nod as if he's answering his own question.

I shake my head. "It's just my accent."

He circles in front of me, and I realize he's walked me to the dance floor.

"It's sexy," he says definitively as he pulls me against his big, tall body.

"I don't dance," I splutter. But what I mean is that Neil hated dancing, so I stopped.

"So what? You paid the cover charge just to look?" he asks, with a raised eyebrow.

My mouth opens and closes.

His upper lip quirks up and he smiles.

"I don't know why I came," I say again.

He nods and begins to move me side-to-side in a gentle sway. "We do these dances every couple months to raise money for the local elementary school. The money's for the kids, but the dances are for grown folks. So if you need to make yourself feel good, just say you came to give back."

The song changes to Smokey's "Cruising," and the near-empty dance floor fills suddenly, the crowd pressing me to him as his hand pulls me even closer. My already warm skin heats.

The tips of his fingers softly touch my wrist, making my breath hitch. His hand moves up my bare arm. His short nails gently scrape over my shoulder. I gasp as his fingers trace my collarbone. That touch is more intimate than anything I've felt in years. Maybe ever.

I grab his wrist with one hand while the other flies to his belt; I hold on tight. He smiles as if he likes my nervous touch on him. We're so close that I feel the low rumble of his laughter in the pit of my stomach. It joins the butterflies going batshit inside me as his thumb moves over my chin and plays at the curve of my bottom lip.

I've never felt anything like his body against mine. Everywhere he touches me is like sensory overload. His stiff jeans scratch my thighs, hard where I'm soft. His vest is so smooth. My nipples tighten as I imagine myself naked, writhing against all that well-worn leather. I hardly know who I am at that thought, but I like it.

He moves my hand from his belt to his chest, right onto that vest, and holds it there, inviting me to touch him if I want.

I want.

"I didn't come to give back." I whisper that admission as he guides me in a circle to the beat.

"That's cool. The kids appreciate your money anyway," he says with a smile and shrug.

"But I do want to feel good," I say and then I swallow, shocked at myself.

I feel his laughter again. "How good?" he asks me, pressing his leg between my thighs and squeezing my ass cheek in his rough hand.

I moan, long and slow, and then grind against his thigh. "We shouldn't—" I gasp, even though I already am.

"Who's gon' stop us?" he asks and helps me dry hump his leg.

I'm wet. "Someone might see," I whisper.

"Who cares?" He laughs.

Who cares? I wonder at that for a second. My therapist once asked me what hurt worse: my husband's betrayal, my best friend's betrayal, or knowing that everyone would know about it. I'd told her that it was Carla's betrayal that cut the deepest, but that wasn't accurate. The painful truth I'd been hiding for months was that the idea of seeing pity in the eyes of the other society wives had near crippled me emotionally. So I signed the divorce papers and ran.

Who cares? Me. I used to care so much.

But as I let this stranger grind me against his stiff jeans and growing erection, I stop caring who'll see me and focus on how good his belt buckle feels digging into my stomach.

As I suck my bottom lip into my mouth, I feel his low, guttural growl reverberate in my chest. My sex quivers. I haven't been with anyone besides Neil in over a decade, but as I stare up at this man—shuddering in his arms—I decide that I'm not leaving this party until I've put my pussy directly on his beard. And the way he's looking at me, I think he's in full agreement with that plan.

"Let me buy you a drink," he rasps in the seconds of silence after the song ends.

I want to tell him that I'm not thirsty—not for anything he could buy at the bar, at least. But I nod and let him lead me away, hoping the short walk will clear my head. It doesn't.

At the bar, I grip the polished wood under my hands and swallow a moan as he settles behind me. His hips press into my ass as I feel his mouth at my right ear. His big hands land on the bar next to mine. His thick fingers are adorned with heavy steel rings on his thumbs and one on his right pinky. I wonder what they'll feel like on my naked body.

He chuckles into my ear as if he knows what I'm thinking.

I shudder from my scalp to deep inside my sex.

"What do you want?" he asks me.

"Is this in your job description as social chair?" I ask instead of answering, pushing my ass back at him.

His hips press forward to meet me. "It's not forbidden in the job description. Let's focus on that." His laugh is a sexy rumble.

I laugh, but it sounds like a moan. Thankfully none of the people around us at the bar seem to notice, or maybe he's right: who cares? We begin to move together to the slow rhythm of the music, his erection growing bigger and harder, my panties wetter, my mouth drier, his breath harsher in my ear.

For a few blissful moments, I don't think about Neil or Carla. I'm not counting the seconds, minutes, or days, because my mind's not running the show. My body is.

"What can I get you, Easy?" the bartender asks, knocking on the bar to get our attention.

He lifts his mouth from my ear, but his erection is still grinding into my ass, his heartbeat pounding against my back. "Give us a second, Trill," he says.

The other man chuckles as he walks away. My face is hot with shame.

"No one here's gonna judge you," he whispers softly.

I turn and make eye contact with him, and immediately get lost in the near-black pools of his eyes and the dirty smirk on his face. My breath hitches as his right thumb strokes the back of my right hand.

"Easy?" I ask.

That small smile grows. "Club nickname."

"And yours is Easy?"

His face moves closer to mine. "Short for Easy Rider," he says, his breath brushing my cheek. He licks his lips.

I don't need to know this man to know what this look means. He licks his lips because he wants to lick me.

"Are you?" I ask in a hoarse voice. "An easy rider?"

He smirks, but his gaze hardens. "I can be," he says.

I turn my head, encouraging him to whisper in my ear again. He laughs as his palm flattens against my stomach and pulls me back to him. His lips touch the shell of my ear, lightly caressing the lobe. "If that's what the situation calls for. But I can also ride hard if I need to." His tongue grazes my skin.

I shiver and moan.

"Lemme finish your tour," he says, roughly turning me from the bar. But when he grabs my hand, his touch and smile are so gentle, it's bewildering. I'm lost in the heady mix of lust and confusion and desire coursing through my veins. I've never known anything could feel like this.

I follow him on shaky legs to the back of the clubhouse, where the sounds of the party are muffled, all the music and human chatter transformed into vibrations through the floorboards and up the walls. Or maybe that's just my body quaking in response to the echoes of Easy's heavy steps in the empty hall and his palm pressed to mine.

He pushes open another door and ushers me through.

I'm expecting a cheap storage room, maybe a cot in the corner. A place where members bring all the women they pick up at these kinds of parties, something sad and pathetic that'll shock me out of this uncharacteristically reckless moment. But the small office seems normal. There's a desk in the corner with an office chair on one side and a couple of hard-backed chairs on the other, a filing cabinet in another corner, and that's it.

He closes the door behind us and locks it.

"I was expecting something else," I admit with a small, nervous smile.

"Let me guess, a dirty rollaway bed and a bowl of condoms?"

I laugh—loud. So loud I shock myself. "Something like that," I admit.

He grins. "We're technically not supposed to fuck in the clubhouse," he says. My body jumps at the word *fuck*. Neil would never.

"So you're breaking the rules?"

He steps closer with that dirty smile back on his face. I expect him to grab me again. I want him to. He doesn't. But he does pin me with his gaze. His eyes travel down my body, and then he begins to move around me, drinking me in with his stare. I shiver. Neil's gaze used to dissect me, but Easy's eyes on me feel like a blanket, a warm covering that holds me together when I want to fly apart.

He moves back in front of me and sucks on that toothpick one more time before plucking it from his lips. His smile sharpens, letting me know he's thinking about putting his mouth on me. I've never known a man with such an expressive and open face, and it makes me squirm in the best way.

"I'm only breaking a few rules," he admits casually, his eyes settling on my hips.

I feel like I'm on display for him. As if I put on this dress and did my hair and makeup all for him.

"But you're worth it," he whispers.

Those words nearly make my knees buckle. For a decade, Neil's criticisms were reminders that no matter what, I'd never be worthy of him. But seeing myself through someone else's eyes for the first time in so long teaches me something I know I need to talk to my therapist about. Was it possible that while I was shearing off parts of myself to fit into the box Neil had created for me, he was the one who wasn't worthy of me?

But that's an exploration for another day. Tonight, I let Easy's firm declaration that I *am* worthy be true, because I want it to be.

I take a deep breath and wait until he raises his eyes to my face. "Ask me what I want again."

He rubs a hand over his beard and smiles. "What do you want, sweetheart?"

"I want you on your knees," I whisper, so nervous to say it aloud that my voice shakes. I expect him to react like Neil did at the beginning of our relationship every time I tried to express a sexual desire, like to teach him how to get me off.

He doesn't.

Easy lowers himself to his knees in front of me. No questions. No hesitation. I feel powerful in a way I never could have imagined four hundred days ago. He smiles up at me and licks his lips. He knows what's coming, he wants it, and that makes me weak. I take a few shaky steps forward. He grabs the backs of my thighs, his fingers digging into my flesh, supporting me.

"Do you want to taste me?" I ask.

"I do," he says in a deep growl that makes my sex flutter.

I reach down and run my hands through his hair. The strands are soft between my fingers, and his eyes close briefly. "Go ahead," I whisper.

He opens his eyes, watching me as his hands move up my legs. His fingers snake under the hem of my short dress, and he pushes the fabric up the curve of my ass. He caresses my left thigh as his other hand grips my right knee. I hold onto him as he lifts my leg over his shoulder.

I begin to rethink this position and open my mouth to tell him so.

But he stops me. "I got you," he whispers desperately, sinking back onto his heels as he lifts my leg higher, setting the sole of my shoe onto his shoulder.

His eyes leave mine. I watch him smile and lick his lips again as his face moves between my legs. Neil never looked at me like that. When he *had* to give me oral sex, he crawled under the covers and licked me with a stiff tongue, poking at me like an experiment. He made me feel dirty for wanting it and deficient for needing it. So I stopped asking. He didn't offer. And I never got off.

But with a single look, Easy makes me so wet I'm nearly ashamed.

He runs a finger along the crotch of my underwear and smiles before pulling the scrap of soaked fabric aside. I moan as the cool air hits my wet sex. He chuckles, the soft gusts of his laughter making my hands flex in his hair.

"I got you," he says again, but this time against my sex, followed by his tongue.

My moan is practically a shout in the quiet office. Easy's wet tongue strokes my lips from clit to opening, swirling at my entrance, teasing me. When his lips cover my clit, I cry out again as I shudder in his hold.

He squeezes my ass, pulling me over his face, encouraging me to grind down onto his tongue. The downy hair of his beard is soft; I whine as it rubs against my sex and inner thighs. He licks and sucks at me like a starving man.

"Oh, god," I groan.

He increases the pressure but not the speed of his tongue, tasting me in unhurried and thorough swipes. Sex with Neil is my barometer and the bar he set was low. But to say that Easy is better than Neil would be a disservice. His mouth covers my pussy, his strong hands massage my ass, his beard strokes my thighs, and the vibrations of his moans against my quivering pussy aren't just better: they obliterate even the memory of all the bad sex with Neil in a second of pounding heartbeats.

I laugh at the freedom of my coming orgasm as I writhe on his mouth. I tighten my grip in his hair and pull. He grunts and groans against my pussy. My legs begin to shake, and I come with a loud moan as I ride Easy's tongue. But he doesn't stop, and the aftershocks of that first orgasm roll through me, building in intensity again. When he sucks my clit into his mouth, I fly all the way apart. It's perfect. I'm only standing because he's still holding me together. On his face.

"Oh, fuck, stop," I finally whine.

He looks up at me with a wet beard and licks his lips.

"I can't take anymore," I admit in panting breaths.

"We'll see," he says, even as he moves my foot from his shoulder. He holds me at the waist until I can stand on my own. He climbs to his feet and moves me back until my butt hits the desk.

"Is that all you need?" he asks.

I quickly shake my head. "Do you have condoms?" I pant.

He dips his head and rubs the back of his neck. I see the smile on his face. "We're not supposed to have sex in the clubhouse," he says as he walks to the filing cabinet and opens the bottom drawer. I watch as he pulls out a half-empty bowl of condoms.

I laugh.

"Things happen," he says. "Better to be safe than sorry."

As Easy walks back to me I appreciate the way he moves, again so unlike Neil. His shoulders are relaxed, his gait long and slow. He's not a man who looks like he's ever been in a hurry or unsure of himself. He walks like he knows who he is and what he has to offer and doesn't need anyone else to validate that. I'm turned on and envious.

And then my eyes settle on the front of his jeans and it's my turn to lick my lips.

"Next time," he laughs. "I need to be inside you."

I've never had someone need me sexually before. Neil had had Carla for that. But this moment isn't about them, so for the first time in four hundred days I force my thoughts to stay in the here and now.

I lock eyes with Easy as I shimmy out of my underwear.

He stops mid-step and groans, "Fuck."

"I'm glad we're on the same page."

"Same paragraph," he says, throwing the condoms onto the desk so he can rip that big belt buckle open.

I step forward and cover his hands. "Let me?"

"Same fucking sentence," he says as his hands fall away.

I keep my eyes on his as I unbutton his pants and slowly pull the zipper open. I push his jeans and boxers just far enough down his legs to free his dick. When I cover him with my hand, his head falls back on a groan. I squeeze and stroke him, just enough to feel him harden in my grasp, and then I reach for a condom.

He tilts his head back to watch as I open the foil wrapper, grab him again, and slowly roll the latex into place.

"What's your name?" he growls at me with a laugh as he grabs my ass and lifts me onto the desk.

"Tysha," I moan. I've never moaned my own name before.

He grabs me behind the knees, spreading my legs wide. I feel obscene and beautiful. He caresses my knee with his thumb as his other hand grips his erection and moves it toward my opening.

"My name's Bobby," he says.

"You don't look like a Bobby." I gasp as he teases my opening with the tip of his dick.

"Short for Roberto."

I grab him at the waist and pull him closer, inside me. "I like Easy."

He smiles. "So do I."

"But I don't want an easy ride," I say as I move a hand to the back of his neck and pull his mouth close. "I want you to fuck me hard. Can you do that, Easy?"

His dark eyes are dancing with arousal and mirth. Neil never looked at me that way.

When he thrusts fully into me, we both groan. "I sure fucking can," he growls and then kisses me.

I can taste myself on his lips.

I wrap my legs around his waist. He starts to fuck me in deep, strong strokes as his tongue and teeth punish my mouth. The room fills with the sounds of our bodies slapping together and the desk banging against the wall. All I can taste is my sex on Easy's lips and the slightly bitter note of tequila underneath. All I can hear is Easy's moans and panting breaths. All I can feel is his hard dick exploring every inch of my pussy, his hands pushing my legs open, and the small tremors of another orgasm on the horizon.

I'm near tears when I come, shuddering around Easy's shaft. He fucks me through that release, dragging it out until I'm an incoherent mess. Then he grips my hips and pounds into me, riding me hard like I demanded, until his shout eventually fills the quiet room, reverberating through my body.

It's been 476 days since I walked in on my husband fucking my best friend. When Easy comes with a growling shout and my name on his lips, I decide that's more than enough time spent wallowing in the past.

SWEATER WEATHER

Elia Winters

Paige was only planning to borrow a sweater. After months of living with her roommate, Lila, sharing a two-bedroom apartment near the university where they both go to grad school, they've developed the kind of casual intimacy where Paige knows borrowing a sweater is no big deal. Lila has always been the friendly sort of "what's mine is yours" roommate, anyway, always willing to share groceries and shampoo. But upon opening the suitcase of not-sweaters from Lila's closet, Paige realizes her mistake. Unfortunately, she's still standing in front of the giant open suitcase of kink and bondage gear when Lila gets home early and walks into her bedroom.

The silence between them stretches out for an uncomfortably long time. Paige knows she's blushing. Fair-skinned and freckled, she blushes at everything, and discovering your roommate is apparently kinky as fuck is *more* than enough to get her blushing.

Lila, though, only smiles. Her body language even *relaxes,* angular shoulders going soft and loose, like she's finally able to let go of some hidden tension.

"I'm sorry," Paige blurts out, taking one step back from the suitcase where it lies open on Lila's bed. "I just wanted to borrow a sweater. I thought these were sweaters. I didn't think you'd mind."

"Those aren't sweaters." Lila is still smiling her enigmatic smile that makes Paige flush all over.

"I can see they're not sweaters." Paige bites her lip. "I. Um. I know what they are."

"Do you?" Lila's eyebrows go up. "That saves a bit of explaining, I guess."

Paige was not planning on having this conversation with her roommate, not now, not ever, but she's accidentally discovered a whole trove of kink gear, so it seems fair to admit a bit of her own habits. "I've seen them on the Internet."

Lila laughs. It's a familiar sound; Paige has heard Lila laugh at television shows and cat videos and sometimes Paige's terrible jokes, and it sets her at ease a bit. She *knows* Lila. They're friends, or at least friendly, and even if they've never delved into this kind of conversation, it's just sex. It's normal and healthy, right? Nothing to be ashamed about.

Lila walks over to stand beside Paige, staring down into the suitcase on the bed. "I haven't taken any of this stuff out in a while." She strokes a hand over the curve of a leather cuff, fingers the suede falls of a flogger. "Lately, I haven't had any sweet submissive girls asking me to tie them up and have my way with them."

Paige sucks in a breath, because Lila is *flirting* and this can't be happening. They haven't had these conversations, haven't crossed these lines, and Paige has always assumed this crush is one-sided and hopeless. She's thought of Lila's full breasts and slender fingers, fantasized about the crushed-berry redness of her lips, imagined the way Lila's blonde, wavy hair would tickle against her soft skin in bed. Now, Lila has opened this door, and Paige's hitching breaths probably tell her all she needs to know.

"I hear you sometimes when you touch yourself." Lila's tone remains matter-of-fact, casually informational, like she's sharing highlights from a podcast. "These walls are terribly thin."

"Oh, my god." Paige turns away; it's too much, and her skin is going to catch fire with embarrassment and wanting. "Lila. Lila, what the *fuck*."

"Do you think about me, Paige?"

Paige wraps her arms around her middle, hugging the curves of her own body. Maybe this is a fever dream. Maybe she's going to wake up in her bed, any moment, soaking wet and trembling, because this can't be happening.

Lila's gentle touch on her arm makes her turn, and Paige forces herself to meet her roommate's eyes. Lila's breathing faster. Her eyes are sharp and intense and filled with—with *desire*. Paige's breath catches in her throat again.

"Yes." Paige forces the word out.

Lila looks back down at the suitcase. "Do you like this sort of thing? Is that why you're looking at it on the Internet?"

Paige nods, and then tries her voice again. "Yeah." It's whisper-quiet and terrified.

Lila turns to face her roommate, running one finger delicately down the side of Paige's cheek, her head tipped to the side like she's considering something.

"I'd love to play with you, Paige. If you want."

Paige is nodding already, but Lila touches her lips with a finger to shush her.

"Not tonight. This weekend. In the meantime, if you want to play with me, email me five or more videos or stories that turn you on between now and Friday night, and include what turns you on about them. I want to know your fantasies. Can you do that?"

Paige presses a hand to her face in embarrassment, but she says "Yes" through her fingers. Lila laughs again.

"I'm starting to think you're into the humiliation." She pats Paige's cheek. "Oh, and one more thing."

"What?"

"No orgasms this week." Lila smiles sweetly. "I like my toys needy."

Paige is still standing there in shock when Lila drags another suitcase out of the closet and pops it open. "Sweaters are in here. Help yourself."

The next four days are torture, but Paige secretly loves it. Each night, she finds another video or two to send Lila, complete with a description of what she finds hot. The process is terrifyingly arousing, and she goes to sleep each night wet and aching. Sometimes she rubs her clit, unable to resist, but she stops short of orgasm. These furtive touches only make her arousal worse, but she can't seem to stop.

Lila acts as though nothing is happening between them. They share meal prep, watch television together sometimes, and enjoy casual conversation, but Lila doesn't bring up a single element of their deal nor does she mention anything about Paige's emails. Paige is burning up inside with the uncertainty of it all, but she wants it, she wants all of it.

Finally, though, on Saturday evening, when they've both finished homework and are crashed in front of the television, Paige's phone vibrates.

Go into my bedroom and take off all your clothes. I want you kneeling on the floor in five minutes when I get in there.

She looks over at Lila, who's got her phone in one hand but is otherwise staring at the television like nothing's happening. When Paige doesn't move right away, though, Lila glances over at her, then at the clock.

"Four minutes," Lila says.

Paige rushes into the bedroom on shaking legs. She's never

done this, never done anything like this. It's all blurry like a dream. When she's taken off all her clothes and set them aside, she kneels on the carpet. Everything's silent but the echo of her heartbeat in her throat.

The seconds tick by into minutes before Lila pushes open the door to her bedroom. Paige stares at the ground, at Lila's bare feet on the carpet, her toenails painted light pink. She's too nervous to look up. Lila's wearing jeans, but then her jeans puddle down around her ankles, and Paige makes a noise in her throat somewhere between a squeak and a gasp.

"You're adorable." Lila's tone is affectionate. She cups the side of Paige's face, turns her chin up to force Paige's eye contact. "I'm sorry I didn't know about this sooner. We could have been having so much fun together."

Paige swallows hard. "Same," she manages to say.

Lila strokes Paige's hair, gently, like she's calming a skittish animal. It feels good but it's also clearly a mark of dominance, and Paige's insides can't settle on their reaction.

"Here's how this is going to work." Lila's tone is direct and calm. "I'm going to ask you some questions tonight, and you're going to answer honestly. If you want me to stop or slow down, you can say stop or slow down, and I will. If you prefer, we can use green, yellow, or red. I'll respond to any of those. Do you understand?"

Paige nods.

"Use your words."

"I understand," Paige says.

Lila takes off her sweater. She's wearing only a matching set of bra and panties now. "Have you ever submitted to anyone before?" she asks.

"No."

Lila nods thoughtfully. "Have you ever slept with a woman before?"

"Yes."

"Did you touch yourself this week?"

Paige squeezes her eyes shut. "Yes."

"Look at me."

Paige forces her eyes open.

"Did you come?" Lila asks.

Paige shakes her head. "No."

Lila smiles. "Good girl."

The praise makes Paige hot all over, embarrassed and pleased all at once.

Lila has her suitcase out, the same one that Paige had discovered earlier this week, and she removes a pair of leather cuffs.

"Have you ever been tied up before?" Lila asks.

"I've . . . tied myself up," Paige admits.

Lila makes a soft noise of admiration. "I'd love to watch that sometime."

The thought of Lila watching her has Paige even more turned on. If Lila were to investigate, she would find Paige dripping wet already, having barely even touched her.

Lila has her hold up her hands, and then expertly fastens the leather cuffs around Paige's wrists. The leather is snug, tight enough that Paige can't pull out of them. Lila clips them together with a simple, small carabiner, the kind with a guard so it can't accidentally unsnap, and Paige's anxiety ramps up as she realizes she can't get the right angle to free herself. Not that she wants to, but the reality that she *can't* crashes down on her and somehow makes her even wetter.

Lila turns her back to Paige and starts poking around in the suitcase. "You sent me such a nice assortment of videos, I had a hard time choosing what to plan for tonight. But I think we're going to have fun. I might even let you come tonight."

Paige sucks in a breath. She hadn't thought of it as a *maybe,* but she knows what she said in some of those emails. She knows she wrote: *I like it when he makes her beg to come* and *sometimes I have chastity fantasies.* She both loves and hates the way Lila is keeping her guessing.

Lila kneels down in front of Paige so they're eye-to-eye. She holds up a pair of nipple clamps so Paige can see them, see their wicked metal bite and the heaviness of the chain.

"Have you ever used these before?" Lila asks. Paige shakes her head before remembering to speak.

"No." She wants to add some honorific after, the word incomplete in her mouth, and Lila notices.

"You can call me Miss if it helps."

Paige might die from embarrassment if desire doesn't kill her first.

Lila holds up the chain, letting the clips dangle.

"Open your mouth and hold this for me."

Paige closes her teeth around the cold, metallic chain, the clips dangling freely, as Lila begins to twist and pinch her nipples. Paige cries out, muffled, nearly opening her mouth out of reflex before Lila tuts.

"Don't drop them, now."

The sharp spikes of pleasure-pain race through Paige's body. Lila is teasing her nipples into tender, aching peaks. It's the first time she's even *touched* Paige, and Paige wants to gasp and cry out but can't drop the clamps.

"Good girl. Open."

When Paige opens her mouth, Lila takes the clamps from her. The bitter taste lingers.

Lila holds Paige's breast, and then carefully closes the clamp on the full, tender peak of her nipple. This time, Paige does cry out, her body jerking in reflex. The pain is *beautiful,* sharp and radiant, and she is breathless with it. Lila watches her reaction with intent.

"I thought you might like that."

Rather than put the other clamp on directly, though, Lila loops it down through the carabiner connecting Paige's cuffs and then back up again. Paige has to lift her hands an inch as Lila attaches the clamp to her other nipple; the pain sears through her once more. Now, if she lowers her hands too far, they tug on the clamps. Lila smiles at her and begins to shimmy out of the rest of her clothing.

She sits on the edge of the bed and spreads her knees wide. "Come here."

Blushing, Paige shuffles forward on her knees, careful not to pull the chain connecting her clamps. They swing anyway, tugging on her sensitive nipples, and she whimpers. How can anything feel so good and hurt so much at the same time?

Lila beckons her all the way to the side of the bed, and then drapes her legs over Paige's shoulders. Her pussy is right there, glistening wet, thick with the heady scent of her arousal, and god, there is *nowhere* Paige would rather be right now.

"Be a good girl."

Paige moans and buries her face in Lila's pussy.

She tastes amazing, sweet and tart at the same time. Paige wants to devour her. If only she could use her hands, she could finger her at the same time. In this position, though, she can only lick and suck at Lila's clit, dragging her tongue across the sensitive bud.

"Fuck, Paige." Lila sounds breathless, rocking her hips into Paige's face. "You're so good at this. I should tie you to the bed and ride your face every day."

Paige moans at the thought.

"I want you to rub your pretty clit," Lila says.

But when Paige reaches down, her cuffed hands pull painfully at her nipples, and she yelps and draws back in response.

Lila chuckles, low and filthy. "Why are you stopping? Don't you want to touch yourself?"

Paige tries again, curling up slightly to make it easier to reach her clit. With her bound hands, the position is awkward; she can barely get a finger on the tender, swollen bud. From here, though, she can't quite reach Lila's pussy. She's forced to kneel up, the clamps tugging fiercely into her nipples, and rub her clit through the pain.

"Good girl. Look at you." Lila strokes Paige's hair, and then uses it as a handle to hold her head in place. "Don't enjoy yourself too much, now. Suck my clit. Make me come, and maybe I'll let you come tonight."

Fuck, Paige wants to come so badly. The pain in her nipples is pulling her right to the edge of orgasm. She has to actually start rubbing more slowly so she doesn't come just from this. She tries to focus on Lila, on her clit, on the soft hitching moans and the way she rubs against Paige's face. Her thighs tremble, tension building, and Paige doubles down on her efforts. She wants to make Lila come, wants to feel her cry out beneath Paige's tongue, wants to *please* her.

Finally, Lila tenses up and comes, clit twitching in Paige's mouth, her hips jerking and body spasming as she cries out. Paige licks her through it, head clamped between Lila's thighs, her own clit and nipples throbbing with desire and pain.

Lila pushes her gently away. Paige falls back, still rubbing her clit because Lila didn't tell her to stop. Lila's juices are wet on her face.

"So good." Lila touches Paige's chin, tilting her face up, leaning all the way down to kiss her on the mouth.

Paige freezes in surprise, and then sighs in pleasure. Lila's tongue sweeps her mouth, tasting herself, before pulling back, leaving her reeling.

"Stop touching yourself," Lila commands. Paige immediately pulls her hands away.

When Lila releases the clamps, Paige cries out with the unexpected surge of pain. It's overwhelming, like knives, yet if she were still touching her clit, she might have come from it.

Lila massages her tender nipples, squeezing them, rolling them, even as Paige whimpers from the pain.

"There we go. So good for me. You're so good for me."

"Thank you, Miss," Paige says.

"I like looking at you like this, all messy and sweet." She brushes her thumb across Paige's bottom lip. "Especially when you're so desperate to come. I can see it in your eyes."

Paige doesn't bother to deny it; her body throbs from thwarted desire.

"Come up here on the bed. Lie on your back."

Paige scrambles to obey. She lets Lila clip her hands up over her head, unfastening the carabiner, and then refastening it around the bar of the metal headboard. This position highlights her vulnerability: she can't cover up, can't free her hands, has to lie there exposed as Lila traces her fingertips lightly over her skin. Paige squirms as Lila reaches her sides.

"Ticklish?" Lila does it again, this time with just her fingernails. Paige writhes and gasps and nods.

"You're so cute." Lila stops tickling her, thank god, and then gets off the bed to grab some rope. "I'm going to finish tying you up now. Would you like that?"

Blushing, Paige nods. "Yes, Miss."

Lila hums to herself as she ties Paige's legs. She first bends them at the knee, binding thigh to calf, and then folding them back toward her chest. Lila works easily, fluidly, running rope from the headboard to Paige's bindings so she can't put her legs down. She's even more exposed now, legs up and back, nothing hiding her pussy from view.

"Look how beautiful you are." Lila strokes the backs of Paige's thighs, smiling at the way she squirms. "Can't go anywhere, can you?"

Paige shakes her head, her throat too tight to speak through.

"What would you like me to do, Paige?"

Paige tries to form words. Saying it out loud is humiliating, exciting, terrifying, a dozen feelings at once.

"I won't do anything unless you ask." Lila's fingers ghost unbearably close to the place Paige wants them, then away. Paige gasps in a breath and finds her voice.

"Oh, please, please touch me. Please fuck me. Please, please make me come." Her face burns with shame and desire, but it's too late for modesty. She *wants*. God, how she wants.

"There. That wasn't so hard, was it?" Lila smiles sweetly.

Paige cries out at the first light touch against her clit. Lila barely brushes her, giving her only the faintest bit of stimulation, torturous contact that does nothing to quell Paige's burning need. Even this feather touch, though, is nearly too much. She quivers at the knowledge that she can't get away, can't hide, and it's *Lila* driving her so crazy.

When she begins pressing harder, circling Paige's clit with firmer, deliberate strokes, Paige lets loose with a broken noise and tries to thrust her hips up against Lila's hand. Lila makes a soft, thoughtful sound and continues rubbing her at the exact same pace. It's perfect, exquisite torture, and if this continues, Paige is going to come. Already, the curl of pleasure builds hot inside her belly, driving her toward that precipice.

Lila leaves her clit, dips fingers down to gather Paige's wetness, and then pushes them into Paige's mouth. "Suck," she commands, and Paige does. "Good girl," Lila croons. Paige's body sings with the double-edged sword of humiliation and desire.

She watches Lila get up off the bed and find a harness, buckling black leather straps around her hips, a practiced motion she's clearly done many times. Under Paige's attentive gaze, Lila selects a deep purple dildo and fits it into the harness. The fake cock is large, but not terrifyingly so, thick and long enough that Paige already aches with need.

Lila settles on her knees between Paige's legs and begins stroking her clit again, almost as an afterthought. "For some girls, I have them suck my cock before we begin, get it nice and wet. But you're absolutely dripping. Are you always this much of a sloppy slut, Paige?"

"Oh, god." Paige squeezes her eyes shut. "I get . . . really wet sometimes . . ."

"I think it's sexy." Lila fairly purrs the words. "Open your eyes and watch me while I fuck you."

She presses the cock slowly into Paige's pussy, pushing just the thick head inside at first. Fuck, that's so *big*. It takes her breath away. It didn't look this big in Lila's harness. It's not painful, but it stretches her out and makes her whimper as Lila gradually slides inside.

"Feel that?" Lila says. "Do you feel how big I am inside you?"

Paige nods, her muscles clenching reflexively around the thick length. "It's so good," she moans.

Stars explode behind her eyes as Lila begins to move. She rocks her hips, fucking Paige, that beautiful cock sliding in and out and sparking pleasure everywhere. It's perfect. *Perfect.* Lila knows just how to fuck, and Paige is her willing subject, helpless in the best possible ways.

"Do you want to come, sweetie?" Lila croons.

Paige nods frantically. "Please," she begs. "Please, touch my clit."

"Do you need that to come?" Lila starts fucking her a bit faster, still just as deep. "Can't come just from my cock in you?"

"I need it," Paige squirms.

"I could fuck you like this all night, then, and you'd never come? That's so tempting."

Lila's expression is devilish, and Paige whimpers.

"Please, no, please make me come." She's done being modest, desperate for release. The pleasure is building with no outlet, and she's burning up from the inside out.

"What will you give me to let you come?" Lila asks.

"Anything," Paige sobs.

"Will you be my little cock slut again?"

"Fuck, yes."

"Will you let me control your orgasms? Make you ask me every time you want to come? Do you like the thought of that?"

Paige sobs. "*Yes,* anything. *Anything.*" Lila sees inside her most private fantasies, somehow, knows exactly what buttons to push.

"So sweet. So obedient. Who wouldn't want a perfect sub like you?"

Like a blessing, Lila begins rubbing her clit in slow, steady circles, still fucking her deep and perfect. Paige tenses, suddenly right on the edge.

"Not yet," Lila orders. "Ask me again."

Her words run together. "Please, Miss, may I come?"

"Beg."

"Please! Please, oh, please, I'll do anything. I'll do—anything, I want you so bad, I've always wanted you, *please,* Mistress Lila, *please!*"

Lila closes her eyes, visibly overcome, and then nods. "You're *such* a good girl. Come for me."

Paige breaks. The pleasure crashes through her, a force of nature that can't be controlled. She pulls at her bonds, but they hold fast, keeping her trapped, helpless to the sensations. It's never been like this, never in her fantasies, and she cries from the pleasure and the possibility and the overwhelming confluence of everything she's ever wanted in bed. Finally, the world dissolves around her.

Paige comes back to herself with Lila carefully unfastening the last of the ropes holding her in place, moving her limbs with a tenderness that belies the intensity of their sex.

"You okay, sweetie?" Lila asks, brushing the hair off Paige's forehead.

Paige is a mess, sweaty and sated and vacillating between embarrassment and happiness. She nods once, then repeatedly.

Lila slips out of her harness, and then she does the unexpected: she curls up with Paige, stretching out alongside her, and wraps their bodies close. Paige settles into the warmth. She's so soft, so perfect. Paige closes her eyes.

At some point soon, they're going to need to define this, but for now, this closeness is enough.

Paige's breathing settles, and she is just beginning to relax when Lila starts to chuckle.

"Oh, you sweet subby girl." She brushes her lips across Paige's forehead. "I'm going to have so much fun with you."

MEAT CUTE

Jane Bauer

Mattie Holloran became a vegetarian at the age of twelve when two things happened. The first was stumbling upon the book *Diet for a New America* among her mother's cookbooks while looking for a recipe for chocolate chip cookies. The center of the book contained black-and-white photos of cows and pigs crammed into too-small pens awaiting slaughter. The idea of death and violence just so she could have a hamburger sickened her. The second was the small war she raged against her developing figure. Her hips were expanding and her breasts, which had been but small protrusions, were now filling out. Reluctantly, she became the first girl in her ballet academy to wear her training bra under her leotard, which she felt may as well have been a neon sign announcing that she would never be a professional dancer. She thought it very unfair to have her dreams dashed so young.

Her diet became a menu of brown rice and vegetables; she explored the world of tofu and tempeh fervently and with a repellent air of superiority to those around her. While this regime didn't stop her from inhabiting her new female form, it did give her a sense of cleanliness and purity. She took great pleasure in declining sweets like birthday cake, sure the offeror admired how pious she must be.

She had been a vegetarian for ten years when on a cold winter day she walked by a Portuguese butcher shop just as an old woman was exiting. The old woman bumped into Mattie and dropped her packages in the space between the door and the road. Mattie bent down to help her retrieve them, offering her apologies. The heat from within the shop billowed out the door in a cloud of salt and seasonings that assaulted Mattie's nose and surprised her by their mix of unfamiliarity and total comfort.

College had not been the sexual awakening Mattie had imagined for herself. She'd taken a couple of lovers, one a fumbling engineer who'd had sex with her as though he were following directions from an outdated manual on lovemaking. The other was a football linebacker she met at a frat party. He'd had quite a bit to drink, and the experience had been more memorable for the way he passed out and how Mattie had needed to extricate herself from his clumsy embrace than any passion between them. Neither experience was repeated.

She'd walked by the butcher's frequently over the years, but since the day she and the old lady collided, she'd become aware of the shop and of the butcher himself, who was often working in the front window so customers could watch him. He wasn't much older than Mattie, but he inhabited a manliness that the boys at college did not. He had a dark head of curly hair and a constant covering of black stubble on the bottom half of his face. His large hands and hairy knuckles were on full display as he pushed hefty pieces of pork belly through the whirling blade of the meat saw. Sometimes he would have his sleeves rolled up to reveal thick biceps and forearm muscles that would flex as he moved his hands and ripped apart sinewy flesh. She found herself wondering about his legs and whether they would display the same brawniness. She started to leave the house earlier in the hopes that she would see him on the street in his regular clothes. She imagined his thighs as muscled and athletic; since much of his day was spent standing, she was sure his lower half would match his upper half.

On her way home she would stop and look into the shop window. The butcher never smiled or raised his head to meet the gaze of his audience. Mattie often found herself hoping someone would go in or out through the door so she might experience the smells from within; she felt cheated when no one did.

Some days he would be stuffing sausage, his robust hands mixing the ground meat in a stainless steel bowl. He would add salt and seasonings with a casual flourish that exuded confidence. Mattie loved to watch his fingers strongly blending everything together. He pressed the meat into the machine to be stuffed into a sausage casing that he would tie off rhythmically, undaunted by the delicateness of the task.

Once she watched him heft an entire pig carcass onto the stainless steel table and without hesitation take a large blade and begin to section it. She felt her thighs burn as he ripped the pieces apart. She began to imagine what it would feel like to have him beside her. She wanted to run her fingers through the dark, curly chest hair that she was sure he kept under his blood-splattered white coat. She hungered to have him on top of her and for him to matter-of-factly open her thighs. She was sure his presence would make her feel small, delicate, and protected. She wanted his mouth on hers, to taste his saliva, which she imagined would taste like bacon.

Watching him carefully separate the skin from the pink meat with a filet knife, she wondered what it would be like to have him unfold her in the same way. She bought steak seasoning to add to her rice and steamed vegetables, but it was a poor substitute for the salty fat she so wanted. Her cravings escalated to the point where she would lie in bed at night and imagine his strong, calloused hands hovering over the soft skin of her body, while her hands gripped the girth of his thick waist, pulling him toward her.

Then one cold day she started to break out into a sweat under her coat as she was walking home from class. It was as though her blood sugar had dropped, and she couldn't hold back any longer. She opened the door to the butcher shop, stepped inside, and was immediately enveloped in the salty air of cured meats and fresh steak. The butcher was completing an order for a pretty young woman whose blonde hair wisped around her red scarf.

Mattie felt a physical ache as she watched the handsome butcher lift a large smoked ham from a ceiling hook. He unwrapped the ham and flicked on the shining industrial meat slicer. The spinning blade made a whirring sound as he moved the ham back and forth. There was a rhythm to the way he caught the thin slices and slapped them on top of one another. Then he flicked off the machine, folded the crisp white butcher paper, and taped it closed. Mattie felt a pang of jealousy as he passed the package over the counter into the hands of the blonde woman. The woman smiled knowingly at Mattie as she exited. Then it was her turn.

"Hello," he said smiling.

He was even more handsome up close.

"Hi," she said, hoping to sound normal.

"What can I get for you?" he asked. His voice was deep and husky, just the way she'd imagined it would be.

Mattie let her eyes travel along the display case to the unfamiliar pieces of meat, wishing she had come more prepared. She didn't even know what to ask for so she pointed awkwardly at a tray holding freshly made sausages.

"This," he said, taking one out and holding it in his hands, "is like a linguica, but it's only lightly smoked. I made it with pork, oregano, chili, garlic, and paprika. It is a little bit spicy. Is that okay?" he asked.

"Yes," Mattie answered, feeling herself blushing as the word came out of her mouth in a breathy sigh.

"One sausage? Or are you cooking for someone else?" he asked.

"Just one," she said as his face softened into a smile.

"Have you cooked fresh sausage before? It's not the same as the crap from the supermarket that's already precooked." He began to wrap the sausage up in butcher paper.

"Um, no, I haven't," Mattie confessed. He reached under the counter and came out with a small jar.

"Here," he said, and as he passed her the jar, their fingers brushed against one another, causing a tightening and pulsing sensation between Mattie's legs. "This is rendered pork fat. I make it myself. You need to heat up a heavy skillet on high and add a spoon of this. Once the fat is bubbling, add the sausage and let it fry the outside completely. Then turn the heat down low, add half a cup of water, and cover for seven minutes so the sausage cooks evenly, firm on the outside and moist inside. Got that?"

Mattie wished she had taken notes, but she'd been too distracted by watching his mouth move to fully absorb the meaning of his words.

"Yes, I think so," she managed to say. He looked uncertain.

He ripped a piece of butcher paper and wrote down an abbreviation of the verbal instructions he'd just given her. He passed her the sausage and the instructions. She paid, once again aware of the proximity of his hands to hers. Receiving her change, she avoided his gaze for fear she might explode. She hesitated for a moment and wondered what would happen if she reached for his hand. As she turned toward the door, she was sure his eyes were following her. Clutching the sausage in her hand, she already missed the warmth of the shop.

"Another thing," he called out, making her turn back. "A good glass of red wine, sip in between bites."

At home, Mattie opened a bottle of red wine and poured herself a generous glass. She unwrapped the sausage, held its coolness up to her face, and smelled it. It was fragrant with oregano and paprika. She heated up a pan and dropped in a generous dollop of the rendered pork fat that only made her remember the way the butcher's fingers had brushed against hers. Once the fat began sizzling, she laid the sausage in the pan and watched as the casing hardened from the heat. She poured in the water, lowered the heat, and covered the pan. She sipped her wine as the kitchen windows steamed up and the small room filled with enticing aromas. As she waited for the sausage to cook she replayed in her mind her interaction with the butcher. She imagined what would have happened if she had reached for him, her hand in his as he pulled her behind the counter and pressed his body onto hers.

Once the sausage was fully cooked, Mattie placed it on a plate. She looked at the knife and fork on the table, but they weren't the tools she needed. She picked up the sausage with her thumb and index finger. It was still hot, but it was a tolerable kind of heat. She brought the tip of the sausage up to her mouth and leaned forward as though she were about to kiss it but then dismissed this idea as well and instead allowed her lips to part and inserted the sausage slowly into her mouth. The taste of the warm, rendered fat was lovely, and it coated her lips like gloss as she moved the sausage in and out. Eventually, she allowed her teeth to sink into the tip; as she ripped into the casing, the filling discharged into her mouth.

She closed her eyes to focus on the texture of the meat. She sucked the piece lightly, releasing all the flavors of oregano, paprika, and the hint of chili. She swallowed, and then opened her eyes before taking a sip of wine and another bite. She ate slowly, savoring each morsel. Her body received this communion like a long lost-friend as an aliveness and heat coursed through her.

When she was done she poured herself another glass of wine. She didn't bother clearing her plate or even putting the pan into the sink to soak. She went to her bedroom and lay down in the dark. She closed her eyes, lifted her shirt, and allowed her hands to rest on her naked belly. She felt liberated after so many years of denying herself. The many times she had said no to Thanksgiving turkey and July Fourth hamburgers now seemed futile. She craved pleasure and could not think what she had gained by denying it. As she lay on her bed she imagined the butcher in the room with her. He would kiss her feet and slowly move his tongue up her leg. He would gently, yet firmly, spread open her thighs; she imagined his calloused palms on the soft skin of her inner thighs.

As she got more excited, she pictured him moving his lips toward her inner left thigh until it almost seemed real. She felt his facial stubble against her skin and then his tongue as he licked, moving higher and higher.

On her bed, Mattie moved her hands down as though reaching for his head, but he wasn't there. She was there, though, wet and uninhibited, ready for something—and perhaps someone—new. She gently moved her fingertips over her moist sex and imagined the pot roasts and suckling pigs in her future.

FAR SIDE OF THE WORLD

Zoey Castile

Graciella Solas knew she was lost again when she saw the same two blue sheep having sex next to the rock formation that resembled a troll.

The sheep in question glanced up only once to bleat a disgruntled sound at her voyeurism. Despite the blisters rubbing against the insides of her hiking boots, Grace adjusted her backpack and trudged through the soggy moors that blanketed the isle of Harris. She jabbed her trekking poles into the soil ahead of her, the muddy ground swallowing the aluminum rod before letting go with an immature slurping sound.

"Great," Grace muttered. She had walked just over a hundred miles, spanning nine of the Western Isles off the coast of Scotland. There were just under fifty miles to go, and Grace was bone tired. She sat down on a moss-covered boulder, her backpack digging nearly permanent red marks on her shoulders. It weighed forty pounds; she was too stubborn to get rid of a paper book to read and overly cautious about her water rations. Hiking across the Outer Hebrides was a lifelong dream. Or rather, a yearlong dream since she'd seen photos of the blue prism waters on a travel Instagram account. Grace's life at home had been at an impasse. She'd quit her banking job of twelve years one morning, broken up with her boyfriend who had more chemistry with a video game console than her, and declined to renew the lease of her overpriced Manhattan apartment. She'd had everything, in a way.

And now she had nothing. No boyfriend. No job. No apartment. She did have a backpack, two rations of dinner, a sleeping bag, two condoms (wishful thinking), three liters of water, three protein bars, a tarp, a gas canister, a portable stove, a first aid kit, a fat paperback novel, her cell phone, a solar charger, headphones fraying at the ends, two changes of clothes (none of them clean), and a map that had seen better days. She'd dropped her phone while coming down a rocky hill. She felt guilt over violating the pristine outdoor space, but it was the final straw.

She took in the smooth crags of rock that peaked beneath choppy stretches of grass. Breathed in so hard it hurt her city-conditioned lungs. All she had to do was follow the trail markers to the main road and hopefully catch the elusive bus that ran every two hours.

"Enough," she said.

In that moment, she'd had enough. The loss of her old life dug into her shoulders worse than her pack. Thirty and on the precipice of the rest of her life, Grace stood up and started the journey back down to the main road. She was getting off the trail.

Finley MacLean was late for work again. His piece of shite car stalled going uphill, and his stomach clenched as Pat from down the road and Marge from the B&B, both eighty-five and giving no fucks, shouted at him as he pulled off on the passing place. To his left was a hill, a fence, sheep. On his right was the outline of the sea, more fence, even more sheep.

He'd spent his whole life in a small house ten minutes outside of Tarbert. His parents had lived there. His grandparents had lived there. The only time he'd ever left was for university over in Edinburgh, where he'd gotten passable grades and a better athletic season. Until his damn ankle became a problem and all of his dreams of football stardom were gone with a one-inch fracture. Now, his days were the same. He knew how Monday–Saturday was going to play out. Wake up and stare out the window. Flip through Instagram to see what his mates were doing, scattered all across Europe and Asia. His longest commute was the ten-minute drive into work at the bar and he was barely managing that.

He gunned the ignition and hollered when his car roared to life. He went to make a left onto the road when he saw a shape run into his path. The figure was a blur—a horse? a sheep?—and he hit the brake hard.

There was a scream. He could *feel* the pressure of the mass he'd hit. Scrambling, struggling, shaking, he fumbled with his seat belt to get out. He prayed to Jesus, Mary, and Joseph that it had been a sheep. But not Pat's sheep because the bastard already had it in for his family. He stepped onto the wet road, drizzle creating a fine mist around everything.

There on the ground was a backpack and a girl attached to it, facedown.

"You hit me!" Grace shouted.

She took a moment to inventory her body. Legs and arms moved. There was sand and gravel on her tongue, which she inhaled as she fell. Her pack, for the albatross it had been the week she'd been wild camping, had saved her. Eating road dirt wasn't fun and the wind had been knocked out of her, but she was otherwise unhurt. The thing wounded the most was her pride. She swatted away his apology and tried to push herself up. Her muscles were like jelly, trembling. Instead, she only rolled onto her back, flailing like a turtle who'd been turned up on its shell and couldn't right itself.

Because of her situation, it took her some time to notice that there was someone trying to help her. His shouts of apology had turned into something else.

"You're *laughing?*" she asked.

"I'm sorry. I'm trying to help you," he said, trying to grab her hand, which she was swatting away. Sheep gathered around. Great, she had an audience. "Will you stop flapping about like a fish in a puddle for one minute?"

She was startled by the playful tenor of his voice and took a moment to calm down. He stood over her. She drank in the sight of this stranger who had nearly run her over. Broad shoulders and muscular biceps clad by a simple black shirt. Raven-dark hair in unruly waves, like coils of a deep black sea. His thick eyebrows frowned and framed blue eyes. He had the kind of beauty that knocked the wind out of her again.

He crouched beside her. "Let me help you."

His mouth was quirked up like he was used to smiling at everything around him.

Grace hated it.

Grace loved it.

"Fine," she said, and took his hand. It was solid and warm. Rough with callouses. Everything about him was rough. The stubble on his sharp jaw. The rough break of his nose that reminded her of the crooked rocks she'd climbed. It was beautiful on his face, imperfect and perfect all at once.

When she was on her feet and grounded, she unshouldered her pack and felt so much lighter.

"Come, I'll take you to the hospital," he said, picking up the strap. His eyes widened. "You've been carrying this about?"

She crossed her arms over her chest, but little eased the strain of her tired muscles. Everything hurt, but everything hurt before she fell on her face. "I'm stronger than I look. And I don't need to go to a hospital. I'm fine, I swear."

"Your hands are bleeding," he said, and walked the pack around to the trunk. "I have a kit in the boot."

For a minute, Grace was too entranced by the lilt of his brogue that she didn't realize she was following at his heels. She cleared her throat and looked at her palms. Bright red blood had bubbled up across the scrapes on the insides of her wrists. It wasn't gushing or anything, but now that her adrenaline had burned through her, she felt the sting.

"Walking the Way, are you?" he asked her as he popped open the boot and dug in there for a first aid kit.

She nodded and bit the inside of her lip because her mind was, once again, taking in the sight of him. When she'd woken up that morning in the caravan, she hadn't thought she'd be on the side of the road getting bandaged up by a beautiful stranger. He glanced up at her. The easy way that he held her hands made her feel heady. She cleared her throat and realized he'd asked a question.

"Was walking," she said. "I've had a series of unfortunate events. Like Murphy's Law or something."

"You're in Scotland, lass. More like Fraser's Law."

Something in her gut tightened when he called her *lass*. She'd had a hundred nice old men refer to her as such, but it was different coming from him.

"This'll bite," he said.

She was going to ask, "What will bite?" when she felt the alcohol pad brush her raw skin. She bit down on her tongue, and he smirked at her bravado.

"What about you?" she asked. The breeze was salty on her tongue and raked her messy brown hair out of her ponytail. "Were you just waiting until I came down the mountain to run me over?"

He laughed and taped the gauze wrap in place. "I'm late for work actually. I work at the bar in town. The Hebrides Hotel."

Grace sat up and examined the job. He wasn't a stranger to healing minor cuts. She grinned hard. "Perfect."

"Don't mention it."

"No, I mean, that you work in town." She opened the passenger door and gave him a look that dared him to deny her. "Saves me the trouble of hitchhiking."

He'd been an hour late but something in his bones told him it had been worth it. Grace. Graciella. The syllables of her name tumbled out of his mouth, tongue wrapping around the curves of the *C* and *L*s. Clumsy at first, but he imagined the more he said it the better it would sound. Some words simply felt good to say, like *fuck* and *whisky* and *Grace. Graciella.*

Even though they didn't have much time to talk in the ten minutes in the car, Finley gathered the following:

Her eyes were infinitely dark and her hair was a right mess, like she'd rolled down a hill and across the moors. But even with the dirt on her cheekbones, the bow curve of her mouth made him dizzy. She was confident and lost all at the same time. A whirlwind with no real direction.

"Do you think they have rooms here?" she asked as he parked in the lot across from the hotel. His ankle hurt from the humidity, but he couldn't stop his leg from shaking with nerves.

"Yeah, it's died down here this time of year," he told her. "Come down for a drink later."

"I should probably get to sleep," she said, but bit her full bottom lip. He wanted to lean forward and suck on her pretty mouth. "Taking the first ferry out of here."

"Without seeing the rest of the islands?" he asked, as he

brought his hand down and hit the horn, scaring Mrs. Brown as she walked her dog.

"The islands have won," she said. "I really did want to see the Callanish Stones, though. I don't know."

"I'll take you."

"What? When?"

"Tomorrow. Hell, tonight. I get off at eight. Sunset isn't until about ten, ten thirty."

"You'd do that?"

He shrugged. Was it so different from a month ago when he'd met a couple of Spanish footballers who were cycling the island and they'd driven to the Butt of Lewis just to go streaking? Or last week when his favorite local band had a concert across the street and he'd stayed up until sunrise getting pissed? Of course it was different because they had all been men and he hadn't been attracted to any of them the way he was attracted to this filthy, beautiful hiker girl.

"I would," he said.

She smelled like sweat and the moors. Her eyes crinkled with a skeptical smile. But she said, "See you in a bit, then."

Within seconds of checking into the Hebrides Hotel, Grace showered and ordered fish and chips from room service. Before she'd left for her hike she'd shaved her legs and bikini. Wishful thinking had her believing she'd meet a beautiful Scottish man on the moors. Sometimes, after trekking twelve miles across a stretch of green, she'd fantasize that when she pitched her tent there would be someone waiting for her. That was the thing about being alone for such a long period of time—her wildest, most ridiculous fantasies came to life.

She hadn't pictured it this way, but she'd found a beautiful Scottish man. Finley MacLean had waited for her after his shift.

His dark curls managed to look windswept even though he'd been inside all day. His blue eyes were the shade of the water that hugged the coastal towns they drove past. He turned onto a highway that cut through sharp green glens with streams trickling through ancient stone. But the sight of him was far more breathtaking.

Her heart felt like it was swelling. Which is why she had to say, "You're not like a serial killer, are you?"

He chuckled and tilted his head to the side to look at her. They were the only ones on the road for long stretches, but she didn't feel anxious about it. "Just a bartender, for both our sakes. I'm a bit squeamish."

"You bandaged my hands all right," she said and held up her wrists as evidence.

"After I got a compound fracture on my leg and saw my own bone sticking out of my leg, I couldn't handle blood. You're the one walking around alone. Maybe you're the one who's a serial killer."

"I'm just an ex–bank teller who went for a long walk looking for adventure," she said. "The only thing I did was kill my feet."

"So why did you choose the Western Isles?"

She looked out the window and had the strangest sensation that she was exactly where she needed to be. "It's as good as any place. I've never been somewhere that has a midnight sun."

"Grand, isn't it?" he said.

They went on that way for the rest of the ride, having the kind of easy conversation that came with feeling like they were the only two people in the world. When they arrived at the stones, the sun was just setting. Red and orange starbursts painted the sky. It was unusually perfect weather, despite the wind.

"Holy fuck," she shouted, racing past him to get a better look at the sky, the lakes ahead of them, the stones that rose from the ground like crooked teeth. When she turned around, he was right there. His smile reached his eyes. A filter of sunset made him look like a painted god.

"Holy fuck is right."

They stood in the ring of stones, older than Stonehenge, a place that was enveloping them. Two lost souls who'd found each other for a moment.

"I want to kiss you," Grace said.

"Then kiss me," he said, his voice deeper with desire.

She went for it, remembering that feeling of running down a mountain with the wind at her back. Gravity slamming her against him. And he caught her. His lips were soft. A rough moan escaped them. His tongue parted her lips, slowly, then hard. He gripped her arms and pressed her to him. Even through the thin material of her sweater, he could feel her rock-hard nipples pressing into his chest.

Her clever fingers roamed his torso, raking nails over the material of his shirt until they found the hem. The cool sensation of her fingers on his hot skin sent chills down his spine. She searched lower, and when she nipped at his swollen lower lip, found his straining hard cock.

Grace pulled back a few inches to look at his face. Her long dark lashes fluttered. "Just think of the orgies that happened here four thousand years ago."

Whatever he thought she'd say, he didn't expect that. It made him want her more. This strange, wild girl who had broken the mundane routine of his day.

"Right now I'm only thinking about you," he said.

"Smooth." She cocked a playful brow. Her heart hammered in her chest. Her skin was hot with desire. She took off her sweater and even still, the cool snap of wind couldn't put out the fire singing through her. "Are you thinking about what you want to do to me?"

There was a depression of stones. A place of ritual. A place that hid them from view at the heart of the ring of stones. She took two steps down and stood at the center, knowing he would follow. He came up behind her, wrapping his arms around her front. One slipped under her tank top. It was like he was trying to familiarize himself with her body before he touched her anywhere else. She reached out a hand to the stone in front of them for balance.

"I want to fuck you against this wall." His warm breath was at her ear. "Can I fuck you, Grace?"

She could hardly speak, nodding as she reached for him and said, "Yes. Please fuck me."

He undid the top button of her jeans and pressed his erection against her. She wiggled against him, hissing when his cold fingers reached into her pants to cup her full ass.

"Commando?" He chuckled against her throat. He could consume her. He was overcome with the need to touch every part of her he could.

Her hand reached up to caress his jaw. "Everything I own is filthy."

"Like you?" He smacked her ass playfully.

"Yes," she said. "I'm fucking filthy."

He sighed hard against her and muttered, "Holy fuck."

She turned around and shoved him a little, testing the waters between them. No one had read her as quickly as he had before. "Well, are you just going to stand there with your dick in your hand?"

Finley felt a growl of lust creep up his throat. He yanked her pants down and buried his face in her slick, wet pussy. She dug her fingers through his hair and tugged. While he ate her, he removed her shoe, finished tugging off her pant leg, and slung her beautiful, thick thigh over his shoulder. He flicked his tongue across the swollen pearl of her clitoris and drove a finger into her hot opening.

Fuck fuck fuck, she thought. Between a rock and a hard place,

Grace had never felt so free. This is what she'd wanted. Not just getting eaten out by a gorgeous Scotsman, but being naked among ancient ruins. Stars blazed above them, but even though it must have been close to midnight, the night wasn't truly dark. There was something sinful about straddling day and night.

She felt herself ready to come undone. But she didn't want it over so soon. She grabbed Finley by his shirt and brought him up to kiss her again.

"You taste divine," he told her.

"I do?" She felt her breath hitch as he traced her lips with the same wet fingers he'd just used to fuck her. Then he kissed her, rougher this time. He picked her up and sat her on top of a bed of moss and grass. She yelped at the cold sensation against how hot she was. She tugged off her tank and sports bra and they laughed at their mountain of clothes. It felt good to laugh with him. She had to admit it was a wild situation. She didn't know him, not the way you're supposed to know someone to make this feel so good.

The metal clink of his belt hit the stone on the floor. In a bold stroke he took off his shirt. She leaned back and drank in his strong form. Muscular and pale as the moon. Freckles dotted his chest, his abdomen. She could see the pearl scars that ran from his knee to his ankle. His thick erection at attention for her. Finley was perfect. Even more perfect with the ease he used to rip the condom packet with his teeth and sheath his dick.

She parted her legs, open to him and the midnight sky. He kissed her, softly. Tasting her lips, licking the swollen parts of her. He traced kisses down her neck, lapping his tongue down until he reached her nipples. He gently nipped at her, and when she moaned, he entered her.

Grace gasped. It had been a long time since she'd been with anyone. She clenched around him, pushing him out with how tight she was. She placed her hands on his smooth, muscular ass and pressed him harder. He moaned and arched his head back like he was ready to howl at the moon.

The feeling of him stretching his way into her made her giddy. She writhed and pushed herself up to meet his steady thrusts, touching all the right places. She raked her nails down his torso and moaned so loudly he thought they would wake the dead.

"I'm coming," she said, followed by a hitched breath and the walls inside her constricting around him until her muscles relaxed.

"God, I'm so glad you ran me over today," she said.

Again with the outlandish things she said. He was glad he hadn't hurt her. He was glad they were together and naked and he was inside of her to the hilt. He wanted to bury himself there and never come out. Fuck the sky above them—when he closed his eyes he could see stars.

He picked her up and pressed her against the standing stone. His dick still inside her. Neither of them moved. He nested into the crook of her neck, and she kissed slow, torturous circles on his neck. She'd leave a mark. She could leave all the marks on him that she wanted if she just kept touching him that way.

Then he felt it—the tight coil of sensation tightening his balls. He was going to come undone.

"I want to watch you," she said.

He pulled out of her, so dizzy with pleasure he could have passed out. She sat back on the throne of moss. He tugged off his condom and pressed her hot mouth to his tip. He jerked forward and took his shaft in his hand, stroking his way to pleasure. Grace watched the ribbons of come spill from him until he was spent.

She thought that when it was over and they put their clothes back on, picking up their soiled remnants, that the spell that had overtaken them might have broken. But back in the warmth of his car he leaned in to kiss her deeply, reverently. The kind of kiss shared by two people on the far side of the world.

INFLATED EGOS

Evie Bennet

The dusk of twilight filters rays of fuchsia on the outside perimeter, red balloons bobbing in anticipation like they're ready to be reunited with the sun. Carla supposes she *should* close the shades. Even though the car lot is reinforced with a huge fence, cameras, and security alarms, the actual sales building has an armored shell in the form of steel curtains.

It'd be such a shame to cover up the view. It's the only thing vaguely *soft* set against a showroom of gorgeous leather and steel where people come with razor-sharp teeth to try to shave away her profits.

Her head throbs from lack of sleep and calculating profit margins for the sale. Her feet are vacuum-sealed into her wedge heels. She has to be a warrior ready to kick into gear at any moment, lest she succumb to lethargy and rest her feet.

She folds her arms and watches the slow bob of balloons in front of a splotch of pink. *No shades tonight.*

The clap of a car door echoes through the open chamber.

"You need these deets?"

At the ridiculous terminology, Carla has to smother an irritated sigh. Aroon is *helpful,* even if he thinks he's way cooler than he is. He's the second hardest worker in their building, always sharply dressed and ready to take on the day—never afraid to stay late and work on paperwork or numbers with her even if he *is* more of a "people person," as he claims. As long as he makes her moan in pleasure more than annoyance, their pseudo-relationship is fine.

The balloons stir as Aroon marches out into the open where he knows she'll see him. He waves a packet until it wobbles like those tacky plastic wind-people with their long, shaky arms. "Where do you want them, babe?"

Terms of affection are fine when the lot's not in operation. They're encouraged when she's got one heel up on a back seat and the other digging into his ass during their lunch break. It's sort of a *fuck and feed* relationship of convenience, but she does *like* him. His thick eyebrows stay raised and ready until she gives him direction. Not that he doesn't take initiative—he just knows how to do it without stepping on her in the process. He doesn't send text messages that say *Good morning, buttercup,* because she finds them annoyingly chirpy and much prefers when he brings her a latte during their shifts instead. Maybe he doesn't even consciously spread his stance behind her every time someone gives her a hard time, but she notices it all the same. They're partners, not just playmates.

That's a rare thing, she thinks, watching the balloons billow gently in a *V* like they're paving his way to her with the breeze.

"Put them on your desk."

"Here?"

She nods. Dropping them in a neat stack, Aroon eyes the top of it to make sure everything is in its place before walking around and leaning on the desk's edge. He pockets his hands in his still-crisp gray slacks and stretches his neck.

"You good, C?"

"Roo, what do you think about the balloons?" She hadn't been *planning* on asking him anything, but she's so tired that it seems like a legitimate question.

He glances at the bundles of buoyant observers in the showroom. "I like 'em. They're cool. Is this about the helium thing? You want to do streamers instead or something? Because I feel like balloons are just kind of the natural way to go. They make people happy."

Her heels clip on the tile as she makes her way toward a balloon bouquet, plucking one from the bunch and wondering how weird it would be to smell it for the hint of latex. "They make me happy, too."

As a kid, she'd always been excited about the emergence of balloon bouquets or archways because it meant the whole family would be in town. They'd be celebrating a wedding or a birthday and everyone would give *her* the extra balloons as the youngest child in the extended family. Life, love, and vitality filled those bouncy packages. Even the pear-shaped, weighted balloon she had punched and kicked as a kid would cushion her when she tackled it to the ground. Only something like a balloon could be so versatile—so supportive and satisfyingly squeezable.

"I daresay I *love* balloons," she tells Aroon, rubbing the firm, round specimen across her breasts. The air prickles with electricity.

He swallows hard, eyebrows raised. "*Oh,* I see."

Eyelids heavy, she smiles. Aroon takes his hands out of his pockets and braces them on the edge of his desk with his eyebrows raised, ready for direction. When she says she *loves* something, she *means* it. He flexes his fingers before tightening his grip. "You wanna show me?"

"*Would* I?"

It's so *bouncy,* so curvy and joyous and squeaky. She's tempted to keep it for herself—rub it along her body and make him get his own to play with. Still, she's drowsy and horny and relaxed enough to want to make every hair on his body stand on end. She stalks to Aroon, slowly tracing her nipples in a circular motion with her free hand on one breast and the balloon on the other.

Both feel *good.* One just makes everything seem more intense. They feed on each other, the sensation of the trade.

Interest piqued, Aroon smiles and spreads his legs for her in an open invitation. She rolls the balloon along the seam of his pants, the fullness of the pressure gradually outlining his thickening dick. Seeing him grow reminds her of inflating—of how it can be squeezed to feel thicker or stretched to near-bursting lightness.

"Interesting," he murmurs, eyes wide and fascinated by the deep purple of her nails indenting the latex sheath.

"You like that, baby?"

He's awestruck, kind of like the first time he saw her boobs in her bra. The absent way his dick twitches for attention is the only indication that he's still in the game. She rubs quickly enough to feel the electric heat in the air mirrored between her legs.

His hips jerk. "Damn, that's fast, C. Let's savor it a little or you might just pop me."

"I won't pop anything unless I mean to."

She pulls the balloon back into two hands, squeezing and stretching it until her insides feel like taffy and Aroon's hand is tickling the back of her thigh to bring her closer.

"You want to share with me?"

Grinning, she places the red balloon on his crotch and climbs onto the desk, forcing his hips back as she straddles both him and the balloon until it's pressed right up against her sex. It's smooth and hot and stiff whenever she rolls her hips. That tiny bit of pressure is so *exciting*—knowing she can anchor it, knowing it could just as easily bounce away. Too much and it could pop—and she doesn't want this swelling need to end so violently.

Aroon's shaking, hoisting her up higher from the crook of her knees. He could just as easily be imploring her to apply more pressure as securing her from toppling off of the desk.

"You're so nervous," she teases, pushing at the short-clipped hair above his ear and rocking on the toy between them. She loves the way it almost butterflies the lips of her lace-covered sex.

"Nervous. Excited." He cants his hips, testing the connection and grinning when it holds up. Maybe he's a popper. He might like that little burst of energy, orgasmic and rippling. She wants to play with it—bounce and rub and test the shape until she's trembling with need.

His knee goes a little too high, and she jolts forward.

"C!"

"I'm fine! It's fine," she assures him, fingers stiff as her palms push off his shoulders to readjust, making sure she doesn't crush the bulging sexy thing. "Maybe, since it's our first time, we should put it somewhere safe."

Aroon frowns at her in confusion as she plucks the balloon from between her thighs, savoring its little squeak of protest, and traps it under her chin. Looping her thumbs into her waistband, she turns over and sits on his uneven lap to slide her underwear down and kick it off the ankle hook of her wedges.

"You are so hot right now."

She shoots a glare over her shoulder, dropping the balloon to her lap where it bounces once and hovers before resettling.

"You're hot all the time," he amends, firmly squeezing her hip. "I just feel like tonight is gonna be extra special. Maybe it's all the electricity." He nuzzles into her hair, and it does feel like a spark passes between them when he presses a kiss into the nape of her neck.

That's what balloons are for, she thinks, holding it close. *Making something extra special.*

She taps his thigh. "Your turn."

The idea of setting her aching feet back on the ground before she has to doesn't seem particularly appealing. Carla scoots off to the side and lets him bare and prepare himself before comfortably straddling him, face-to-face once more.

"You feelin' good, C?"

"I will be."

She places his tip at her clit, closing her eyes and pressing the balloon between their chests. They move forward in their rhythm, Carla sinking down with each pass and taking more of him in. The pressure and poise of the rubber make her feel stretched and warm and magnetic—drawn to this feeling, drawn to her partner, who fills her in a similar, less visceral way.

Every time she sinks down, the shape changes. It curves. It extends. It's blowing up and expanding into something full and tight and overwhelming.

The squeak of latex and the pressure from within inspire her to ride him harder. There's so much stimulating her nerves beyond just the grinding at her clit. The bulbous compression against her chest combined with the way Aroon gathers and grips her hair makes her feel like she's rising beyond her aching body and into a plane of pleasure amidst the smeared pink sky.

Bobbing, rubbing, she's stretched and shaking. The shutters of her mind crumble and clatter to make way for pure feeling.

As the crash recedes, she registers Aroon's hand on the small of her back, the warmth of his breath on her neck and the stillness of his hips. Her eyes feel dewy as she leans forward and pecks him on the lips, lingering long enough to feel lethargy setting in. The balloon drifts to the side, barely caught by her arm.

"Hey, C?"

"Yeah?" All she wants to do is eat something and go to sleep.

"You think we could take some of these home?"

Unexpcctedly, she giggles, the sound shallow and vibrant. "Sure. Then we can tie you up in Shibari with one of the car ribbons."

"Really?" He jerks his head in the direction of the giant bows and red satin sheets.

"No, not *really*. Those belong to the company."

Sighing, he stretches his neck and looks longingly at the glossy car covered by stark red.

Biting her lip, Carla plucks at the wavy hair by the nape of his neck, wondering just how much she should reveal about her toy trunk at home. "I could invest in some . . . *personally*."

"You could invest in me."

She jerks back, surprised. "Aroon . . ."

"Just saying," he offers, planting a quick, strong kiss on her cheek. "If you were ever looking for something more than coffee and balloons, I'm a decent boyfriend, I think."

"You think?" she repeats dryly.

Huffing, he rolls his head back. "I'm tired of selling things today. Let's clean up and crash. If you want, you can stay at my place."

His place *is* closer than hers. She tugs the collar of his crisp white button-down for an excuse to feel the flush of his dark skin. "Okay."

She grunts in stiff protest and clambers off of him to put the balloon back by its cluster, caressing it one last time. The whole school of them bobs in an effortless farewell.

As her heels clip against the showroom floor, her hips sway with the easy camaraderie of her floating friends. The warm pink hues behind the glass seem to glow, reflecting shiny cars, handsome partners, and, of course, a sea of floating reds.

MAGIA

D. L. King

I had always heard that there were strange people who lived in the desert. I grew up in southern New Mexico, near the Arizona border. Yes, that's the desert too, but I live in a town in the desert, not in the middle of nowhere. Were there really such people out there? Who knew? But my *abuela* always warned me not to go too far from home or the *magia* would get me. Was that magic or magic people? She never answered my questions. She'd just cross herself and shoo me out of the kitchen.

I suppose I wondered my whole life about who or what, if anything, was really out there. I mean, think about it: what about all the alien sightings, and Roswell, and the fact that we *are* known as the "Land of Enchantment"? Yeah, they say that's about the landscape, and it is beautiful here, but legends have to come from somewhere, right?

I graduated from college with a degree in anthropology and no job prospects. I found work waiting tables at the best café in town, not that there were many to choose from. It made my parents happy that I wasn't just lying around doing nothing with my college education, and it gave me enough money to not be a total drain on them.

The conversation, lately, had turned to immigrants illegally crossing the border from Mexico and how hard it must be for them in the desert. Some people were on "the harder the better" side, but more were on the "humanitarian" side. But in the last few days, people were talking about seeing strange glows out past the places locals considered safe.

"Maybe they're campfires made by aliens," one of my customers said.

"You mean little green men or migrants?" I asked.

"You think you're so smart with your college and books. I mean migrants, missy, and you know it."

"Well, maybe not," another guy piped up. "Could be real aliens." He got a few guffaws. "Well, it could be," he insisted. "Or maybe it could be the *magia*."

There was a general chorus of "Oh, please" and "Really?"

"It could be, man," he doubled down. "Those stories have been around forever; even Apache legends talk about strange spirit people in the desert."

The conversation slowly wound down after that, but it made me wonder what really was out there. My anthro gene was buzzing with excitement. I decided to go investigate. After all, I'd grown up in this place; I knew how to handle myself in the desert, and I wouldn't go far—no more than a mile past the "safe zone." I'd bring plenty of water, some beef jerky, and a compass, maybe even an apple or two.

I decided to hike out on the next Monday I had off. Turned out I had the following Tuesday off, too, which was good—just in case. As far as I'd heard, you could come upon the *magia* during the day just as easily as at night. Because I didn't feel like getting lost in the desert at night, I opted for day.

It was hot. I wore desert camo shorts, hiking boots and thick socks, a short-sleeved, cotton button-up shirt, and a wide-brimmed hat. I put on sunblock and brought it with me. I had my supplies in a backpack and a walking stick to discourage snakes and scorpions. I'd put my long, dark hair up with a clip in an attempt to stay cool. I'd left a note about where I was headed and why, in my bedroom, in case anything happened and I didn't make it back that evening. I didn't want to tell anyone what I was doing before I left because I knew they'd try to stop me and I didn't want the drama. My only thought was, *Fieldwork, here I come!* It would probably be nothing more than a dehydrating walk in the desert.

I walked west-northwest until I couldn't see the buildings of the town. Another mile would take me to the limits of safety, as laid out by the elders of the town—and my *abuela*. Actually, she thought that even that was too far, but she was very protective of me. I checked my compass to make sure I was still on the right heading and continued on. Not too far after that, I decided to take a break and had a seat on a natural outcrop of flat rocks. I drank more water and ate an apple, leaving the core in the sand for the water-starved desert creatures. I took another look at my compass, which showed I was heading due north. I had no idea how I'd gotten off course, as I'd been checking it every fifteen minutes or so.

I climbed off the rocks, still looking at my compass, and slowly circled around counterclockwise, searching for the right heading. It was weird, but the needle never moved from north. This was not good. Now that the town was no longer visible, if my compass crapped out, I could become well and truly lost. I had no idea what was wrong. Maybe there was too much iron in the rocks. Maybe there was too much uranium in the ground from nuclear tests. I wasn't a scientist.

"Don't panic," I said to my apple core. "Okay. I should just head home now." Maybe this was the reason people had said don't wander too far out in the desert. Maybe it had nothing to do with *magia,* just with getting lost—and dying in the middle of nowhere! "Okay, don't panic."

I was pretty sure I knew which way I'd come and decided to retrace my steps. I set off in the direction I thought was correct but became unsure of that a while later. My compass was still no help. "Don't panic!" I said aloud again. I stood there, looking around for something I remembered seeing on my way in but nothing came to me. "This is how migrants die in the desert. This is how anyone dies in the desert." There weren't even any rocks to sit on. I stood there and drank some water, then wondered if I should be rationing my water, just in case.

It was then I saw it: a slight shimmer just ahead of me. *Oh, great, a mirage,* I thought. But it grew bigger, and then I saw a person walking toward me in the short distance. *I'm saved,* I thought. *He can tell me how to get back!*

"Hi," I yelled and waved. He waved back, but as he came closer, something didn't seem right. He was wearing a jacket and scarf. Why would anyone wear a jacket and scarf in this heat? Maybe I was hallucinating. But on he came.

I could see he was real and not an apparition as he stood before me. He was beautiful. I don't usually say that about guys, but this guy really was beautiful. He had wind-tossed sandy hair, a little on the longish side. It was odd because there wasn't any wind. He was tall and beautifully proportioned with a straight nose, brown eyes, and long fingers.

"Hi, I'm Anita. Can you help me?" I stammered. "I seem to be lost, and my compass won't work." I held it out to him as illustration. "I just want to get back to town."

He smiled—a really warm and inviting smile—and in a liquid

baritone said, "I've been watching you, hoping you'd find the way home. But you haven't. Here, take my hand and I'll help you."

His melting brown eyes seemed slightly more golden. I took his proffered hand. It was cooler than I expected, and when I grasped it, I began to fall.

I woke in a house by the sea. I could see the waves on the beach a short way past the windows. The ocean breeze was cool. I looked around and found my rescuer leaning against the wall by the door, watching me with that same smile on his lips. That's when I panicked.

"Don't worry, you're safe. I won't hurt you."

When I stood up, he wrapped me in his arms. I started to struggle, but he felt safe and warm and, somehow, right. I began to relax.

"You're a goddess, Anita. May I kiss you?" he asked.

He said it so sweetly. He was as beautiful as the hero of any romantic novel and I felt so safe, I nodded before I could even think about what I was doing. His lips met mine and I melted into them—into him—into his eyes, his touch, his mouth. It was like swimming in a vat of caramel, and I was lost in his touch. I clawed at him, at his clothes. I wanted to see more, to see all of him; he complied. He picked me up and carried me to the bed before removing first his scarf, then his jacket. His shirt followed.

His chest was taut and muscled. I could see the *V* of his hips, disappearing into his low-slung leather pants. I hadn't noticed they were leather. *What was he doing in the desert in leather pants?* I wondered just before he pulled me into his arms for another kiss. Before I knew what I was doing, I was unbuttoning my shirt and shrugging it off. His cool hands reached behind me and unhooked my bra, and as soon as my breasts were free, he cradled them in his hands and gently kissed the top of first one and then the other, making his way slowly down the slope to the nipple, each of which he bathed with his tongue until I thought I couldn't stand it anymore.

He squeezed and then caressed my breasts before exploring further. His hands roamed my stomach and sides, then shifted over to my back, up to my shoulders, and slowly down the curve of my spine to the waistband of my shorts. As his fingers slid inside the waistband, his eyes met mine, questioning. I wanted him, and I trusted him. I knew it was illogical, but I really wanted this. I undid my shorts and let his hands glide down my ass to rim the edge of my underwear before sliding underneath to cup my buttocks and squeeze me to him. I briefly wished I were wearing nicer panties before he slid both shorts and underwear down my legs.

When I laughed, he looked a bit hurt. "No," I said, "I wasn't laughing at . . . I was laughing about not taking my boots off first." I looked down at my bare feet and then noticed the boots neatly lined up next to the bed with my socks folded on top. "Is this heatstroke? Am I dying?" I asked.

"No, love, you are here with me." His voice had a strange lilt to it. "You are safe," he replied before moving his hands over my hips and sliding them down to my pussy. He played in the trimmed hair before bending down to kiss me there, just above my opening. His fingers parted me, and then he gently tasted me with the tip of his tongue before laving my entire slit up and down and settling in for what I would call a major session of expert oral sex. I must have come at least three times, maybe more; I lost count. All the while his hands explored my body, ranging up and down from buttocks to breasts, never stopping. It was as though he couldn't get his fill of me. It was definitely swoon-worthy, though I never lost consciousness, not for an instant.

When he stopped, I was boneless, as relaxed as I think I've ever been. I was seesawing between wakefulness and sleep when he stood up and began to undo his pants. That brought me to full attention. I rose up on my elbows to catch the full show. As the leather slowly parted, his cock emerged, already full and hard. It wasn't any different from those of most men I knew. I don't know what I was expecting, size-wise, but he was averagely endowed. It wasn't the size that drew my attention, but the perfection of form.

I've never really found cocks to be all that attractive. Don't get me wrong: I like them. They're useful and fun to play with but not my aesthetically favorite part of the male body. But he really was beautiful. It's difficult to describe why, but he was perfect, like a statue by Michelangelo, one that was made especially for me.

I watched the contours of his body come into view as he slid his pants down and stepped out of them. The curve of his back as it met his ass, the curve of his ass as it met his thighs, the roundness of his muscular legs, perfectly formed, both thighs and calves, his thin ankles and beautiful feet. Actually, I think the male foot might be my favorite part, slender, all the bones and sinews on view, with long, perfectly shaped toes.

It wasn't until he knelt back on the bed, between my legs, and kissed me one more time that I snapped out of it. I could feel his hard cock brush against my stomach. "Is it all right, my beauty?" he asked, looking into my eyes. In answer, I wrapped my hand around his cock, still staring into his amber and brown eyes, and guided him to my opening.

I was wet from all the oral sex, but just the sight of him made me gush. His entry was smooth and final, like a high diver attempting the perfect jackknife. We fitted perfectly, and when he started to move inside me, it felt like coming home. I don't know how long we made love (because this was way beyond simple fucking). It felt like he could go on and on forever, but he knew time was short. He stroked my clit while I stroked his balls. As I reached climax again, I felt them contract in my hand and he came inside me.

I must have passed out, because the next thing I remember, I was in his arms, fully dressed, and we were in the desert. My *magia* man kissed me and set me on my feet. “My beautiful Anita. You are even more beautiful than the lovely Consuelo.” He kissed me again and turned me a little to my right. “Walk straight ahead for only a few minutes and you will see your village. You will not find me again, so you mustn’t return to the desert looking.”

He gave me a gentle push. A few steps later, I looked over my shoulder, but he was gone, as I knew he would be.

Consuelo. My grandmother’s name was Consuelo.

ADULT TIME

Jeanette Grey

I give myself exactly thirty seconds to stand there and wave.

Penny can't even see me from her car seat, but it doesn't matter. I hold my breath, watching my mom drive away with my two-year-old in her care.

We're on the second day of our trip to New York to see her. The ritual of lunch in Chinatown has just been accomplished. Now I'm supposed to be relaxing and enjoying a little adult time, but I've never felt so stressed out in my *life*.

Annoyingly perceptive, my husband, Drew, wraps his arms around me from behind. "Ming."

I shush him, still watching as the car turns onto Canal Street. It merges left, and then disappears behind a truck, out of view.

"Ming," Drew says again, hugging me tighter. "They'll be fine."

"I know."

"It's only a few hours."

"I *know*."

Pulling me closer, Drew puts his lips to the corner of my jaw.

His hot breath washes over my skin, making me shiver. "Then why are your shoulders up around your ears?"

Shit, he's right. I relax my posture, pretending like he never caught me being a total worrywart. Again.

Can he blame me, though? This is the first time we've let anybody else take care of our kid. My mom's been trying to get us to let her babysit since the moment Penny was born, but I've resisted.

She and Drew finally ganged up on me this time, though.

"You two should go see New York," my mom insisted.

What do I need to see? I grew up in Queens. But this is the first time Drew's ever set foot outside the airport.

"We should," he agreed. Catching the instant refusals that rose to my lips, he squeezed my hand, and warmth shot all the way up my arm. "Come on. It'll be an adventure."

And there was something to the way his fingers grazed my knuckles. A heat in his gaze as he worked to convince me.

Ten years of marriage and my husband can still make me weak in the knees.

So I said yes, and here we are, on our own for the entire afternoon.

And we're not going to waste it.

"Okay." I nod to myself and tug away from Drew's embrace, reaching into my purse to grab the guidebook pages I printed to help us get the most from our time.

Only for Drew to yank them right out of my hand.

"Hey—"

He's so tall, all he has to do is lift them overhead to keep them out of my reach. I put my hand on his muscled chest anyway, clawing at his arm to try to get him to relent.

Instead, he reels me in with his free hand.

"Ming." His voice drops into a low purr that I feel where my breasts are pressed against his chest. In the neglected, achy place between my legs.

I fight to hide my reaction, though. "Drew—"

"No guidebooks."

"But—"

"No perfectly efficient walking tours." He raises a brow. "No timing us through a museum to make sure we hit every highlight."

That's a low blow.

"One time," I grumble.

Instead of arguing, he leans down to kiss me, and I can't help it. I melt into him. He sucks at my bottom lip with a dirty promise, his slick tongue sweeping past my teeth and pushing all thought from my mind.

When he pulls away, I'm breathless.

"Just relax today, please." Intensity colors his words. "Let us take our time and *enjoy* it."

All at once, I understand where he's going with this.

Parenthood has sent my type A personality spinning into high gear. The rigid schedule I've adhered to has kept our busy household running like a well-oiled machine, but it's spilled over into every aspect of our lives—including our breaks and our vacations.

Even our meager sex life has been carefully slotted in.

But there was a time, back when Drew and I were dating, when we would stay up all night talking or making love. We were both new to San Francisco, and we explored it with relish, wandering it endlessly, just taking it all in. Enjoying each other's company.

Tearing each other's clothes off any time—and any*where*—the impulse struck.

When was the last time we did that?

When was the last time I let go of my compulsive control long enough to even try to?

Making out on a crowded city street is the closest we've come in literal years.

Drew gently massages the back of my neck in that persuasive, oh-so-sexy way of his. Pulling back by a fraction, he raises a brow. "So?"

Nervous energy prickles along my skin. Going off-script is terrifying. The script has served me so well for so long.

But the combination of Drew's seductive touch and his liquid eyes makes up my mind. "Okay." I manage a small smile and a nod. "Let's try it."

"Good."

He releases me just long enough to pitch my itinerary for the afternoon in a trash can. I wince but suppress the impulse to dig it right back out.

Wrapping his arm around me, he sets off, heading north. He's more confident in his sense of direction than he has any right to be. It occurs to me that he may have done more planning than I did, but I refuse to get derailed by that. His embrace is too warm.

Excitement bubbles in my chest.

Drew's deferred to me about so many things these past couple of years. He reminds me now that he's perfectly capable of taking control.

He reminds me how much I used to *like* him taking control.

Especially when the first place he leads us is a bar.

The place isn't much bigger than a hole in the wall, one of those trendy hipster spots that's started moving into Chinatown.

I raise a brow at my husband but don't complain as he holds the door. My body rubs up against his, maybe more than it needs to. Tingles light me up inside, and he puts a possessive hand on my hip.

We grab a couple of seats, and a bartender asks for our orders.

Drew speaks before I can open my mouth. "Two of whatever's your house special."

"Coming right up."

Normally, that kind of thing would piss me off, but today, Drew's confidence just turns me on.

Worse, he knows it.

Within minutes, two elaborate cocktails land on the bar in front of us. Drew hands me one glass while raising the other. Our fingers brush.

And this man is the father of my child. We've been together for half our lives. A simple touch shouldn't send shivers of interest humming through all my wanting places, but it does.

Something about this day, about being alone together outside our house for the first time in years, about being utterly free of responsibility . . .

It makes me feel young in a way I'd forgotten I could be.

Holding my husband's gaze, I take a sip of my drink. It's surprisingly complex, fruity but rich, with just enough of an afterburn on the way down to prove its potency.

I whistle and set it back on the bar. "That's going to be dangerous."

Drew smiles crookedly. "Perfect."

So we drink and talk. By some unspoken agreement, parenting is off-limits. We steer away from the logistics for the rest of the trip, too.

And yet there are no awkward silences.

Having the freedom to hold an actual, adult conversation opens something in my chest—or maybe that's the alcohol.

It's not enough to make me impaired, but I feel my inhibitions leaving my body.

As we talk, the place begins to fill up. When someone settles into the barstool beside mine, I lean into Drew's space even farther. He welcomes me in, putting a broad, hot palm on my knee.

That hand slowly creeps higher and higher. I pretend I don't notice, but the rubbing motion of his thumb on my upper thigh sends heat blooming through me.

Then he closes the gap between us. Right beside my ear, he whispers, "I wish you were wearing a skirt."

A firework goes off inside me. My pussy throbs almost painfully, and I grab onto his arm—both because I need to steady myself and because I'm suddenly desperate for his touch.

I can picture it so easily, his hand on my bare skin. He could dip beneath the hem, let his fingertips trace along the edge of my panties. Nobody would be able to see. He could practically finger me right here in the middle of this bar.

How far would he push it? Would he brush my wet opening? Or go right for it and plunge inside, stroke his thumb across my achy, swollen clit?

Would the people around us hear my gasp?

A thrill of arousal shoots through me.

I haven't worn a short skirt since my kid started crawling. I don't even know if I have any that fit.

But that's a problem I know how to fix.

Lifting my gaze to meet his, I lick my lips. "What do you say we go find me one?"

His dark eyes smolder. Standing, he grabs his wallet and pulls out a couple of bills. He places them on the bar and reaches for my hand. He hauls me to my feet and leans down to capture my lips in a wet, dirty kiss. The growing hardness at the front of his jeans presses into my body in the most tantalizing tease.

Then he pulls away. "I'd say I fucking love my wife."

Fueled by our drinks, we set back out on the streets. Drew wraps his arm around me tightly, a strong hand resting on my hip, and I lean into him with my whole body. It's like we're new lovers all over again, intoxicated by each other, unwilling to stop touching for a second.

Despite having a goal, we keep wandering. There's no shortage of places that sell clothing in lower Manhattan, but nothing in particular catches my eye until Drew stops. He points across the street.

"There."

I follow his gaze, my eyes flying wide.

Drew wants us to go into a sex shop. Sure enough, though, there are mannequins in the window dressed in leather and lace. Some of the garments are a cross between fetish wear and lingerie, but others could pass as regular clothes.

It's not a place I'd dare walk into normally, but today, with my husband wrapped around me like a possessive, horny scarf . . . with my pussy dripping with excitement and my lungs full of bright city air . . .

I swallow down my doubts and nod. "Okay."

No one in New York cares what anyone else is doing, and two thirtysomethings walking into an adult store won't even make the top ten list of weird things on this street in this moment. My skin still flushes as if a thousand eyes are on us. I squirm inside, breathless arousal building between my thighs.

Drew holds the door for me and guides me in, then toward the clothing section on the right. My gaze lingers on the far wall, though, taking in displays covered in huge silicone cocks and brightly colored vibrators. I swallow hard at the racks of lube. Plugs and harnesses and handcuffs and god only knows what else.

"Later," Drew murmurs, and a tremor ripples along my spine.

Right.

I stay tucked in tightly against his side as we peruse the racks. Drew pulls out a black leather skirt that would barely hit mid-thigh on me. A few other options in scratchy lace and shining satin follow.

He pauses for a second at the edge of the display. Then he reaches out and grabs a pair of black thigh highs and a garter belt. More wetness floods my pussy.

I thought I'd lost the version of myself who ever wore those kinds of things. The one who dressed and *felt* like a sexy woman.

But just like that, she's back.

Without a word of argument, I let him lead me to the dressing rooms in the rear corner of the store. The people I imagined were staring at us out on the street might have been figments of my imagination, but the salesperson is entirely too real. Her face is utterly blank as she hands me a number and opens a curtain for me.

I look to Drew expectantly. Surely he'll want to watch me try these on. Maybe he'll even want to help.

But he waves me in. "Come back out in your favorite."

Oh. Something in me falls. I worry the edge of one of the skirts between my fingers and look to the floor. I don't want to have to ask him to come with me. I don't want to lose this intoxicating sexual energy that's been buzzing between us since he first put his hand on my leg at the bar.

"Ming," he says, voice rough and low.

I jerk my gaze up.

"Don't keep me waiting."

His eyes burn with undisguised lust.

And in a flash, my confidence is back. He trusts me. He wants me to do this for him.

So who am I to doubt anything now?

With a nod and a gulp, I close the curtain between us.

Studiously avoiding my reflection, I start to strip. The outfit I wore to take my mother to lunch wasn't meant to be seductive.

The top is a basic black number, though, so I leave it on. The package for the hose crinkles in the silent air. Sitting on the bench, I pull them on.

A shiver hums through me. The silky fabric glides over my skin, hugging it tightly. My pale legs disappear beneath it, and it's like I'm transforming into another person. Another being. My breathing shallow, I stand. Impulsively, I take off my underwear, revealing my wet, needy flesh to the air. I get on the garter belt and put the panties back on over it.

I still refuse to look at myself. I try on each of the skirts we picked out. One is too tight and another too large. Two fit perfectly, though. I tuck my top into the leather one and turn around.

And it suddenly doesn't matter that I've spent the last two years in a sexless haze. It doesn't matter that I'm two sizes bigger than I used to be or that my makeup is barely there and my hair unstyled.

The skirt is *obscene*. The tops of the thigh highs and the straps of the garter belt show beneath the hem. With my shirt tucked in, my breasts look huge and my waist tiny.

My dark eyes, flushed cheeks, and wet lips are all the makeup I need.

I turn around. I shove the curtain to the side.

And there's my husband. One look at me, and I swear to god he's going to eat me alive.

Then I spot the tube of lube and the purple anal plug in his hands.

My throat clamps down.

Sense memory crashes into me out of nowhere. My nipples twist and my clit *throbs*.

Nothing's come anywhere near my ass in ages, but I used to love it. Drew would eat my pussy out and gently open my rear entrance. He'd shove a plug in there and fuck my cunt—or sometimes the other way around. With a huge dildo keeping me full, he'd slowly work his thick cock into my ass, and I'd come so hard I'd wake the neighbors.

Gripping the wall just to keep myself upright, I gaze back at him in utter rapture.

I suddenly need him so desperately I can hardly stand. My knees are jelly, my pussy swollen and wet, and I don't know how I'm going to wait another second to get my husband buried deep inside me.

And then it strikes me.

Who says we have to wait?

We crash through the door of the store's bathroom as one. Shoving it closed behind us, he flips the lock. His hot mouth descends on mine, and I open for him easily, ecstatically. I rake my fingers through his hair, groaning at the heat of his hands as they palm my ass through my brand new skirt. The package containing our *other* purchase crinkles in his jacket pocket, and aching need spreads through me, my clit pulsing hard.

Pressing me into the wall, he takes command, dominating and demanding in a way he hasn't been in ages. Desperate heat floods my pussy, while at the same time my ribs squeeze around my heart.

Where has this Drew *been* all these years?

My husband is so kind, so caring, and so considerate. He's deferred to my maternal instincts and meticulous research as we've raised our child together, but what has he been holding back? What have I been subtly asking him to keep under wraps?

What have we both been denying ourselves, and *why?*

He yanks his mouth from mine.

"Stop thinking," he growls, pulling me out of my spiral. His dark gaze burns into me, full of lust and need. "Just be here. With me. Now."

"Drew—"

I want to obey so badly, but I don't know how to be spontaneous. How to let go and have an adventure, how to be present in the moment.

Fortunately, my husband does.

"Not another word," he warns.

With that, he twirls me around. All the air is knocked out of my lungs as he marches me the handful of steps to the little sink in the corner. He grabs my hands and places them on the counter. Meeting my gaze in the mirror, he pushes firmly at the space between my shoulder blades.

My heart thunders, but I let myself be moved. I grasp on tightly to the edges of the sink, sticking my ass out as I'm bent over the porcelain. He reaches under my barely there skirt to grab my panties and tear them down to my knees. Cool air hits my backside, followed by my husband's rough, hot palms.

Shuddering, I close my eyes and push into his touch. The threads of my anxiety melt away, one by one. He traces the edges of the garter straps then palms my ass fully, pulling the cheeks apart.

"Just as perfect as ever," he swears.

I drown out the voice inside that wants to remind him that my ass used to be an awful lot smaller, but I refuse to ruin this. He told me to stop thinking, to just enjoy the moment, and I'm going to do that, goddammit all.

His thumbs graze the swollen lips of my pussy. I'm so wet that they glide easily over that aching flesh. I clench down inside, my clit twitching with need, my trapped nipples twisting themselves into tight points.

"You want my cock here?" he asks, low and gravelly. He dips a fingertip just inside my pussy, only to drag it farther back. When he brushes my tight rear entrance, I light up with dirty, illicit sparks. "Or here?"

"Fuck," I breathe out. "Anywhere. Everywhere."

"Just might take you up on that."

Then he's dropping to his knees, right there on the bathroom floor. I grip the edges of the sink so hard I swear the porcelain will crack. There's the quiet rustling of plastic somewhere in the distance, but all I can concentrate on is his heat behind me, his breath in this tiny, public room.

All the people outside who might be able to hear me begging for my husband's cock.

The next thing I know, he's pulling my ass cheeks apart again. His fingertip returns to my asshole, slick and cool, and bless me but he doesn't mess around. He rubs and rubs, getting me used to his touch there after so long without, and then between one breath and the next he presses inside.

I suck in a ragged breath. Jesus—it really has been forever, hasn't it? The sting of being stretched open mixes with the impossible pleasure of being filled like this until everything feels good. I'm holding on as tightly as I can to the sink, but in my head, I'm letting go for the first time in as long as I can remember.

He fucks in shallowly with that one finger at first, opening me up for him. This man knows me so well, he feels when I'm ready for him to go deeper, when he can press another finger in.

So he does.

A jolt of something sharp forces a gasp from between my lips, but then I'm yielding inside. He makes space inside me for himself, just like he always has. He finds new parts of me.

Maybe parts I'd forgotten.

Out of nowhere, stinging tears threaten the corners of my eyes, but they're of the very, very best kind. Bent over a sink in a public bathroom in a sex store, I'm having some kind of epiphany.

Blinking my eyes open, I meet my own blurry gaze in the mirror.

I love my life. I love my family. I wouldn't trade any of the sacrifices I've made for them.

But I missed *this*.

And we can make room for it. We will.

Because every time I forget to, every time I forget *myself* . . .

This man will remind me. Over and over and over again.

Before I can get too carried away in sentimentality, Drew crooks his fingers deep inside my ass. With his free hand, he passes me the plug he bought.

I don't need to ask for instructions. I force my fingers to unclench and accept the curved silicone, then turn the water on. I wash the toy and hand it back.

When he pulls his fingers out, my knees nearly buckle. The sudden emptiness howls inside me, but he doesn't make me wait. He presses the plug in to fill that searing gap. My pussy clenches, and I go up onto my toes as he shoves the toy in to the hilt.

Then he's spinning me around to face him. Grabbing me and holding me and lifting me.

Slamming me into the wall.

For a second, I'm winded.

But I get with the program fast.

Kicking off what's left of my underwear, I wrap my legs around his trim hips. He's had the foresight to get himself unbuckled and unzipped. Together, we shove his boxer briefs down until his huge, bare cock pops free. I groan at the searing heat of him and kiss his mouth again.

My wetness has spread so far, his cock slides slickly against my skin. Bucking, I try to get him closer to my needy center. Sparks shoot through me as he finally grinds against my clit. When I flex inside, I'm met by the resistance of the plug in my ass, only it's not enough.

"Come on," I beg. "Please, I need—"

"Believe me." His gaze bores into mine. "I know exactly what we need."

Without another word, he fits himself to my opening, the blunt head of him spreading my pussy wide.

Staring right into my eyes, he slams himself home.

I howl, digging my nails into the back of his neck. Drew's always been well endowed, but the sudden fullness is insane, everything magnified by the plug in my ass, the chill of the plaster wall behind me, the clench of my legs around his hips.

The people outside who can hear us fucking.

The *freedom*.

After years of tucking our passion away on a shelf, we've gotten one afternoon to let it run wild, and we are.

Wasting no time, Drew lets our unleashed sexual energy consume him, and it just about devours me, too. He crushes his lips to mine, holding me up with his hands beneath my thighs. I cling to him and tilt my hips, but I have no leverage. As he draws back, all I can do is grasp onto him and feel the magnitude of that retreat.

He leaves me almost empty for a fraction of a second. Then he thrusts back in deep. Hot pleasure sweeps through me, and I cry out again.

Hard and fast, he fucks me into the wall. Every slide in pummels at the most sensitive parts of me, while every withdrawal leaves me scrabbling at his shoulders, kicking at his ass with my heels, trying to get deeper, better, *more*.

Over and over, we crash together. The wet, messy sounds of flesh slapping on flesh fill the room, drowned out only by our groans of absolute pleasure. Desperate need for release builds up inside me until I swear I'll explode, only I can't get there.

"Please," I gasp. "Drew—"

Grunting with effort, he shifts his grip. His muscles strain, biceps bulging beneath his shirt. Somehow, he manages to hold me up with just the force of his hips and the wall and one hand. He dips the other into the place where our bodies are joined.

His thumb finds my clit, and colors flash before my eyes.

"Oh, Jesus—"

"That's it, gorgeous," he growls. "Come on, come on my cock—"

Orgasm swallows me up out of nowhere. I scream and bite his lip, and crack my head back against the wall. Darkness eclipses my vision as I pulse and pulse.

My husband fucks me through it, almost savage in the way he batters me with his cock.

The second and third wave are just as blinding, my pleasure seeming to go on forever now that I've finally given into it.

But the instant I start to come down, he pulls out.

I sob, the emptiness too much, but of course I shouldn't have doubted him for even a second.

He sets me down on my feet, and then turns me around. I put my arms up to brace myself against the wall. He kicks my legs apart, spreading me wide.

He shoves his cock back into my pussy without a word of warning. It's just as shocking as that first entry, just as electric. My climax still has me tingling everywhere, my legs shaking with the force of keeping myself up when all I want to do is collapse.

Letting my cheek press into the wall, I arch my back.

"Fuck," Drew groans. "Ming—"

I glance back over my shoulder at him. His beautiful face is red with exertion, his temples damp with sweat, and my heart swells to the point of bursting. Gripping the wall, I pant out, "I love you."

And in the middle of this filthy bathroom fuck, that's what sends my husband over the edge.

He shouts in triumph as his cock swells inside me. Hot come fills my pussy. I slip a hand down to mash at my clit until the pleasure is too much to hold. A final orgasm rolls through me as I milk him for every drop.

Wrapping his arms around me from behind, he presses his brow into the back of my shoulder. He shudders, and then goes still.

For a long minute, we stay there just like that, breathing hard and holding onto each other. My body sings with satisfaction. Freedom and love swirl inside my chest.

Then Drew pulls back. Pushing my hair to the side, he kisses the nape of my neck. He laughs and says, "Well, that was something."

I can't help but smile. "It really was."

We disengage enough to clean ourselves up. Come and my own juices streak the inside of my new skirt. I crinkle up my nose.

"Go ahead and take it off," Drew tells me.

"Guess it's not really the right outfit for heading back to my mom's house, huh?"

My fingers tighten on the fabric all the same. I don't want to turn into boring, uptight old me again. I don't want him to retreat back into his shell.

I don't want to *lose* this.

As if he can sense my conflict, Drew reaches for me. He grabs my chin and tilts my face up. "Take off the skirt," he insists. His eyes flash. "But leave in the plug."

My sore pussy and ass both clench as one. Heat flares across my face.

But in my chest I'm soaring.

Trembling and aroused, I cover his hand with mine. "Why? What are you planning to do with it?"

"Anything I want," he insists.

His mouth meets mine, and just like that I know.

Our time together as irresponsible adults is almost over.

But this new phase of our adventure together has only just begun.

CREAM

Saskia Vogel

Jacinda settled in to watch some porn. She only did this when Ben was not at home. She liked the surreptitious feeling of masturbating all alone in their shared apartment, especially on a day like this when there was a chance he'd come home from work before she climaxed. If she heard his key in the door, she'd stop what she was doing to greet him with a kiss and guide his hand between her legs. "You're so wet," he'd say. And she'd respond with a smile. She'd stay slick through dinner, enjoying the tension between her legs, and when they'd make love, again he'd whisper: *You're so wet*. Perhaps this was why she liked keeping her daytime masturbation a secret. She liked that he didn't seem to know why she was so wet, even after seven years of coupledom, and she longed to hear the bright surprise that entered his voice when he said it—you're so wet—as though she were proffering an incredible gift.

Her daytime masturbation was, in part, about desire. But Jacinda worked from home, and the long hours by the computer often led her to this type of procrastination. When she felt her mind drift but needed to press on, she masturbated. When she felt particularly pleased with the work she'd done, she masturbated. When she needed to clear her mind, she masturbated. Despite the frequency of her masturbation, what she masturbated to was much the same. There was one fantasy she'd had since she was a teen. It involved a bathhouse full of women pleasuring themselves with strategically placed phalluses, both mounted to things and loose. The phalluses were large: they stretched the women; the women wanted to feel full. It was a vision of eager bodies, together and alone, pursuing pleasure, and the only gaze shaping the scene was hers. Jacinda had always taken her bathhouse fantasy as an indicator that she was open to all things so long as they were pleasurable. She hadn't given much thought to the fact that her fantasy had always trod a similar path.

Still images didn't do it for her, but sometimes writing did: sex scenes in novels, a paragraph she'd read again and again until she couldn't read anymore; the words would slip inside her mind like a chant, and she'd shut her eyes and let go. There was one bit of pulp erotica she kept coming back to, a naughty secretary story, but she preferred being taken by surprise by a sex scene in a novel. There were three lines in a Bret Easton Ellis novel that did it for her, to her chagrin, and a paragraph in Judith Krantz's *Scruples* where the mistress of the house fucks the pilot in her employ because it's what her dead husband would have wanted. There was something extraordinarily kind and generous in that fuck. Most of all she liked how it began: with a flicker of desire that caught her off guard.

When Jacinda watched porn, she liked to see a woman filled, too. She liked finding videos at random, that element of surprise again, and this meant wading through scenes where she didn't get the feeling that the woman was enjoying it or the men were too much in charge. Sometimes she felt guilty and couldn't separate her thoughts about labor conditions and performer agency from the scenes. She and her friends would break down their feelings about porn late into the night on the balcony, with a sneaky cigarette and a glass of red wine, when it was her turn to host book club. They never really seemed to reach a conclusion, other than committing to each other that they would try to pay for the porn that they liked to encourage more of its production.

What she liked in porn was the look in the woman's eyes. She liked watching her strain. Jacinda sought out scenes of women testing their physical limits—one cock, two cocks, three—with a look in their eyes that asked for more. It was a delicate spell.

Masturbating to porn, she would feel greedy, wanting more than one orgasm. First she'd use her fingers—thinking of Ben, who'd later say, "You're so wet"—then a variety of toys: a vibrator to encourage multiple orgasms, a dildo she'd slide in and out of her to the rhythm of the cock or cocks on screen, that same dildo plus one of her fingers for variation. Some days the very sight of her office chair made her excited, thinking about all the orgasms she'd had there.

On this particular day, Jacinda had found a new video, and after vetting it by clicking at random points in the stream to look at the woman's face deep into action, she returned to the beginning of the video and settled in. She lifted her skirt and slid her hand into her cotton panties, leaned back in her desk chair, and let her legs spread. She started to rub, dry at first, then came the wetness, her fingers slipping around, lubing up her clit. Her eyes followed a familiar path. Watching the woman's face, seeing her eyes widen when the first cock slid in, the determined frown when the second pushed his dick in, filling two holes. The shot from behind, showing the cocks rubbing against each other as they found their rhythm, in and out, the woman's face, the reverse shot . . . but today it wasn't working. Her eyes wanted something new. But what? She had been treading the same path of fantasy for so long. Why this change? Why today? She decided not to question it. She would follow the feeling wherever it took her.

Jace stuck with this video but allowed her gaze to rove. Across the slim but muscular men, the dark pucker of one man's anus, the space between the cock and balls . . . She kept rubbing, wondering what it was her eyes were trying to connect with, still wet. She tried to find her spark in the men's strong arms, the woman flexing and pointing her toes, the way her breasts bounced, her quivering breath, those muscular thighs. Jacinda's attention roved, and when her gaze finally settled on a part of the screen, it settled on a pair of balls.

Jacinda couldn't take her eyes off them: round and smooth, slapping as he sped up his fucking in time with the woman's calls for more, his vulnerable soft organs. She wanted to touch them, she wanted to lick them, she wanted to feel them slap against her, too. She thought about Ben and their sex, trying to remember if she had ever noticed his balls slap against her. Ben and their sex. Ben's balls. Round and smooth, his dark curls. Why did she never spend much time with them? In their seven years together, surely this wasn't the first time she'd thought about his balls in this way? But it was. She glanced at the man on the screen again, just to cement the visual, and then she shut her eyes and imagined what she would do to Ben.

"You're so wet, Jace," Ben said when he came home from work. Jacinda nodded and instead of guiding his hand down between her legs, she slid her hand between his. The heat of his blue jeans. She worked one hand down his waistband, into his briefs and cupped him, weighing his balls, giving them a gentle squeeze. With her other hand, she stroked him through the fabric with her nails. As she drew her hand out of his pants, she stroked his stiff cock, hard arc. She licked her thumb and ran it along his glans, which stuck up from the elastic band.

"Jace," he sighed, and took a step back so he was leaning against the front door. She pulled his trousers to his ankles, and right there, she took him in her mouth. Jacinda sucked. She lapped at his glans, the shaft, sliding her tongue all the way down, then up. *How could so many years with Ben have passed without me loving his balls like this?* she thought as she took them in her mouth—one, then the other, rubbing them with her tongue. She tried to fit both in her mouth, just for sport, then spit on her hand and squeezed his slick shaft. He moaned, told her to keep going, keep jerking him off. She lapped at his balls, pressed a knuckle against his perineum, like she knew he liked, and stroked his cock until he fell to his knees. "I want to be inside you, let me be inside you," Ben said, taking her in his arms.

They kissed on the hardwood floor until they found it too hard, then they scrambled to the nearest soft place, the living room sofa. He sat at the edge of the cushion, and she straddled him, facing away, riding him, cupping his balls as she did, his strong thighs spread. When she felt that he was about to come, she slid off him and caught as much semen as she could in her hands. With that hot, sticky come between her fingers, Jacinda had the strange and new sensation of having milked him. Pulling out had always been their method of birth control, but this time Jacinda was almost sorry to see his semen go to waste, rinsed down the drain in the bathroom sink. A clatter came from the kitchen. Pots and pans. Ben was cooking tonight. He was humming. It was likely to be grilled cheese.

Balls. She couldn't stop thinking about them. Jace fell asleep spooning Ben, her hand between his legs. The skin of his balls had been so thick and tight as he'd neared orgasm, and now it was loose and soft. Careful not to wake him, she traced the egg shapes with one finger, sensing the difference in temperature between where his thighs met and the bristled sac. What would it feel like if they were smooth? Could she ask him to shave, just to see? These were new thoughts. She liked how they made her feel.

After coffee the next morning but before she sat down to work, she took out her sex toy chest, made of pine with iron hinges and a lock she never used. She kept it under her bedside table, safe in the knowledge that no one, no curious little hands, would disturb it. Around her, the large apartment was suddenly very quiet, like there was something missing. Jacinda had the sensation that she was being watched. Jacinda thought about how long she'd been masturbating to the same things. She wondered if it was a lack of imagination or simply the comfort of the familiar. She was thirty-three now: life was stable, she and Ben were in love still. Jacinda had worked so hard to be in this state, which had felt full, but now the silence she was hearing made it feel . . . roomy. She didn't quite understand why. She took out each of her dildos and lined them up in a row.

There was the clear silicone rabbit vibrator with its rotating pearls, a hand-blown glass dildo that had been a gift from another lover long before, a hard, red plastic torpedo-shaped vibrator that had been given to her at her bachelorette party, and the realistic dick that could be used on its own or slipped into a strap-on.

She picked each one up and examined them closely, paying attention to how each made her feel, the kinds of orgasms they could give her. She took the realistic dick in her hand and squeezed. The exterior was soft and pliable, but inside there was a harder core. She stood it up on the floor. The balls were tight and ridged. She stroked them. Jacinda liked the way they felt to the touch.

She remembered Ben's balls and dragged her nail up the seam that ran along the sac between the testicles, imagining them contracting. She wanted to bite that skin, run her teeth along it as though it were fruit leather, the taste of Ben there. She fingered herself, enjoying the softness inside, circling her G-spot to get herself going. She could be like the women from her bathhouse fantasies and mount this curved cock right there on the floor. And so she did.

She opened her legs and teased herself with the dildo's head, her grip tight at its base. Just the tip, just the tip. The sentence made her giggle. Just the tip could be so wonderful, no compromise at all. In and out, feeling the head slide in and out, that delicious ridge. Once she was so wet there was no longer any friction, she did something she would never do to Ben. She slid her hands down the shaft of the dildo and pressed the heels of her palms hard down on the balls. She squished them, she pressed them down, kneading them like a happy cat, the cat that got the cream. The curved cock hit her right in the sweetest spot as she ground into it, rubbing her clit against her wrists as she pinned the balls down. She ground and she ground, wanting more, the idea of those balls slapping against her. She lay back, and as she ran her thumbs over those firm testicles, she fucked herself, stoking the furnace inside, feeling the heat build from her core. She sped up her fucking, gripping the balls, digging her nails into the silicone, wanting more, more, more. As she came, she imagined herself full of come. She imagined holding it inside her. She imagined her belly growing large, new life.

Jacinda stopped what she was doing and opened her eyes. So far, this was something she and Ben had been trying to avoid, but suddenly the desire was there: this new wanting. The desire had announced itself, and Jacinda, to her surprise, welcomed it in. Jacinda sat there, feeling it all. The idea was thrilling; it seemed a little dangerous. She thought of all the sex she'd had, all the things she'd done, the pleasures of leather cuffs and women, of days in bed with a lover whose name she couldn't remember, but this new desire felt like the kinkiest of them all. Almost taboo. What would it be like to have sex with Ben and for him not to pull out? Slowly, she started up again, working the cock inside her. When she was finished, she kissed the balls of the dildo sweetly and lay on the floor with them pressed to her cheek, thinking of the line that she and Ben might cross together, the fresh intimacy that was available for them to explore.

In this dreamy state, Jacinda decided that she would put off working for some hours. She opened her favorite cookbook and planned a three-course meal: Middle Eastern-inspired, something light with a nice amount of spice, salad, and rice. In the grocery store, she lingered by the avocados, taking longer than usual to find the perfect one. She gave the fruit a gentle squeeze, feeling its ridged skin, and then moved on to the tomatoes. She liked the earthy texture of them, the scent that rose from the vine. She put a peach to her cheek. The firm fuzz against her skin reminded her of him, and she kissed it without thinking. Blushing, she added it to her cart. Back home, she took the eggs out of their cardboard box and arranged them in a bowl. She held one in her hand, let it grow warm, rocking it gently, aware of the movement inside. Jacinda looked at the clock and told herself it would be silly to start work now, so late in the day. She might as well write today off and start fresh tomorrow. No one would mind. *Maybe,* Jacinda thought, *I should go back to bed.*

Her laptop propped up beside her on a pillow, Jacinda found the video from the day before, wondering what she would see this time around. Not the woman so much, but the men. She watched the swing of their balls; she was seeing how much they wanted her. Their cocks strained to be inside her, their balls ached to spill their seed. The very idea was making Jacinda's skin electric to touch. She ran her hands along her arms, she hugged herself, she felt the curve of her wide hips, she squeezed the meat of her thighs. Her breasts, nipples puckered and hard, rubbery like his. She heard Ben's key in the door, but she didn't run to meet him. When he called for her, she responded, "I'm in here."

Ben laughed when he saw her still in bed. She invited him to undress, taking pleasure in what was hard and soft about his body. Jacinda thought about what she wanted to do to him: lick his balls, run her teeth along the skin, taste every inch of him. Suddenly she felt shy. How could she bring it up, what she wanted them to do next? How could she tell him that she wanted him to come inside her?

Ben climbed into bed and snuggled up tight against her. He squeezed her breasts and ran his hands over her body, an echo of what she had just done: arms, hips, grabbing the meat of her thighs, her breasts. The pleasure of synchronicity. He parted her from behind, and as just the tip began to push inside her, Ben gasped with surprise.

"You're so wet," he said.

She smiled. This time she'd tell him why.

THE ESCAPE ROOM

Elizabeth SaFleur

"Ready to give me my birthday present, Ava?" The fabric of the blindfold dragged down her face, and she blinked moisture from her lashes. The room was shrouded in darkness, but Bret's eyes glowed like the Caribbean blue waters. His stiff length pushed into her crotch, and her knees widened further. They'd always split wide for him.

"Mhmmm. Decide what kind of exploit you want?" she asked.

He'd been nibbling on her neck for five panty-ruining minutes, so whatever he wanted, he'd get. Besides, what else do you give your husband for his birthday when he already owned resorts and a private jet and kept you living on a Caribbean island ten months of the year? Another Hawaiian shirt he'd never wear?

"Yes." His breath warmed her neck as he sucked on her earlobe. "I'd like you to test out our new entertainment for our resort guests—the escape room."

"It's ready? Is that where we are?" She glanced around. The room looked like an ordinary office to her, nothing like the adventure-of-his-choosing she'd gifted him.

"It is, and we are." His hands moved to her inner thigh,

thumbs brushing against her captive pussy folds. Goosebumps chased each other up and down her spine as they always did when he got anywhere *there*. Lordy, please keep doing *that*. His thumb made lazy circles over her clit, imprisoned behind soaked thong underwear, the scratch of lace feeling oh so amazingly good.

"As the resort owner's wife, I believe you should try it out before the room goes live. If you're game."

"Game?" A spangle of pleasure pushed the word out of her mouth.

"Otherwise, I open the door and we'll go to dinner."

Hell, his games beat food any day. "I'm not hungry."

"Is that a yes?" His face split into that grin she loved.

"Yes." She returned his smile with a swipe of her tongue to her top lip.

His hands moved to her ass, and he yanked her closer, her sodden panties mashing into his trousers, instantly wetting them. As his lips returned to just under her earlobe, her molecules lit up like a fireworks display. So long as he kept making love to her neck with his mouth and his hands stayed on her, he could have whatever he wanted—her heart, her soul, her internal organs.

"You can say no," he murmured against her skin.

"No, or rather, yes. I want to play." When he pulled back, she purposefully pouted. His eyes narrowed with a stern dominance that drilled right through her mischief. *Oh.* He wanted to *play.* Her pussy clenched, ready to rock and roll with whatever he had planned. He had the *best* ideas, so, yes, yes, yes!

His fingers inched under her dress and hooked on either side of her panties—ones she didn't give a fig about. When married to this man, a girl had to be prepared for lingerie-ruining fun. She held her breath, waiting for the yank and the ripping sound of the fabric succumbing to his will. *Oh, please.* He chuckled because, of course, she'd whispered that aloud.

"First you have to solve the clues," he said. "Then you get your reward."

She ground her hips against his cock, as hard as she was wet. "Want to wager how long it will take me to find them?"

"No need. I'm giving them to you. You have to guess what they mean and what you need to do with them. Guess correctly, do it, and you earn the next one. One hour. Four clues. Four puzzles to unravel."

"Only four?" She slipped her fingers between her legs and cupped his erection in her palm.

He gently removed her hold. "If you don't behave, you don't get your present."

"But it's *your* birthday, Mr. Wright."

"Which means I get to give you things, and today, I have something special."

Sure, hit her up. His gifts usually involved her screaming his name loud enough to scare the birds out of the trees on the nearby islands. Wait. What did he mean by something "special"? *Oh, shit.* "You know I was kidding about getting me a puppy, right?"

"Not a puppy. Now . . ." He pushed off.

At the release of the pressure from his cock against her lit-up clit, a small whimper of protest escaped.

He snapped his fingers, and slowly, light bloomed in the crown molding near the ceiling.

"You're such a drama king," she teased.

"One hour, Ava. Now, first riddle." He lifted her hand and placed a tiny silver key into her palm. "This is the only time it's going to be easy. This key opens something near and dear to me that only I can unlock. What does it unlock?"

He strode to the other side of the room and leaned against the door frame, his face cracking into that megawatt smile that three years ago had melted off every stitch of her clothing, and had done so every day since.

"A lock that only you can unlock? Let's see." She eased off the desk, enjoying the way her thong tightened up her ass. With an exaggerated sway of her hips, she sauntered around the room. She could tease, too. "Hmmm, an office. Lock. Key."

A cheap metal desk monopolized the center of the room. To the knowing, it was at the perfect height for bending over. A large executive chair sat behind it. The perfect stage for reverse cowgirl. A tall hat rack stood bolted to the floor in the corner, adorned with hat, umbrella, and trench coat. The perfect frame for bondage. *Ava, center yourself.* Her overactive libido was all his fault, and she'd bet money his earlier foreplay had been conducted to throw her off her game.

She paused at a large painting of a familiar ocean view hanging against the far wall. She grinned at him. "The scene of the crime."

"Marrying you overlooking that view was hardly a crime. Fifty-five minutes left, Ava."

"Plenty of time."

The single door in the room had a keyhole, but it was too large for the tiny key in her hand. Besides, the idea was to earn her way out, despite the fact she didn't want out. Never did when it came to Bret. *Oh.* She held out the key to him.

"Mr. Wright, I do believe this is yours. I'm the lock. Care to insert your key?" Such a bad metaphor but one she'd live with if it meant he'd engage in some *inserting.*

"My smart Ava." He pocketed it in his ruined trousers, because yep, wet stain.

"Second clue," he said. "You can play with this object yourself, but it's better when I do it."

Her gaze swept the room. She pointed at the trench coat and arched her eyebrow. She could play the femme fatale and he the private dick she came to see. Or . . . she turned and presented her back to him. "My zipper?" Please let it be her zipper. If so, she'd fricking love this game.

He laughed. "No. By the way, you only get three guesses per riddle. That was one. Don't get them, game over."

She spun to face him, on-purpose pout in place. "Then I'll get them right."

"I know you will, smart girl. When you win, I win. Remember that. Again, the object you seek can be used by you, but it's better if used by me."

She circled the desk and faced the set of drawers. She found they held papers, pens, and—oh, hello—a Ping-Pong paddle. She lifted it up because if the zipper wasn't it, she so, so wanted this item to be *it*. She climbed up on the desk, presented her ass, and held out the paddle.

"My favorite position." He took the paddle and laid it by her hand. He pushed her dress up around her waist. "Much better. Continue."

Okay, he wanted her to spank herself. Game on. Her breath shot from her lungs at the first blow. He was right. This would be so much better if he wielded this thing because the angle wasn't really hitting her right. She adjusted her hand grip and landed a second slap, this one deliciously waking up her backside. The third time, she gave herself a stronger whack. The sting vibrated straight to her clit. Oh, yes, she'd have to remember this. She struck her own ass a fourth and fifth time, her hot pants echoing in her ears. Her thighs ached to spread wider but couldn't. She was at the edge of the desk. They were going to need bigger furniture in here. She startled when his fingers touched her backside. *Oh, good.* The nerves she'd lit up were ready for more.

"Are you thinking of me, Ava? When you spank yourself?" He

slid her panties to the side. The brush of fabric over her swollen clit loosened a bleat from her throat. The paddle clattered to the desk, and she pushed her ass back, trying to capture his fingers as the need for penetration took over.

He tsked. "I asked you a question. Did you think of me?"

Think? How could she think when his fingers were running up and down her inner lips like that? Oh, god, and *that*.

"Yes, I always think of you," she managed to rasp. "Is that the answer? Spanking me?"

"No, and the paddle wasn't the right object, but I appreciate the effort." He lifted a dime-store ruler to her face, his other hand continuing to brush around her clit. "This was the one I wanted, but I enjoyed the show."

Bastard that I love.

"The spanking was correct, so we'll let the paddle choice slide." On the word *slide,* his finger swiped up and down. "So wet for me, Ava."

"Yes, sir. F-for you. Ohhh . . ."

In one long, delicious thrust, his finger slid into her all the way, and the air in her lungs released in a rush.

"You know why it's better when I spank you?" His other hand held her hips as he fingered her *there,* deep inside her. "Do you?" His finger curled inside her, hitting that exquisite spot that only he had ever discovered.

His finger pulled out halfway, and she whimpered with the need to thrust backward.

"Tell me why, Ava. Mmm, you're very close, love."

Her clit throbbed so hard she swore she could hear it. "You make me come," she managed. *Please make me come.*

"What do you do before you come?"

Yes, desperately close. "Permission, sir, please?"

"Good girl. Permission is the correct answer." His finger

withdrew and his grip loosened. His chortle was diabolical. "But, no. You may not come."

"But I guessed right." It came out a whine . . . but whatever.

"Third clue next. Off the desk." He slid her lace thong back into place.

Was he kidding her? Maybe she wouldn't love this game.

"Turn around. On the edge of the table. Leave your dress up. Keep those dripping panties on display."

Fine. It did feel good to be off her knees, though her thighs were so slick she was shocked her panties didn't slither off by themselves when she twisted to sit in the slick of her own desire.

He held out a book to her. Please be the *Kama Sutra*, and she had to do all the positions to get to the next clue.

"*War and Peace?*" She peered up at him. "You hate this book. You said it never ends."

He yanked her knees open wider, and a new trickle of juice ran down to hit the desk. They were going to need to sanitize the ever-loving fuck out of this room before opening it to their resort guests.

"Is this a game that never ends?" she groaned. If he didn't let her come tonight she'd die of frustration—right after she killed her husband.

"Lie back." His eyes darkened with lust.

Her panties ripped to shreds when he yanked them down her legs—finally. Okay, he wasn't so wicked. She may have rushed to judgment. Best. Game. Ever.

"So this clue means"—she kicked off her pumps, hooked her bare feet on the edge of the desk, and spread her thighs wide—"peace now, right?"

His low laugh was not encouraging. "Touch yourself, and no coming, Ava."

Her head fell back. She managed to keep, "*Good thing it's your birthday,*" to herself.

"Ava." His growl broke through her runaway exasperation.

Right. Her hand slipped to her bare sex. She ran her middle and ring fingers alongside her slick pussy lips, trying to avoid her aching clit and failing. She gulped air and dipped her fingers down farther until she could curl them inside. He wanted a show? He was going to get one.

She tensed her muscles around her fingers and imagined they were Bret's. His cock would be even better. She scissored her fingers, imagining his width, his length. Just like that, her insides needed more, so much more. A moan broke from her throat, and her spine arched up, as if asking for him to just get on with it already. A full-on plundering, that's what she needed. She closed her eyes and disappeared into a place where she was nothing but twisting fingers and wet and nerves and swollen flesh and . . . If she came, would the punishment be so bad?

"Stop." His rumble broke through her need to just pitch over that edge.

Her fingers stilled.

"Tune into your breathing. Hear yourself."

She was panting like a dog in heat. A whole pack of wild dogs . . .

"I love hearing that, Ava. Hearing how close you are." His large hands curled around her ankles, and he pulled her legs together. *Together.*

"Now, what do you think the *War and Peace* clue means?" he asked.

"You're never letting me come again."

"Try again. Remember, you only get three tries."

She rose up on two elbows. "Forever frustrated?"

"That's two."

"You aren't letting me come right now, but it's not forever. *Sir.*"

"Half right. Because I'm not a sadist, I'll take it. The correct answer is forever."

She'd take issue with the "not a sadist" part, but okay—forever—whatever the hell that meant.

"Fourth clue." He pointed to the clocks. "You have twenty minutes left."

She sat up, instantly sobered. She was not getting beaten by an escape room in her own resort. If marketing got ahold of her failure, she'd die. *Resort owner's wife couldn't figure it out* made pretty good ad copy.

He pulled her off the desk to standing, and she didn't bother to straighten her dress. Juices trailed down her inner thighs. Maybe seeing her glowing pussy would make him rethink his choices.

He smiled. "I see I need to repeat myself. Focus, Ava."

"I am working on half my normal quota of brain cells. The other half is down here." She pointed to her crotch.

He, however, pointed to the five clocks on the wall.

She shimmied her dress back over her ass and hips and gazed at the clock faces. "Four o'clock. Two o'clock. Seven. One. Nine." She grinned. "We got married on April 27th."

"Yes, and remember Jonathan and Christiana's wedding here last year? They got married on April 27, too. And . . . they did more."

Why the hell was he bringing up anyone else? She was right here. Pussy ready. Waiting for him to nail her against anything in this room. Oh, Jesus, did he want a threesome? Or foursome? Once released, would she find someone on the other side of the door? Or *someones?*

"Ava?"

She turned to him and blinked.

"Think of all the objects and clues you've had so far." He

circled her waist with his arm and pressed his hard cock against her hip as if that would help her concentrate.

She huffed a centering breath. "A key that only you can use. A paddle. Excuse me, a *ruler,* and permission requested and denied." Thank you fucking much. "Forever. Though I don't know what that means. And our anniversary, the wedding, and the collaring." She sucked in air. They'd had a fight over her offhand joke at the wedding about Christiana's collar and how Ava was the only one in the room without one that day. Well, except for Sarah but she was a femme domme and . . .

"Ava." His hand circled the back of her neck. "The next object you have to guess. What did I tell you the first time we got together?"

"You weren't a serial killer."

He laughed aloud. Well, it was true. After downing too much tequila in the bar as a guest the first time she'd ever been here, he'd taken her out on the beach to sober up. Turned out he was the resort owner and the best man she'd ever met. The last night of that vacation he'd said something to her about men—and who she should be involved with.

"You told me to hold out for the man who'd move the island for me. That's what you said." Before Bret, she'd had terrible taste in men. Worse, she'd chased them.

His strong hands cupped her cheeks. "Because my baby deserves everything—all the islands and the stars hanging over them."

"Moving the island. That's the final clue."

He dropped his hold. "Clever girl." His eyes shone with pride.

She strode to the painting of the view of the Caribbean islands. When she fingered the edge, a soft click sounded. The painting easily swung away from the wall like a door. "A hidden safe." When the dial accepted 4-2-7-1-9 as the correct combination, a sense of triumph joined her aching pussy. *We are so going to get that orgasm.*

She lifted out the only item inside, a long, rectangular box. "A clue or present?"

"Your gift. Open it."

Please let it be a vibrator. She took the velvet box to the desk, careful to avoid the wet smear. The black ribbon fell free, and she lifted the top. Inside, on a velvet bed, lay a necklace of three interwoven silver strands dotted with various colored jewels. A little silver lock dangled where the clasp should be.

She swallowed and raised her head to find Bret's deep blue eyes smiling down on her. "Please tell me this isn't a collar for a puppy."

"Not a puppy." He took it from her and placed a finger on a clear stone. "Those jewels represent the planets and how they were aligned the day you were born. The diamond represents Earth. The ruby, Jupiter . . . Hey, you okay?"

"It really is a . . ."

"Collar. When you win, I win, remember?" He straightened and adopted a rare serious face. "Or it can be just a necklace. Think about it. Don't answer right away."

"Yes. My answer is yes."

His lips came down on hers. His tongue worked the inside of her mouth to the point where her pussy begged even more, as if that was possible. When he broke his kiss, she blinked little black spots from her sight and panted anew.

"We'll discuss your well-thought-out answer over dinner, Mrs. Wright, after you've had a chance to come down."

"Still not hungry."

"I am. Lie back."

Best. Man. Ever. "With pleasure, sir."

When his lips met her pussy—finally—she gripped the sides of the desk so as not to shoot to the ceiling. She was vaguely aware of calling out his name a hundred or so times as he ate at her as if he, not her, had been waiting an eternity. *Forever.* Yes, she could do that. When he murmured *mine* into her swollen clit, she detonated, losing sight of the ceiling tiles, awareness of the slickened metal under her, or her wrists clamped down by his big hands. A giant neon billboard erupted in her mind: *Resort Owner's Wife Never Escaped* because . . . Best. Game. Ever.

ABOUT THE AUTHORS

JANE BAUER (janebauer.info) is a restaurant owner and the editor of *The Eye,* a local English magazine in Mexico. She has previously been published in the *New York Times* Modern Love column.

SHELLY BELL (ShellyBellBooks.com) is the award-winning author of the popular Benediction and Forbidden Lovers series. When she's not working her day job, taking care of her family, or writing, you'll find her reading the latest romance or thriller.

EVIE BENNET is a narrative designer who writes fiction and visual novels. Currently, she's expanding on the Rattler Romance motorcycle club series that starts with a tortured, obsessive mechanic falling for a wordsmith gang member in *We Belong.* Bennet is also pursuing a *Master's in Game Design.*

ZOEY CASTILE was born in Ecuador and raised in Queens, New York. For nearly a decade, she worked as a bartender, hostess, and manager in New York City's nightlife. When she's not writing, she can be found backpacking and hiking. You can follow her on Twitter and Instagram @ZoeyCastile.

AMY GLANCES is a New York-based writer who doesn't believe in mermaids, except, of course, for the ones she's met.

RITA-finalist author **JEANETTE GREY** (jeanettegrey.com) started out with degrees in physics and painting, which she dutifully applied to stunted careers in teaching, technical support, and advertising. Now she writes sexy, smart, heart-squeezing romance. When she's not at her keyboard, she's probably crafting, gaming, or chasing after her husband and toddler.

MIA HOPKINS (miahopkinsauthor.com) writes lush romances starring fun, sexy characters who love to get down and dirty. She's a sucker for working-class heroes, brainy heroines, and wisecracking best friends. Her favorite form of procrastination is baking. She lives in Los Angeles with her family.

BRIT INGRAM lives in southern Ontario, Canada. She writes short erotic stories, personal essays, and poetry, and is working on her first novel. She can be found writing in the pre-dawn hours, with plenty of breaks for coffee, her cat, and Twitter.

KATRINA JACKSON is a college history professor. She writes diverse erotica and erotic romance in her very limited spare time. She's the queen of telling awkward, sarcastic jokes at the absolute worst time.

D. L. KING (dlkingerotica.blogspot.com) is the editor of fifteen anthologies and the author of novels and novellas, as well as a collection of shorts. More than one hundred anthologies have included her short stories. She has acquired multiple literary awards, including a Lambda, a Golden Crown, several IPPYs, and NLA-I awards.

MARGOT PIERCE is a romance novelist and smut enthusiast based in upstate New York.

ELIZABETH SAFLEUR (elizabethsafleur.com) writes award-winning romance that dares to "go there" from twenty-eight wildlife-filled acres, which she shares with her husband and a seventeen-pound Westie (the real Dom in the family). When not immersed in books she can be found burlesque dancing or drinking good Virginia wine.

Published since 2009, *USA Today* bestselling author **NAIMA SIMONE** (naimasimone.com) writes sizzling romances with heart, a touch of humor, and snark. She is wife to her non-Kryptonian Superman and mother to the most awesome kids ever. They live in perfect, domestically challenged bliss in the southern United States.

LEAH W. SNOW writes at the attic window of the eighteenth-century stone farmhouse she shares with her husband and two gentle hounds of uncertain heritage. By day she writes corporate magazine articles, executive speeches, and white papers. By night she writes erotica, which she finds far more engaging.

KYRA VALENTINE spends her time dancing to the throbbing beat on a darkened dance floor, sleeping on the beach in the sultry heat of summer, or on the bench in her courtroom. She loves cheese, dark chocolate, and moody French films.

ANUJA VARGHESE (anujavarghese.com) is a Canadian writer whose work has appeared in several journals and literary magazines. She is currently working on a collection of short stories while pursuing creative writing at the University of Toronto. She has been to a lot of terrible conferences.

SASKIA VOGEL (saskiavogel.com) is a writer and literary translator from Los Angeles and based in Berlin. Her debut novel, *Permission* (Coach House Books, 2019), is a story of love, loss, and BDSM set between Hollywood and the crumbling LA coastline.

OLIVIA WAITE (oliviawaite.com) is a former bookseller and *Jeopardy!* champion who writes historical romance, fantasy, science fiction, and essays. She is the Kissing Books columnist for the *Seattle Review of Books,* where she reviews romance both new and old with an emphasis on insightful criticism and genre history. She lives in Seattle with her husband and their stalwart mini dachshund.

ALEXIS WILDER lives near a lake with her patient husband, their mermaid children, and a deranged dog. She loves movies, beer, and complaining about Michigan's weather. An active fangirl, she restricts her stanning to her various aliases and does not chase down celebrity men for sex in real life. Seriously.

ELIA WINTERS (eliawinters.com) is a fat, tattooed, polyamorous bisexual who loves petting cats and fighting the patriarchy. A sex educator and kink-positive feminist, Elia reviews sex toys, speaks at kink conventions, and writes geeky, kinky, cozy erotic romance. She lives in western Massachusetts with her loving husband and weird pets.

ABOUT THE EDITOR

RACHEL KRAMER BUSSEL (rachelkramerbussel.com) is a New Jersey-based author, editor, blogger, and writing instructor. She has edited over sixty books of erotica, including *Best Women's Erotica of the Year, Volumes 1, 2, 3, 4,* and *5; Best Bondage Erotica of the Year, Volume 1; Dirty Dates; Come Again: Sex Toy Erotica; The Big Book of Orgasms; The Big Book of Submission, Volumes 1* and *2; Lust in Latex; Anything for You; Baby Got Back: Anal Erotica; Suite Encounters; Gotta Have It; Women in Lust; Surrender; Orgasmic; Cheeky Spanking Stories; Bottoms Up; Spanked; Fast Girls; Going Down; Tasting Him; Tasting Her; Please, Sir; Please, Ma'am; He's on Top; She's on Top;* and *Crossdressing.* Her anthologies have won eight IPPY (Independent Publisher) Awards, and *The Big Book of Submission, Volume 2, Dirty Dates,* and *Surrender* won the National Leather Association Samois Anthology Award.

Rachel has written for *AVN, Bust, Cosmopolitan, Curve,* The Daily Beast, Elle.com, Fortune.com, *Glamour,* The Goods, Gothamist, *Harper's Bazaar,* Huffington Post, *Inked, InStyle,*

Marie Claire, MEL, Men's Health, Newsday, New York Post, New York Observer, The New York Times, O: The Oprah Magazine, Penthouse, The Philadelphia Inquirer, Refinery29, *Rolling Stone,* The Root, Salon, *San Francisco Chronicle, Self,* Slate, Time.com, *Time Out New York,* and *Zink,* among others. She has appeared on "The Gayle King Show," "The Martha Stewart Show," "The Berman and Berman Show," NY1, and Showtime's "Family Business." She hosted the popular In the Flesh Erotic Reading Series, featuring readers from Susie Bright to Zane, speaks at conferences, and does readings and teaches erotic writing workshops around the world and online. She blogs at lustylady.blogspot.com and consults about erotica and sex-related nonfiction at eroticawriting101.com. Follow her @raquelita on Twitter.